THE PRIDE
OF CHANUR

THE PRIDE
OF CHANUR

C.J. Cherryh

DAW Books   New York

Published by arrangement with
DAW Books, Inc.
1633 Broadway
New York, New York 10019

Manufactured in the United States of America

THE PRIDE
OF CHANUR

i

There had been something loose about the station dock all morning, skulking in amongst the gantries and the lines and the canisters which were waiting to be moved, lurking wherever shadows fell among the rampway accesses of the many ships at dock at Meetpoint. It was pale, naked, starved-looking in what fleeting glimpse anyone on *The Pride of Chanur* had had of it. Evidently no one had reported it to station authorities, nor did *The Pride*. Involving oneself in others' concerns at Meetpoint Station, where several species came to trade and provision, was ill-advised—at least until one was personally bothered. Whatever it was, it was bipedal, brachiate, and quick at making itself unseen. It had surely gotten away from someone, and likeliest were the kif, who had a thieving finger in everything, and who were not above kidnapping. Or it might be some large, bizarre animal; the mahendo'sat were inclined to the keeping and trade of strange pets, and Station had been displeased with them in that respect on more than one occasion. So far it had done nothing. Stolen nothing. No one wanted to get involved in question and answer between original owners and station authorities; and so far no official statement had come down from those station authorities and no notice of its loss had been posted by any ship, which itself argued that a wise person should not ask questions. The crew reported it only to the captain and chased it, twice, from *The Pride*'s loading area. Then the crew got to work on necessary duties, having settled the annoyance to their satisfaction.

It was the last matter on the mind of the noble, the distinguished captain Pyanfar Chanur, who was setting out down her own rampway for the docks. She was hani, this captain, splendidly maned and bearded in red-gold, which reached in silken curls to the middle of her bare, sleek-pelted chest, and she was dressed as befitted a hani of captain's rank, blousing scarlet breeches tucked up at her waist with a broad gold belt, with silk cords of every shade of red and orange wrapping that about, each knotted cord with a pendant jewel on its dangling end. Gold finished the breeches at her knees. Gold filigree was her armlet. And a row of fine gold rings and a large pendant pearl decorated the tufted sweep of her left ear. She strode down her own rampway in the security of ownership—still high-blooded from a quarrel with her niece—and yelled and bared claws as the intruder came bearing down on her.

She landed one raking, startled blow which would have held a hani in the encounter, but the hairless skin tore and it hurtled past her, taller than she was. It skidded around the bending of the curved ramp tube and bounded right into the ship, trailing blood all the way and leaving a bloody handprint on the rampway's white plastic wall.

Pyanfar gaped in outrage and pelted after, claws scrabbling for traction on the flooring plates. *"Hilfy!"* she shouted ahead; her niece had been in the lower corridor. Pyanfar made it into the airlock, hit the bar of the com panel there and punched all-ship. "Alert! *Hilfy!* Call the crew in! Something's gotten aboard. Seal yourself into the nearest compartment and call the crew." She flung open the locker next to the com unit, grabbed a pistol and scrambled in pursuit of the intruder. No trouble at all tracking it, with the dotted red trail on the white decking. The track led left at the first cross-corridor, which was deserted—the intruder must have gone left again, starting to box the square round the lift shafts. Pyanfar ran, heard a shout from that intersecting corridor and scrambled for it: *Hilfy!* She rounded the corner at a slide and came up short on a tableau, the intruder's hairless, red-running back and young Hilfy Chanur holding the corridor beyond with nothing but bared claws and adolescent bluster.

"Idiot!" Pyanfar spat at Hilfy, and the intruder turned on *her* suddenly, much closer. It brought up short in a staggered crouch, seeing the gun aimed two-handed at itself. It might have sense not to rush a weapon; might . . . but that would turn it right back at Hilfy, who stood unarmed behind. Pyanfar braced to fire at the least movement.

It stood rigidly still in its crouch, panting from its running and its wound. "Get out of there," Pyanfar said to Hilfy. "Get back." The intruder knew about hani claws now, and guns, but it might do anything, and Hilfy, an indistinction in her vision which was focused wholly on the intruder, stayed stubbornly still. *"Move!"* Pyanfar shouted.

The intruder shouted too, a snarl which almost got it shot, and drew itself upright and gestured to the center of its chest, twice, defiant. *Go on and shoot,* it seemed to invite her.

That intrigued Pyanfar. The intruder was not attractive. It had a bedraggled gold mane and beard, and its chest fur, almost invisible, narrowed in a line down its heaving belly to vanish into what was, legitimately, clothing, a rag almost nonexistent in its tatters and obscured by the dirt which matched the rest of its hairless hide. Its smell was rank. But a straight carriage and a wild-eyed invitation to its enemies . . . that deserved a second thought. It knew guns; it wore at least a token of clothing; it drew its line and meant to hold its territory. Male, maybe. It had that over-the-brink look in its eyes.

"Who are you?" Pyanfar asked slowly, in several languages one after the other, including kif. The intruder gave no sign of understanding any of them. "Who?" she repeated.

It crouched slowly, with a sullen scowl, all the way to the deck, and extended a blunt-nailed finger and wrote in its own blood which was liberally puddled about its bare feet. It made a precise row of symbols, ten of them, and a second row which began with the first symbol prefaced by the second, second with second, second with third . . . patiently, with increasing concentration despite the growing tremors of its hand, dipping its finger and writing, mad fixation on its task.

"What's it doing?" asked Hilfy, who could not see from her side.

"A writing system, probably numerical notation. It's no animal, niece."

At the exchange, the intruder looked up—stood up, an abrupt move which proved injudicious after its loss of blood. A glassy, desperate look came into its eyes, and it sprawled in the puddle and the writing, slipping in its own blood in trying to get up again.

"Call the crew," Pyanfar said levelly, and this time Hilfy scurried off in great haste. Pyanfar stood where she was, pistol in hand, until Hilfy was out of sight down another corridor, then, assured that there was no one to see her lapse of dignity, she squatted down with the gun in both hands held loosely between her knees. The intruder still struggled, propped itself up with its bloody back against the wall, elbow pressed against that deeper starting point of the scratches on its side, which was the source of most of the blood. Its pale-blue eyes, for all their glassiness, seemed to convey some sense. It looked back at her warily, with seeming mad cynicism.

"You speak kif?" Pyanfar asked again. A flicker of those eyes, which might mean anything. Not a word from it. It started shivering, which was shock setting in. Sweat had broken out on its naked skin. It never ceased to look at her.

Running broke into the corridors. Pyanfar stood up quickly, not to be caught thus engaged with the creature. Hilfy came hurrying back, the crew approaching from the other direction, and Pyanfar stepped aside as they arrived and the intruder tried to scramble off in retreat. The crew laid hands on it and jerked it skidding along the bloody puddle. It cried out and tried to grapple with them, but they had it on its belly in the first rush and a blow dazed it. *"Gently!"* Pyanfar yelled at them, but they had it then, got its arms lashed at its back with one of their belts, tied its ankles together and got off it, their fur as bloody as the intruder's, who continued a feeble movement.

"Do it no more damage," Pyanfar said. "I'll have it clean, thank you, watered, fed, and healthy, but keep it restrained. Prepare me explanations of how it got face to face with me in the rampway, and if one of you bleats a word of this outside the ship I'll sell you to the kif."

"Captain," they murmured, down-eared in deference. They were second and third cousins of hers, two sets of sisters, one set large and one small, and equally chagrined.

"Out," she said. They snatched the intruder up by the binding of its arms and prepared to drag it. "Careful!" Pyanfar hissed, and they were gentler in pulling it along.

"You," Pyanfar said then to Hilfy, her brother's daughter, who lowered her ears and turned her face aside—short-maned, with an adolescent's beginning beard, and now with an air of martyrdom. "I'll send you back shaved if you disobey another order. Understand me?"

Hilfy made a bow facing her, duly contrite. "Aunt," she said, and straightened, contriving to make it all thoughtfully graceful; looked her straight in the eyes with offended worship.

"Huh," Pyanfar said. Hilfy bowed a second time and padded past as softly as possible. In common blue breeches like the crew's was Hilfy, but the swagger was all Chanur, and not quite ludicrous on so young a woman. Pyanfar snorted, fingered the silk of her beard into order, looked down in sober thought at the wallowed smear where the Outsider had fallen, obliterating all the writing from the eyes of the crew.

So, so, so.

Pyanfar postponed her trip to station offices, walked back to the lower-deck operations center, sat down at the com board amid all the telltales of cargo status and lines and grapples and the routine operations *The Pride* carried on automatically. She keyed in the current messages, sorted through those and found nothing, then delved into *The Pride*'s recording of all messages received since docking, and all that had flowed through station communications aimed at others. She searched first for anything kif-sent, a rapid flicker of lines on the screen in front of her, all operational chatter in transcription—a very great deal of it. Then she queried for notice of anything lost, and after that, for anything escaped.

Mahendo'sat? she queried then, staying constantly to her own ship's records of incoming messages, of the sort which flowed constantly in a busy station, and in no wise sending any inquiry into the station's comp system. She recycled the whole record last of all, ran it past at eye-blurring speed, looking for any key word about escapes or warnings of alien presence at Meetpoint.

So indeed. No one was going to say a word on the topic. The owners still did not want to acknowledge publicly that they had lost this item. The Chanur were not lack-witted, to announce publicly that they had found it. Or to trust that the kif or whoever had lost it were not at this moment turning the station inside out with a surreptitious search.

Pyanfar tuned off the machine, flicked her ears so that the rings on the left one jangled soothingly. She got up and paced the center, thrust her hands into her belt and thought about alternatives and possible gains. It would be a dark day indeed when a Chanur went to the kif to hand back an acquisition. She could justifiably make a claim on it regarding legal liabilities and the invasion of a hani ship. Public hazard, it was called. But there were no outside witnesses to the intrusion, and the kif, almost certainly to blame, would not yield without a wrangle . . . which meant court, and prolonged proximity to kif, whose gray, wrinkle-hided persons she loathed; whose naturally dolorous faces she loathed; whose jeremiad of miseries and wrongs done them was constant and unendurable. A Chanur, in station court with a howling mob of kif . . . and it would go to that extreme if kif came claiming this intruder. The whole business was unpalatable in all its ramifications.

Whatever it was and wherever it came from, the creature was educated. That hinted in turn at other things, at cogent reasons why the kif might indeed be upset at the loss of this item and why they wished so little publicity in the search.

She punched in intraship. "Hilfy."

"Aunt?" Hilfy responded after a moment.

"Find out the intruder's condition."

"I'm watching them treat it now. Aunt, I think it's *he,* if there's any analogy of form and—"

"Never mind zoology. How badly is it hurt?"

"It's in shock, but it seems stronger than it was a moment ago. It—he—got quiet when we managed to get an anesthetic on the scratches. I think he figured then we were trying to help, and he quit fighting. We thought the drug had got him. But he's breathing better now."

"It's probably just waiting its chance. When you get it safely locked up, you take your turn at dock work, since you were so eager to have a look outside. The others will show you what to do. Tell Haral to get herself to lower-deck op. Now."

"Yes, aunt." Hilfy had no sulking in her tone. The last reprimand must not have worn off. Pyanfar shut down the contact and listened to station chatter in the interim, wishing in vain for something to clarify the matter.

Haral showed up on the run, soaking wet, blood-spattered and breathless. She bowed shortly in the doorway, straightened. She was oldest of the crew, tall, with a dark scar across her broad nose and another across the belly, but those were from her rash youth.

"Clean up," Pyanfar said. "Take cash and go marketing, cousin. Shop the second-hand markets as if you were on your own. The item I want may be difficult to locate but not impossible, I think, in such a place as Meetpoint. Some books, if you will —a mahendo'sat lexicon, a mahendo'sat version of their holy writings. The philosopher Kohboranua or another of that ilk, I'm completely indifferent. And a mahendo'sat symbol translator, its modules and manuals, from elementary up, as many levels as you

can find . . . above all, that item. The rest is all cover. If questioned—a client's taken a religious interest."

Haral bowed in acceptance of the order and asked nothing.
Pyanfar put her hand deep into her pocket and came up with a
motley assortment of large-denomination coinage, a whole stack
of it.

"And four gold rings," Pyanfar added.

"Captain?"

"To remind you all that *The Pride* minds its own business. Say
so when you give them. It'll salve your feelings, I hope, if we have
to miss taking a liberty here, as well we may. But talk and rouse
suspicion about those items, Haral Araun, and you won't have an
ear to wear it on."

Haral grinned and bowed a third time.

"Go," said Pyanfar, and Haral darted out in zealous applica-
tion.

So. It was a risk, but a minor one. Pyanfar considered matters
for a moment, finally walked outside the op room and down the
corridor, took the lift up to central level, where her own quarters
were, out of the stench and the reek of disinfectant which filled the
lower deck.

She closed the door behind her with a sigh, went to the bath
and washed her hands—seeing that there remained no shred of
flesh in the undercurve of her claws—checked over her fine silk
breeches to be sure no spatter of blood had gotten on them.
She applied a dash of cologne to clear the memory from her nostrils.

Stupidity. She was getting dull as the stsho, to have missed a
grip on the intruder in the first place; *old* was not a word she pre-
ferred to think about. Slow of mind, woolgathering, that she
struck like a youngster on her first forage. Lazy. That was more
like it. She patted her flat belly and decided that the year-old com-
placent outletting of her belt had to be taken in again. She was
losing her edge. Her brother Kohan was still fit enough, planetbound as he was and not gifted with the time-stretch of jump; he
managed. Inter-male bickering and a couple of sons to throw out
of the domicile kept his blood circulating, and there was usually a
trio of mates in the house at any one time, with offspring to chas-
tise. About time, she thought, that she put *The Pride* into home
dock at Anuurn for a thorough refitting and spent a layover with
her own mate, Khym, high in the Kahin hills, in the Mahn estates.

Get the smell of the home-world wind in her nostrils for a few months. Do a little hunting, run off that extra notch on the belt. Check on her daughter Tahy and see whether that son of hers was still roving about or whether someone had finally broken his neck for him. Surely the lad would have had the common courtesy to send a message through Khym or Kohan if he had settled somewhere; and above all to her daughter, who was, gods knew, grown and getting soft hanging about her father's house, among a dozen other daughters, mostly brotherless. Son Kara should settle himself with some unpropertied wife and give his sister some gainful employment making him rich—above all, settle and take himself out of his father's and his uncle's way. Ambitious, that was Kara. Let the young rake try to move in on his uncle Kohan and that would be the last of him. Pyanfar flexed claws at the thought and recalled why all her shore leaves were short ones.

But this now, this business with this bit of live contraband which had strayed aboard, which might be kif-owned . . . the honorable lord Kohan Chanur, her brother, was going to have a word to say about his ship's carelessness in letting such an incident reach their deck. And there was going to be a major rearrangement in the household if Hilfy got hurt—brotherless Hilfy, who had gotten to be too much Chanur to go following after a brother if ever her mother gave her one. Hilfy Chanur *par* Faha, who wanted the stars more than she wanted anything, and who clung to her father as the one who could give them to her. It was Hilfy's lifelong awaited chance, this voyage, this apprenticeship on *The Pride*. It had torn Kohan's doting soul to part from his favorite; that was clear in the letter which had come with Hilfy.

Pyanfar shook her head and fretted. Depriving those four rag-eared crew of hers of a shore leave in the pursuit of this matter was one thing, but taking Hilfy home to Anuurn while she sorted out a major quarrel with the kif was another. It was expensive, curtailing their homeward routing. More, Hilfy's pride would die a death, if she were the cause of that rerouting, if she were made to face her sisters in her sudden return to the household; and Pyanfar confessed herself attached to the imp, who wanted what she had wanted at such an age, who most likely *would* come to command a Chanur ship someday, perhaps even—gods postpone the hour—*The Pride* itself. Pyanfar thought of such a legacy . . . someday, someday that Kohan passed his prime and she did. Others in the house of Chanur were jealous of Hilfy, waiting for some chance to

vent their jealousy. But Hilfy *was* the best. The brightest and best,
like herself and like Kohan, and no one so far could prove otherwise. Whatever young male one day won the Chanur holding from
Kohan in his decline had best walk warily and please Hilfy, or
Hilfy might take herself a mate who would tear the ears off the in-
terloper. That was the kind Hilfy was, loyal to her father and to
the house.

And ruining that spirit or risking her life over that draggled
Outsider was not worth it. Maybe, Pyanfar thought, she should
swallow the bitter mouthful and go dump the creature on the
nearest kif ship. She seriously considered it. Choosing the wrong
kif ship might afford some lively amusement; there would be riot
among the kif and consternation on the station. But yielding was
still, at bottom, distasteful.

Gods! So that was how she proposed teaching young Hilfy to
handle difficulties. *That* was the example she set . . . yielding up
what she had, because she thought it might be dangerous to hold
it.

She *was* getting soft. She patted her belly again, decided against
shore leave at voyage's end, another lying-up and another Mahn
offspring to muddle things up. Decided against retreat. She drew
in a great breath and put on a grim smile. Age came and the
young grew old, but not too old, the gods grant. This voyage,
young Hilfy Chanur was going to learn to justify that swagger she
cut through the corridors of the ship; so, indeed she was.

There was no leaving the ship with matters aboard still in flux.
Pyanfar went to the small central galley, up the starboard curve
from her quarters and the bridge, stirred about to make a cup of
gfi from the dispenser and sat down at the counter by the oven to
enjoy it at leisure, waiting until her crew should have had ample
time to deal with the Outsider. She gave them a bit more, finally
tossed the empty cup in the sterilizer and got up and wandered
belowdecks again, where the corridors stank strongly of antiseptic
and Tirun was lounging about, leaning against the wall by the
lower-deck washroom door. "Well?" Pyanfar asked.

"We put it in there, Captain. Easiest to clean, by your leave.
Haral left. Chur and Geran and *ker* Hilfy are out doing the loading. Thought someone ought to stay awhile by the door and listen,
to be sure the creature's all right."

Pyanfar laid her hand on the switch, looked back at Tirun—

Haral's sister and as broad and solid, with the scars of youth well weathered, the gold of successful voyages winking from her left ear. The two of them together could handle the Outsider, she reckoned, in any condition. "Does it show any sign of coming out of its shock?"

"It's quiet; shallow breathing, staring somewhere else—but aware what's going on. Scared us a moment; we thought it'd gone into shock with the medicine, but I think it just quieted down when the pain stopped. We tried with the way we handled it, to make it understand we didn't want to hurt it. Maybe it has that figured. We carried it in here and it settled down and lay still . . . moved when made to move, but not surly, more like it's stopped thinking, like it's stopping doing anything it doesn't have to do. Worn out, I'd say."

"Huh." Pyanfar pressed the bar. The dark interior of the washroom smelled of antiseptic, too, the strongest they had. The lights were dimmed. The air was stiflingly warm and carried an odd scent under the antiseptic reek. Her eyes missed the creature a moment, searched anxiously and located it in the corner, a heap of blankets between the shower stall and the laundry . . . asleep or awake—she could not tell—with its head tucked down in its forearms. A large container of water and a plastic dish with a few meat chips and crumbs left rested beside it on the tiles. Well, again. It was carnivorous then and not so delicate after all, to have an appetite left. So much for its collapse. "Is it restrained?"

"It has chain enough to get to the head if it understands what it's for."

Pyanfar stepped back outside and closed the door on it again. "Very likely it understands. Tirun, it *is* sapient or I'm blind. Don't assume it can't manipulate switches. No one is to go in there alone and no one's to carry firearms near it. Pass that order to the others personally—Hilfy too. Especially Hilfy."

"Yes, Captain." Tirun's broad face was innocent of opinions. Gods knew what they were going to *do* with the creature if they kept it. Tirun did not ask. Pyanfar strolled off, meditating on the scene behind the washroom door, the heap of deceptive blankets, the food so healthily consumed, the avowed collapse . . . no lackwit, this creature who had twice tried her ship's security and on the third attempt succeeded in getting through. Why *The Pride,* she wondered. Why her ship, out of all the others at dock? Because they were last in the section, before the bulkhead of the dock seal might force the creature to have left cover somewhat, and it was the last available choice? Or was there some other reason?

She walked the corridor to the airlock and the rampway, and out its curving ribbed length into the chill air of the docks. She looked left as she came out, and there was Hilfy, canister-loading with Chur and Geran, rolling the big cargo containers off the station-side dolly and onto the moving belt which would take the goods into *The Pride*'s holds, paid freight on its way to Urtur and Kura and Touin and Anuurn itself, stsho cargo, commodities and textiles and medicines, ordinary stuff. Hilfy paused at the sight of her, panting with her efforts and already looking close to collapse, stood up straight with her hands at her sides and her ears back, belly heaving. It was hard work, shifting those cans about, especially for the unskilled and unaccustomed. Chur and Geran worked on, small of stature and wiry, knowing the points of balance to an exactitude. Pyanfar affected not to notice her niece and walked on with wide steps, nonchalant, smiling to herself the while. Hilfy had been mightily indignant, barred from rushing out to station market, to roam about unescorted, sightseeing on this her first call at Meetpoint, where species docked which never called at homeworld . . . sights she had missed at Urtur and Kura, likewise pent aboard ship or held close to *The Pride*'s berth. The imp had too much enthusiasm for her own good. So she got the look at Meetpoint's famous docks that she had argued to have—now, this very day—but not the sightseeing tour of her young imaginings.

Next station call, Pyanfar thought, next station call her niece might have learned enough to be let loose unescorted, when the wild-eyed eagerness had worn off, when she had learned from this incident that there were hazards on dockside and that a little caution was in order when prowling the friendliest of ports.

Herself, she took the direct route, not without watching her surroundings.

ii

A call on Meetpoint station officials was usually a leisurely and pleasant affair. The stsho, placid and graceful, ran the station offices and bureaus on this side of the station, where oxygen breathers docked. Methodical to a fault, the stsho could be tedious, full of endless subtle meanings in their pastel ornaments and the tattooings on their pearly hides. They were another hairless species—stalk-thin, tri-sexed and hanilike only by the wildest stretch of the imagination, if eyes, nose and mouth in biologically convenient order constituted similarity. Their manners were bizarre among themselves. But stsho had learned to suit their methodical plodding and their ceremoniousness to hani taste, which was to have a soft chair, a ready cup of herbal tea, a plate of exotic edibles and an individual as pleasant as possible about the forms and the statistics, who could make it all like a social chat.

This stsho was unfamiliar. Stsho changed officials more readily than they changed ornament. Either a different individual had come into control of Meetpoint Station, Pyanfar reckoned, or a stsho she had once known had entered a New Phase. New doings? Pyanfar wondered, at the nudge of a small and prickly instinct—new doings? Loose Outsiders and stsho power shuffles? All changes were suspect when something was out of pocket. If it was the same as the previous stationmaster, it had changed the pattern of all the elaborate silver filigree and plumes—azure and lime now, not azure and mint; and if it were the case, it was not at all polite to recognize the refurbished person, even if a hani suspected identity.

The stsho proffered delicacies and tea, bowed, folded up *gtst* stalklike limbs—he, she, or even it, hardly applied with stsho—and seated *gtst*-self in *gtst* bowlchair, a cushioned indentation in the office floor. The necessary table rose on a pedestal before *gtst*. Pyanfar occupied the facing depression, lounged on an elbow to reach for the smoked fish the stsho's lesser-status servant had placed on a similar table at her left. The servant, ornamentless and no one, sat against the wall, knees tucked higher than *gtst* head, arms about bony ankles, awaiting usefulness. The stsho official likewise took a sample of the fish, poured tea, graceful gestures of stsho elegance and hospitality. Plumed and cosmetically augmented brows nodded delicately over moonstone eyes as *gtst* looked up—white brows shading to lilac and azure; azure tracings on the domed brow shaded to lime over the hairless skull. Another stsho, of course, might read the patterns with exactitude, the station in life, the chosen Mood for this Phase of *gtst* existence, the affiliations and modes and thereby, *gtst* approachability. Nonstsho were forgiven their trespasses; and stsho in Retiring mode were not likely to be filling public offices.

Pyanfar made one attempt on the Outsider topic, delicately: "Things have been quiet hereabouts?"

"Oh, assuredly." The stsho beamed, smiled with narrow mouth and narrow eyes, a carnivore habit, though the stsho were not aggressive. "Assuredly."

"Also on my world," Pyanfar said, and sipped her tea, an aroma of spices which delighted all her sinuses. "Herbal. But what?"

The stsho smiled with still more breadth. "Ah. Imported from my world. We introduce it here, in our offices. Duty free. New cultivation techniques make it available for export. The first time, you understand. The very first shipment offered. Very rare, a taste of my very distant world."

"Cost?"

They discussed it. It was outrageous. But the stsho came down, predictably, particularly when tempted with a case of hani delicacies promised to be carted up from dockside to the offices. Pyanfar left the necessary interview in high spirits. Barter was as good to her as breathing.

She took the lift down to dock level, straight down, without going the several corridors over in lateral which she could have taken. She walked the long way back toward *The Pride*'s berth, strolled casually along the dockside, which stretched upward before and behind, unfurling as she moved, offices and businesses on the one hand and the tall mobile gantries on the other, towers which aimed their tops toward the distant axis of Meetpoint, so that the most distant appeared insanely atilt on the curving horizon. Display boards at periodic intervals gave information of arrivals, departures and ships in dock, from what port and bearing what sort of cargo, and she scanned them as she walked.

A car shot past her on the dock, from behind: globular and sealed, it wove along avoiding canisters and passersby and lines with greater speed than an automated vehicle would use. That was a methane-breather, more than likely, some official from beyond the dividing line which separated the incompatible realities of Meetpoint. Tc'a ran that side of the station, sinuous beings and leathery gold, utterly alien with their multipartite brains—they traded with the knnn and the chi, kept generally to themselves and had little to say or to do with hani or even with the stsho, with whom they shared the building and operation of Meetpoint. Tc'a had nothing in common with this side of the line, not even ambitions; and the knnn and the chi were stranger still, even less participant within the worlds and governments and territories of the Compact. Pyanfar watched the vehicle kite along, up the horizon of Meetpoint's docks, and the section seal curtained it from view as it jittered along in zigzag haste, which itself argued a tc'a mind at the controls. There was no trouble from *them* . . . no way that they could have dealt with the Outsider; their brains were as unlike as their breathing apparatus. She paused, stared up at the nearby registry boards, sorting through the improbable and untranslatable methane-breather names for more familiar registrations—for potential trouble, and for possible allies of use in a crisis. There was scant picking among the latter at this apogee of *The Pride*'s rambling course.

There *was* one other hani ship in dock, *Handur's Voyager*. She knew a few of the Handur family, remotely. They were from Anuurn's other hemisphere, neither rivals nor close allies, since they shared nothing on Anuurn's surface. There were a lot of stsho ships, which was to be expected on this verge of stsho space. A lot of mahendo'sat, through whose territory *The Pride* had lately come.

And on the side of trouble, there were four kif, one of which she knew: *Kut,* captained by one Ikkukkt, an aging scoundrel whose style was more to allow another ship's canisters to edge up

against and among his on dockside, and to bluff down any easily
confused owners who might protest. He was only small trouble,
alone. Kif in groups could be different, and she did not know
about the others.

"Hai," she called, passing a mahendo'sat docking area, at a
ship called *Mahijiru,* where some of that tall, dark-furred kind
were minding their own business, cursing and scratching their
heads over some difficulty with a connection collar, a lock-ring
disassembled in order all over the deck among their waiting canisters. "You fare well this trip, *mahe?*"

"Ah, Captain." The centermost scrambled up and others did
the same as this one stepped toward her, treading carefully among
the pieces of the collar. Any well-dressed hani was captain to a
mahendo'sat, who would rather err by compliment than otherwise.
But this one by his gilt teeth was probably the captain of his own
freighter. "You trade?"

"Trade what?"

"What got?"

"Hai, *mahe,* what need?"

The mahendo'sat grinned, a brilliant golden flash, sharp-edged.
No one, of course, began trade by admitting to necessity.

"Need a few less kif onstation." Pyanfar answered her own
question, and the mahendo'sat whistled laughter and bobbed
agreement.

"True, true," Goldtooth said, somewhere between humor and
outrage, as if he had a personal tale to tell. "Whining kif we wish
you end of dock, good Captain, honest Captain. *Kut* no good.
Hukan more no good; and *Lukkur* same. But *Hinukku* make new
kind deal no good. Wait at station, wait no get same you course
with *Hinukku,* good Captain."

"What, *armed?*"

"Like hani, maybe." Goldtooth grinned when he said it, and
Pyanfar laughed, pretending it was a fine joke.

"When do hani ever have weapons?" she asked.

The *mahe* thought that a fine joke, too.

"Trade you two hundredweight silk," Pyanfar offered.

"Station duty take all my profit."

"Ah. Too bad. Hard work, that." She scuffed a foot toward the
ailing collar. "I can lend you very good hani tools, fine steel, two
very good hani welders. Faha House make."

"I lend you good quality artwork."

"Artwork!"

"Maybe someday great *mahen* artist, Captain."

"*Then* come to me; I'll keep my silk."

"Ah, ah, I make you favor with artwork, Captain, but no, I ask you take no chance. I have instead small number very fine pearl like you wear."

"Ah."

"Make you security for lend tools and welders. My man he come by you soon borrow tools. Show you pearl same time."

"Five pearls."

"We see tools you see two pearls."

"You bring four."

"Fine. You pick best three."

"All four if they're not of the best, my good, my great *mahe* Captain."

"You see," he vowed. "Absolute best. *Three.*"

"Good." She grinned cheerfully, touched hand to hand with the thick-nailed *mahe* and strolled off, grinning still for all passersby to see; but the grin faded when she was past the ring of their canisters and crossing the next berth.

So. Kif trouble had docked. There were kif and kif, and in that hierarchy of thieves, there were a few ship captains who tended to serve as ringleaders for high-stakes mischief, and some elect who were very great trouble indeed. Mahendo'sat translation always had its difficulties, but it sounded uncomfortably like one of the latter. Stay in dock, the mahendo'sat had advised; don't chance putting out till it leaves. That was mahendo'sat strategy. It did not always work. She could keep *The Pride* at dock and run up a monstrous bill, and still have no guarantee of a safe course out; or she could pull out early and hope that the kif would *not* suspect what they had aboard—hope that the kif, at minimum, were waiting for something easier to chew than a mouthful of hani.

Hilfy. That worry rode her mind. Ten quiet voyages, ten voyages of aching, bone-weary tranquility . . . and now this one.

The docks looked all quiet ahead, up where *The Pride* had docked, her people working out by the loading belt as they should be doing, taking aboard the mail and the freight. Haral was back, working among them; she was relieved to see that. That was Tirun outside now, and Hilfy must have gone in; the other two were Geran and Chur, slight figures next to Haral and Tirun. She found no cause to hurry. Hilfy had probably had enough by now, retreated inside to guard duty over the Outsider, gods grant that she stay outside the door and refrain from meddling.

But the crew caught sight of her as she came, and of a sudden expressions took on desperate relief and ears pricked up, so that her heart clenched with foreknowledge of something direly wrong. "Hilfy," she asked first, as Haral came walking out to meet her: the other three stayed at their loading, all too busy for those looks of anxiety, playing the part of workers thoroughly occupied.

"*Ker* Hilfy's safe inside," Haral said quickly. "Captain, I got the things you ordered, put them in lowerdeck op, all of it; but there were kif everywhere I went, Captain, when I was off in the market. They were prowling about the aisles, staring at everyone, buying nothing. I finished my business and walked on back and they were still prowling about. So I ordered *ker* Hilfy to go on in and send Tirun out here. There are kif nosing about *here* suddenly."

"Doing what?"

"Look beyond my shoulder, Captain."

Pyanfar took a quick look, a shift of her eyes. "Nothing," she said. But canisters were piled there at the section seal, twenty, thirty of them, each as tall as a hani and double-stacked, cover enough. She set her hand on Haral's shoulder, walked her companionably back to the others. "Hark, there's going to be a small stsho delivery and a mahendo'sat with a three-pearl deal; both are true . . . watch them both. But no others. There's one other hani ship docked far around the rim, next the methane docks. I've not spoken with them. It's *Handur's Voyager*."

"Small ship."

"And vulnerable. We're going to take *The Pride* out, with all decent haste. I think it can only get worse here. Tirun, a small task: get to *Voyager*. I don't want to discuss the situation with them over com. Warn them that there's a ship in dock named *Hinukku* and the word is out among the mahendo'sat that this one is uncommonly bad trouble. And then get yourself back here fast. . . . No, wait. A good tool kit and two good welders—drop them with the crew of the *Mahijiru* and take the pearls in a hurry if you can get them. Seventh berth down. They'll deserve that and more if I've put the kif onto them by asking questions there. Go."

"Yes, Captain," Tirun breathed, and scurried off, ears back, up the service ramp beside the cargo belt.

Pyanfar cast a second look at the double-stacked canisters as she turned. No kif in sight. *Haste,* she wished Tirun, *hurry it.* It was a quick trip inside to pull the trade items from the automated delivery. Tirun came back with the boxes under one arm and set out directly in the kind of reasonable haste she might use on her captain's order.

"Huh." Pyanfar turned again and looked toward the shadow. There. By the canisters after all. A kif stood there, tall and black-robed, with a long prominent snout and hunched stature. Pyanfar stared at it directly—*waved* to it with energetic and sarcastic camaraderie as she started toward it.

It stepped at once back into the shelter of the canisters and the shadows. Pyanfar drew a great breath, flexed her claws and kept walking, round the curve of the canister stacks and softly—face to face with the towering kif. The kif looked down on her with its red-rimmed dark eyes and long-nosed face and its dusty black robes like the robes of all other kif, of one tone with the gray skin . . . a bit of shadow come to life. "Be off," she told it. "I'll have no canister-mixing. I'm onto your tricks."

"Something of ours has been stolen."

She laughed, helped by sheer surprise. "Something of *yours* stolen, master thief? That's a wonder to tell at home."

"Best it find its way back to us. Best it should, Captain."

She laid back her ears and grinned, which was not friendliness.

"Where is your crewwoman going with those boxes?" the kif asked.

She said nothing. Extruded claws.

"It would not be, Captain, that you've somehow found that lost item."

"What, *lost,* now?"

"Lost and found again, I think."

"What ship *are* you, kif?"

"If you were as clever as you imagine you are, Captain, you would know."

"I like to know who I'm talking to. Even among kif. I'll reckon you know my name, skulking about out here. What's yours?"

"Akukkakk is mine, Chanur Captain. Pyanfar Chanur. Yes, we know you. Know you well, Captain. We have become *interested* in you . . . thief."

"Oho. Akukkakk of what ship?" Her vision sharpened on the kif, whose robes were marginally finer than usual, whose bearing had precious little kifish stoop in dealing with shorter species, that hunch of shoulders and thrusting forward of the head. This one looked at her the long way, from all its height. "I'd like to know you as well, kif."

"You will, hani. . . . No. A last chance. We will redeem this prize you've found. I will make you that offer."

Her mustache-hairs drew down, as at some offensive aroma. "Interesting if I had this item. Is it round or flat, this strayed object? Or did one of your own crew rob you, kif Captain?"

"You know its shape, since you have it. Give it up, and be paid. Or don't—and be paid, hani, be paid then too."

"Describe this item to me."

"For its safe return—gold, ten bars of gold, fine. Contrive your own descriptions."

"I shall bear it in mind, kif, should I find something unusual and kif-smelling. But so far nothing."

"Dangerous, hani."

"What ship, kif?"

"*Hinukku.*"

"I'll remember your offer. Indeed I will, master thief."

The kif said nothing more. Towered erect and silent. She aimed a dry spitting toward its feet and walked off, slow swagger.

Hinukku, indeed. A whole new kind of trouble, the mahendo'sat had said, and this surly kif or another *might* have seen . . . or talked to those who had seen. *Gold,* they offered. Kif . . . offered ransom; and no common kif, either, not that one. She walked with a prickling between her shoulderblades and a multiplying apprehension for Tirun, who was now a small figure walking off along the upcurving docks. No hope that the station authorities would do anything to prevent a murder . . . not one between kif and hani. The stsho's neutrality consisted in retreat, and their law in arbitrating after the fact.

Stsho ships were the most common victims of marauding kif, and still kif docked unchecked at Meetpoint. Madness. A bristling ran up her back and her ears flicked, jingling the rings. Hani might deal with the kif and teach them a lesson, but there was no profit in it, not until moments like this one. Divert every hani ship from profitable trade to kif-hunting? Madness too . . . until it was *The Pride* in question.

"Pack it up out here," she told her remaining crew when she reached them. "Get those last cans on and shut it down. Get everything ready to break dock. I'm going to call Tirun back here. It's worse than I thought."

"I'll go after her," Haral said.

"Do as I say, cousin—and keep Hilfy out of it."

Haral fell back. Pyanfar started off down the dock—old habit, not to run; a reserve of pride, of caution, of some instinct either good or ill. Still she did not run in front of witnesses. She widened her strides until some bystanders—stsho—did notice, and stared. She gained on Tirun. Almost, almost within convenient shouting distance of Tirun, and still a far, naked distance up the dock's up-curving course to reach *Handur's Voyager*. *Hinukku* sat at dock for Tirun to pass before she should come to the hani ship. But the mahendo'sat vessel *Mahijiru* was docked before that, if only Tirun handled that extraneous errand on the way, the logical thing to do with a heavy load under one arm. Surely it was the logical thing, even considering the urgency of the other message.

Ah. Tirun did stop at the mahendo'sat berth. Pyanfar breathed a gasp of relief, broke her own rule at the last moment and sprinted behind some canisters, strode right into the gathering which had begun to close about Tirun. She clapped a startled mahendo'sat spectator on the arm, pulled it about and thrust her way through to Tirun, grabbed her arm without ceremony. "Trouble. Let's go, cousin."

"Captain," Goldtooth exclaimed from her right. "You come back make new bigger deal?"

"Never mind. The tools are a gift. Come *on,* Tirun."

"Captain," Tirun began, bewildered, being dragged back through the gathering of mahendo'sat. Mahendo'sat gave way before them, their captain still following them with confused chatter about welders and pearls.

Kif. A black-clad half ring of them appeared suddenly on the outskirts of the swirl of dark-furred mahendo'sat. Pyanfar had Tirun's wrist and pulled her forward. "Look out!" Tirun cried suddenly: one of the kif had pulled a gun from beneath its robe. *"Go!"* Pyanfar yelled, and they dived back among cursing and screaming mahendo'sat, out again through a melee of kif who had circled behind the canisters. Fire popped after them. Pyanfar bowled over a kif in their path with a strike that should snap vertebrae and did not break stride to find out. Tirun ran beside her; they sprinted with fire popping smoke curls off the deck plates ahead of them.

Suddenly a shot came from the right hand. Tirun yelped and stumbled, limping wildly. More kif along the dock-front offices, one very tall and familiar. Akukkakk, with friends. "Earless bastard!" Pyanfar shouted, grabbed Tirun afresh and kept going, dragged her behind the canisters of another mahendo'sat ship in a hail of laser pops and the reek of burned plastic. Tirun sagged in shock—a curse and a jerk on the arm got her running again, desperately: the burn ruptured and bled. They darted an open space, having no choice: shrill harooing rang out behind and on the right, kif on the hunt.

A second shout roared out from before them, another flash from guns, multicolor, at *The Pride*'s berth; *The Pride*'s crew was returning fire, high for their sakes but meaning business. Station alarms started going off, bass-tone whooping. Red lights flashed on the walls and up the curve till the ceiling vanished. Higher up the curve of the dock, station folk scrambled in panic, hunting shelter. If there were kif among them, they would come charging down from that direction too, at the crew's backs.

And Hilfy was out there at that access, fourth in that line of their own guns—laying down a berserk pattern of fire. Pyanfar dragged Tirun through that line of four by the scruff of the neck. Tirun twisted and fell on the plates and Pyanfar helped her up again, not without a wild look back, at a dockside where enemies fired from cover at her crew who had precious little. *"Board!"* she yelled at the others with the last of her wind, and herself skidded on the decking in turning for the rampway. Haral retreated and grabbed Tirun's flailing arm from the other side and Hilfy suddenly took Pyanfar's. Pyanfar looked back again, willing to turn and fight. Geran and Chur were falling back in orderly retreat behind them, still facing the direction of the kif and firing—the kif had been pinned back from advance into better vantage. Hilfy pulled at her arm and Pyanfar shook free as they reached the rampway's first door. "Come *on*," she shouted at Geran and Chur, and the moment they retreated within, still firing, she hit the door seal. The massive steel clanged and thumped shut and the pair stumbled back out of the way; Hilfy darted in from across the door and rammed the lock-lever down.

Pyanfar looked round then at Tirun, who was on her feet, though sagging in Haral's arms, and holding her upper right leg. Her blue breeches were dark with blood from there to the fur of her calf and threading down to her foot in a puddle, and she was muttering a steady stream of curses.

"Move," Pyanfar said. Haral took Tirun up in her arms and outright carried her, no small load. They withdrew up the rampway curve into their own lock, sealed *that* door and felt somewhat safer.

"Captain," Chur said, businesslike, "all lines are loose and cargo ramp is disengaged. In case."

"Well done," Pyanfar said, vastly relieved to hear it. They walked through the airlock and round the bend into the main lower corridor. "Secure the Outsider; sedate it all the way. You—" She looked aside at Tirun, who was trying to walk again with an arm across her sister's shoulders. "Get a wrap on that leg fast. No time for anything more. We're getting loose. I don't imagine *Hinukku* will stand still for this and I don't want kif passing my tail while we're nose-to-station. Everyone rig for maneuvers."

"I can wrap my own leg," Tirun said. "Just drop me in sickbay."

"Hilfy," Pyanfar said, collected her niece as she headed for the lift. "Disobedient," Pyanfar muttered when they were close.

"Forgive," said Hilfy. They entered the lift together; the door shut. Pyanfar fetched the youngster a cuff which rocked her against the lift wall, and pushed the mainlevel button. Hilfy righted herself and disdained even to clap a hand to her ear, but her eyes were watering, her ears flattened and nostrils wide as if she were facing into some powerful wind. "Forgiven," said Pyanfar. The lift let them out, and Hilfy started to run up the corridor toward the bridge, but Pyanfar stalked along at a more deliberate pace and Hilfy paused and matched her stride, walked with her through the archway into the curved-deck main operations center.

Pyanfar sat down in her cushion in the center of a bank of vid screens and started turning on systems. Station was squalling stsho language protests, objections, outrage. "Get on that," Pyanfar said to her niece without missing a beat in switch-flicking. "Tell station we're cutting loose and they'll have to cope with it."

A delay. Hilfy relayed the message in limping stsho, ignoring the mechanical translator in her haste. "They complain you killed someone."

"Good." The grapples clanged loose and a telltale said they had retracted all the way. "Tell them we rejoice to have eliminated a kif who started firing without provocation, endangering bystanders

and property on the dock." She fired the undocking repulse and
they were loose, sudden loss of *g* and reacquisition in another direction . . . fired the secondaries which sent *The Pride* out of
plane with station, a redirection of up and down. Ship's *g* started
up, a slow tug against the thrust aft.

"Station is mightily upset," Hilfy reported. "They demand to
talk to you, aunt. They threaten not to let us dock at stsho—"

"Never mind the stsho." Pyanfar flicked from image to image
on scan. She spotted another ship loose, in about the right location
for *Hinukku*. Abruptly the scan acquired all kinds of flitter on it,
chaff more than likely, as *Hinukku* screened itself to do something. "Gods rot them." She reached madly for controls and got
The Pride reoriented gently enough to save the bones of those
aboard who might not yet be secured for maneuvers . . . warning
enough for those below to dive for security. "If they fire on us
they'll take out half the station. Gods!" She hit general com.
"Brace. We're backing hard."

This time things came loose. A notebook sailed across the section and landed somewhere forward, missing controls. Hilfy spat
and curses came back from com. *The Pride* was not made for such
moves. Nor for the next, which hammered against that backward
momentum and, nose dipped, shot them nadir of station (the
notebook flew back to its origins) and braked, another career of
fluttering pages.

"Motherless bastards," Pyanfar said. She punched controls,
linked turret to scan. It would swivel to any sighting, anything
massive. *"Now* let them put their nose down here." Her joints
were sore. Alarms were ringing and lights were flashing on the
maintenance board, cargo having broken loose. She ran her
tongue over the points of her teeth and wrinkled her nose for
breath, worrying what quadrant of the scan to watch. She put *The
Pride* into a slow axis rotation, gambling that the kif would not
come underside of station in so obvious a place as the one in line
with last-known-position. "Watch scan," she warned Hilfy, divert-
ing herself to monitor the op board half a heartbeat, to see that all
the telltales were what they ought to be. *"Haral, get up here."*

"Aunt!" Hilfy said. Pyanfar swung her head about again. A little dust had appeared on the screen, some of the chaff spinning
their way from above. She had the scan-linked fire control set
looser than that and the armament did not react. The lift back
down the corridor crashed and hummed in operation. Haral had

not acknowledged, but she was coming. "We fire on anything that shows solid," Pyanfar said. "Keep watching that chaff cloud, niece. And mind, it could be outright diversion. I don't trust anything."

"Yes," Hilfy said calmly enough. And then: *"Look out!"*

"Chaff," Pyanfar identified the flutter, her heart frozen by the yell. "Be specific to quadrant. Number's enough."

Running feet in the corridor. Haral was with them. Hilfy started to yield her place at scan; Haral slid into the third seat, adjusted the restraints.

"Didn't plan to do so much moving," Pyanfar said, never taking the focus of her eyes from scan. "Anyone hurt?"

"No," said Haral. "Everything's secure."

"They're thinking it over up there," Pyanfar said.

"Aunt! 4/2!"

Turret was swiveling. Eye tracked to the number-four screen. Energy washed over station's rim: more chaff followed, larger debris.

"Captain, they hit station." Haral's voice was incredulous. "They *fired.*"

"Handur's Voyager." Pyanfar had the origin mapped on the station torus and made the connection. "O gods." She hit repulse and sent them hurtling to station core shadow, tilted their nose with a second burst and cut in main thrust, shooting them nadir of station, nose for infinity. Pyanfar reached and uncapped a red switch, hit it, and *The Pride* rocked with explosion.

"What was *that?*" Hilfy's voice. "Are we hit?"

"I just dumped our holds." Pyanfar sucked air, an expansion of her nostrils. Her claws flexed out and in on the togglegrip. *G* was hauling at them badly. *The Pride of Chanur* was in full rout, having just altered the mass/drive ratio, stripped for running. "Haral, get us a course."

"Working," Haral said. Numbers started coming up on the comp screen at Pyanfar's left.

"Going to have to find us a quiet spot."

"Urtur's just within singlejump range," Haral said, "stripped as we are. Maybe."

"Has to be." Beyond Meetpoint in the other direction was stsho space, with a great scarcity of jumppoints to help them along, those masses by which *The Pride* or any other jumpship steered; and on other sides were kif regions, and knnn, and unexplored regions, uncharted, without jump coordinates. Jump blind into those and they would never come back again . . . anywhere known.

She livened another board, bringing up jump-graphs. Urtur. That was the way they had come in, two jumps and loaded—a very large system where mahendo'sat did a little mining, a little manufacture, and licensed others. They *might* make that distance in one jump now; kif were not following . . . yet. Did not have to follow. They could figure possible destinations by dumped mass and the logic of the situation. *O my brother,* she thought, wondering how she would face Kohan. He would be affected by this disgrace, this outrage of lost cargo, of flight while a hani ship perished station-bound and helpless. Kohan Chanur might be broken by it; it might tempt young males to challenge him. And if there were enough challenges, and often enough. . . .

No. Not that kind of end for Chanur. There was no going home with that kind of news. Not until kif paid, until *The Pride* got things to rights again.

"Mark fifteen to jumppoint," Haral said. "Captain, they'll trace us, no question."

"No question," she said. Beyond Haral's scarred face she caught sight of Hilfy's, unmarred and scant-bearded—frightened and trying not to show it. Pyanfar opened allship: "Rig for jump."

The alarm started, a slow wailing through the ship. *The Pride* leapt forward by her generation pulses, borrowed velocity at the interface, several wrenching flickers, whipped into the between. Pyanfar dug her claws in, decades accustomed to this, did that mental wrench which told lies to the inner ears, and kept her balance. *Come on,* she willed the ship, as if intent alone could take it that critical distance farther.

iii

The Pride came in, a sluggish, nightmare arrival, pulsed out and in again, a flickering of jump-distorted instruments which showed them far out on the Urtur range, not close enough to pick up more than an indication of a stellar mass.

Near miss. They had stretched it as far as it could be stretched. Pyanfar struggled to move in her cushion, fighting to aim the fingers of her hand, to shut down all scan, running lights, the weak locational and ID transmission, every emission from the ship, forgetting nothing in the mental confusion which went with emergence. Then she started the sequence to bleed off their velocity, an uncomfortable ride, even as nightmare-slow as they were moving on their emergence. She kept her mind focused, trying not to let her thoughts stray to the horror at the back of it, how fine they had cut it.

Hilfy threw up, not an uncommon reaction to the shift. It did not help Pyanfar's own stomach.

"We're dumping down to systemic drift velocity," Pyanfar said on allship. "Possibly the kif stayed to sort through what we jettisoned, but they'll be here in short order. Or they're already here . . . with likely more kif here to help them. I'll be very surprised otherwise. We've shut down all transmission, all scan output. No use of the main engines either. Everyone still all right down there?"

There was prolonged delay in response. "Looks to be," Tirun's voice came back from lowerdeck op, which had lost most of what it was primarily designed to monitor when the holds blew. "Chur and Geran are starting a check by remote, but it looks like it was a clean separation when we blew it out. All working systems are clean."

The velocity dump went on. Hilfy moved about, cleaning up in shame. Haral stayed her post. Pyanfar occupied herself with feverish calculations and sorted and calculated on that one arrival image they had gotten before scan shut down, and on what they had on passive recept. She did a delicate attitude adjustment, trimmed up relative to the flow they were trying to enter, to present the least surface and the least delicate portion of them to hazard—put *The Pride* into synch with the general rotation of the system, one with the debris and the rock and gas which made Urtur, spread out over the orbits of ten planets and fifty-seven major moons and uncounted planetoids and smaller hazards, one of the more difficult systems for the rapid passage of any ship into its central plane. *The Pride* was picking up decayed signal from a mahendo'sat installation further in . . . at least that station should be the origin of it, chatter meaningless not only in the distance but in elapsed time since its sending. Some might be scatter from ships operating in the system, traders, countless miners in ships of all sizes from the great ore carriers down to single-seat skimmers. In due course they themselves ought to announce presence and identity, but she had no intention of doing so. There was an excellent chance that their arrival had been far beyond the capacity of the longest scan from outsystem relay, and she saw no profit in bringing the mahendo'sat of Urtur in on a private quarrel with the kif. The kif could have arrived days ago, bypassing them in the between, which could happen with a more powerful ship—system chatter might reveal that. She kept listening to it with one ear, finished up the dump, pulling them finally into trim, counting to herself and hoping her position was what she thought it was.

The Pride drifted then, still maintaining rotation for *g*, but nothing else of movement. She kept counting. Debris suddenly rang off the unshielded hull, distant battering, a few crashes and squeals of larger objects. Target dead on; she had it, a mob of rocks a little off their velocity, cold mass swarming about them, a screen between them and the kif's possible arrival. She feathered directional jets and trimmed up again. The battering diminished to an occasional patter of dust. Hilfy, standing by the com console counter, looked about her as if she could expect to see the impacts with all their sensor eyes dark; met Pyanfar's face and looked then at Haral, who grimly sat her post and kept trying to plot their position; and Hilfy composed her own face, managed not to flinch when another rock shrilled down the forward-thrusting bow.

Pyanfar heaved her aching body out of the cushion, staggered in walking around the dividing console to put her hand on the back of Haral's cushion. "Put the pagers in link," she told Haral. "Keep it channel one and see that someone's always on it. Tie into lowerdeck op: they'll be working down there a while yet. The kif will show, never doubt it. So we lie still, rest up. We receive signal; we don't send; we don't maneuver. We don't do anything now but drift."

"Aye." Haral started making the links, shunting over some of com function, an operation which Hilfy should have done. Her broad, scarred face was without disturbance at this insanity. Haral knew the game; they had done it a time or two, this prolonged dark silence, waiting out a kif or an unknown—but not in Urtur's debris-cluttered field, not where other ships were likely and collision was possible. Haral knew. It was Hilfy for whom she offered instructions.

Pyanfar took her own pager from the wall by the exit and went back to give one to Hilfy, who was leaning against the counter, nostrils slitted and ears laid back. Pyanfar clapped her on the shoulder and thrust the pager into her hand. "Out. Go. Everything's about to go under automatic here, and there's nothing you can do." She passed by Hilfy and headed out her own way down the corridor outside, with a foul headache, a worry in her gut, and an obsessive desire for a bath.

Her quarters, left unsecured, were not as bad as they might have been. The spring covers had held on the round bed, and the only casualty was a pile of charts now randomized. She gritted her teeth against the throbbing in her skull and picked them up, straightened the edges and slapped the unsorted pile back onto the desk, then stripped off her bloody clothes, brushed dried blood from her fur and a cloud of shed fur, too. She always shed in jump . . . sheer fright. Her muscles were tight. She flexed her cramped shoulders and an arm strained from fighting g, a stitch all the way into her rib muscles; and she picked up the pager again and took it with her into the bath, listening to it, which had nothing but static—set it on the bathroom counter before getting into the shower cabinet.

The shower was pure delight, warm and soothing. She lifted her face to it, letting the stream from the jet comb her mane and beard into order, turned her back and let the spray massage the pain out of her tired shoulders.

The pager went off, emergency beep. She spat a curse and flung the shower door open, skidded on the floor and ran out of the bath and out of her quarters naked and dripping as she was. She met Haral and Hilfy returning separately and beat them to the central console.

A ship was out there all right, some way distant, where no ship had been previously—an arrival out of jump. Pyanfar leaned over the board, wiped a bit of water off the screen, trying to avoid dripping. The newcomer was closer to Urtur than they, a good distance inward and zenith—had actually arrived a while ago; passive recept picked it up from its inherent noise.

"Better part of an hour backtime," Haral calculated. "I can fine it down."

"Do that."

They watched it a while, while Pyanfar dripped a cold puddle on the decking and the counter. "Going inward," she pronounced finally on the figures Hilfy passed her, checked against current reception. "If that's the kif, they overjumped us and now they've got a bit of hunting to do. We have a wave just getting to them, but it's got nothing for them, nothing they're going to know from all the rest of the junk out here. Good." She recalled her condition and straightened from bending over the board. "Mop that," she said to Hilfy, who was juniormost. She strode off, pricklish in her dignity.

"Captain," Haral's voice came over the pager, and Pyanfar crossed the cabin in two strides to reach the com by her bedside . . . punched it with a forefinger, comb clenched in the same hand. "Receiving you."

"Got some chatter that doesn't sound good," Haral said. "I think there are kif here, all right. What came into the system a while ago isn't certain, but it could be mahendo'sat; and I'm getting kif voices and kif signal out of system center."

"Doesn't surprise me. Pity the *mahe* who dropped into *this* pond, if that's what's happened. But it might cover any noise we made in entry, if that's what it is."

"Might do," Haral said. "Gods, Captain, no telling how many

kif there may have been at Urtur to start with. They're going to swarm all over the mahendo'sat."

"Gods know how much kif trouble they've already had here. That bunch from Meetpoint could have gotten as much as five, six days' jump on us. Forget it. Let it rest. Our business is our own business."

"Aye," Haral said reluctantly.

"Shut it down, Haral. Until they come after us, we're snug."

"Aye, Captain."

The contact broke off. Pyanfar drew a long breath and let it go, stood in front of the unit and after a moment punched in the image they *could* get, from the telescope in the observation dome. Urtur was a glorious sight . . . at a distance, a saucer of milky light. A shadow passed the image, a bit of rock, doubtless, part of the swarm with which they traveled. She shut it down again. They rolled along blind, getting a tap on the hull now and again from debris, muted this far into *The Pride*'s core, as they played their part as a mote in Urtur's vast lens. This silence was an old trick. It worked . . . sometimes.

She continued her combing, and finally, pelt dried, mane and beard combed and silky again in their ringlets, changed to her third-best trousers, of black silk, with green and gold cuffing and belt, a round-the-hips dangle of real gold chains. She changed her pearl earring for an emerald, inspected her claws and trimmed a roughness. A tip had broken. Hardskinned, the kif. But she had got him, that bastard on the dock. That was at least some consolation for the lost cargo and Tirun's misery. For hani lives—that was yet to collect.

She strolled out again, into controls, where Hilfy was standing lone watch. They had far more room when they were under rotation, with the ship's *g* making the crew's private quarters and a great deal of the storage accessible, as well as that large forward ell of the control area itself which was out of reach during dock. Some of the crew ought to be offshift now, eating, sleeping. They arranged such details among themselves when things were tight, knowing best when they needed rest and balancing the ship's needs against their own. Hilfy had a bruised look when she turned to face Pyanfar as she came up behind her in the semishadow of the bridge, amid dead screens and virtually lightless panels. She stood there as if there was something she could hope to do, ears pricked up and eyes wide-irised with her general distress.

"Haral left you on watch, imp?"

"Haral said she was going below."

"I thought I dismissed you."

"I thought it wouldn't hurt to be here. I can't rest."

"Can't rest is a cheat on the ship. Can't rest is something you learn to remedy, imp. It's going to be too long a wait to wear ourselves to rags up here. Nothing we can do."

"Com keeps coming in. It's them—it's the same kif. They're asking the mahendo'sat ships where we are and they're making threats. They call us thieves."

Pyanfar spat dryly and chuckled. "What tender honor. What are the mahendo'sat doing about it?"

"Nothing. It *is* a mahendo'sat station, after all; there are other ships—all over the place—there's help for them, isn't there? I'd think they'd *do* something, not just let the kif do what they please."

"There may be a lot of kif, too." Pyanfar leaned forward and checked the boards herself, the little data the computer got off passive recept. A rock hit them, a slow scream down the metal; a screen flickered to static and corrected itself, an impact on one of the antennae. "I won't tell you, imp, just how close we came to losing our referents in that jump. If that kif ship did get here ahead of us, it's considerably more powerful than we are. All power and precious little cargo room. That tell you anything?"

"It's not a freighter."

"Kif runner. Got a few false tanks strapped on, all shell and no mass to speak of, masking what she is. You understand? Ships like that do the kill; the carrion eaters come after, real freighters, that suck up the cargoes and do the dockside trading when they do get to some port. That's what we're probably up against. A runner. A hunter ship. They overestimated our capacity . . . overjumped us, more than likely, and incoming traffic may have been good enough to confuse the issue further. If that's the case we've just used up all the luck we're entitled to."

"Are we just going to sit here?" Hilfy asked. "Ship after ship is going to come into this system not knowing what they're running into . . . all those ships from Meetpoint that don't go the stsho route—"

"Imp, we're blind at the moment. We've dumped velocity . . . and maybe some of those hunting us haven't; and maybe some are yet to come. You know what kind of situation that puts us in. Sitting target."

"If they all stay to centerward," Hilfy suggested cautiously, "we could just jump out again . . . be gone before they could catch us, take the pressure off these *mahe* before someone else gets hurt. Maybe we could get away with it again at the next jumppoint, get to Kirdu . . . after Urtur, couldn't we maybe make Kirdu in two jumps? Get out of here. After this place, there are other choices. Aren't there?"

Pyanfar stared at her. "Been doing some research, have you?"

"I looked."

"Huh." It was a sensible idea, and one she had had even before the jump, but there were loose pieces in this business. Moves not yet calculated. It remained to measure how upset the kif were. And why. "Possible." She jabbed a finger at Hilfy. "First we take account of ourselves. We go down, shall we, and see what we have left of cargo."

"I thought we dumped it all."

"Oh, not what the kif want, not that, niece." She leaned over the console, checked the pager link. "I think we can leave it a while. Come along. It's all being recorded, all the com and scan up here. We'll check it. Can't live up here." She set her hand on Hilfy's shoulder. "We go ask some questions, that's what."

Their uninvited passenger had settled after jump—cocooned in blankets and sedated for the trip, now let go again, to huddle in that heap of blankets in the corner of the washroom. It had curled up in a knot and thrown one of the blankets over its head, showing nothing but the motions of its breathing.

"The ankle restraint is back on it," Chur said as they watched it from the doorway. "It's been docile all along . . . but let me call Geran and we'll be sure of it." Chur was smallest of the crew, smaller than Geran, her sister, who was herself of no great stature —with a thin beard and mane and a yellowish tint to her fur; delicate, one might say, not knowing Chur.

"There are three of us," Pyanfar said, "already. Let's see how it reacts." She walked into the washroom and came near the heap of breathing blankets. Coughed. There was movement in the blankets, the lifting of a corner, a furtive look of a pale eye from beneath them. Pyanfar beckoned.

It stopped moving.

"It quite well understands me," she said. "I think, Chur, you're going to have to get Geran. We may have to fetch it out and I don't want to hurt it."

Chur left. Hilfy remained. The blankets stirred again, and the creature made a faltering effort to get its back into the angle of the corner made by the shower stall and the laundry.

"It's just too weak," Hilfy said. "Aunt, it's just too weak to fight."

"I'll stand here," Pyanfar proposed. "There's a mahendo'sat symbol translator and some manuals and modules; Haral said she put it in the lower-deck op. I want the elementary book. Gods forbid someone put it into cargo."

Hilfy hesitated, cast a look at the Outsider, then scurried off in haste.

"So," Pyanfar said. She dropped to her haunches as she had before, put out a forefinger and traced numbers from one to eight on the flooring. Looked up from time to time and looked at the creature, who watched her. It reached out of its nest of blankets and made tentative movements of writing on the floor, drew back the arm and watched what she was doing until she stopped at sixteen. It tucked the blankets more closely about itself and stared, from bleak, blue eyes. Washed, it looked better. The mane and beard were even beautiful, silken, pollen-gold. But the naked arm outthrust from the blankets bore ugly bruises of fingered grips. There had been a lot of bruises under the dirt, she reckoned. It had a reason for its attitude. It was not docile now, just weak. It had drawn another line, staked out its corner. The blue eyes held a peculiar expression, analysis, perhaps, some thought proceeding at length.

She stood up, hearing Chur and Geran coming, their voices in the corridor—turned and motioned them to wait a moment when they arrived. She watched the Outsider's pale eyes take account of the reinforcements. And Hilfy came back with the manual. "It was in the—" Hilfy broke off, in the general stillness of the place.

"Give it here," Pyanfar said, holding out her hand without looking away from the Outsider.

Hilfy gave it. Pyanfar opened the book, turned the pages toward the Outsider, whose eyes flickered with bewilderment. She bent, discarding her dignity a moment in the seriousness of the matter, and pushed the manual across the tiles to the area the creature could reach. It ignored the open book. Another ploy failed. Pyanfar sat still a moment, arms on her knees, then stood up and brushed her silk breeches into order. "I trust the symbol translator made it intact."

"It's fine," Hilfy said.

"So let's try that. Can you set it up?"

"I learned on one."

"Do it," Pyanfar said and motioned to Geran and Chur. "Get it on its feet. Be gentle with it."

Hilfy hurried off. Geran and Chur moved in carefully and Pyanfar stepped out of the way, thinking it might turn violent, but it did not. It stood up docilely as they patted it and assisted it to its feet. It was naked, and *he* was a reasonable guess, Pyanfar concluded, watching it make a snatch after the blankets about its feet, while Chur carefully unlocked the chain they had padded about its ankle, Geran holding onto its right arm. Pyanfar frowned, disturbed to be having a male on the ship, with all the thoughts *that* stirred up. Chur and Geran were being uncommonly courteous with it, and that was already a hazard.

"Look sharp," Pyanfar said. "Take it to the op room and mind what you're doing." She stooped and gathered up the symbol book herself as they led it out toward the door.

The Outsider balked of a sudden in the doorway, and Chur and Geran patted its hairless shoulders and let it think about it a long moment, which seemed the right tack to take. It stood a very long moment, looked either way down the corridor, seemed frozen, but then at a new urging—"Come on," Geran said in the softest possible voice and tugged very slightly—the Outsider decided to cooperate and let itself be led into the hall and on toward operations. Pyanfar followed with the book under her arm, scowling for the cost the Outsider had already been to them, and with the despondent feeling that she might yet be wrong in every assumption she had made. They had paid far too much for that.

And then what? Give it back to the kif after all, and shrug and pretend it had been nothing?

The Outsider balked more than once in being moved, looked about it at such intervals as if things were moving too fast for it and it had to get its bearings. Chur and Geran let it stop when it would, never hurrying it, then coaxed it gently. It walked for them —perhaps, Pyanfar thought sourly, biding its time, testing their reflexes, memorizing the corridors, if it had the wit to do so.

They brought it into the op room, in front of all the boards and the glowing lights, and it balked again, hard-breathing, looking about. Now, Pyanfar thought, they might have trouble; but no, it let itself be moved again and let itself be put into one of the cushions at the dead cargo-monitor console, near the counter where Hilfy worked over the translator, running a series of figures over the screen. The Outsider slumped when seated, dazed-looking and sweating profusely, tucked in its blanket which it clutched about itself. Pyanfar walked up to the arm of the cushion; its head came up instantly at her presence and the wariness came back into its eyes. More than wariness. Fear. It remembered who had hurt it. It knew them as individuals, past a clothing change. That at least.

"Hai," Pyanfar said in her best friend-to-outsiders manner, patted its hairless, sweating shoulder, swept Hilfy aside in her approach to the translator, a cheap, replaceable stickered keyboard unit linked by cable into one of their none so cheap scanners. She pushed *wipe,* clearing Hilfy's figures, then the Bipedal Sentient button, with a stick figure of a long-limbed being spread eagled on it. The same figure appeared on the screen. She pushed the next, which showed a hani in photographic image, and indicated herself.

It understood. Its eyes were bright with anxiety. It clutched its blanket tighter and made a faltering attempt to get its feet back on the floor and to stand, reaching toward the machine. "Let it loose," Pyanfar said, and Chur helped it up. It ignored them all, leaned on the counter and poised a trembling hand over the keyboard. The whole arm shook. It punched a button.

Ship. It looked up, its eyes seeking understanding.

Pyanfar carefully took its alien hand, oh, so carefully, but it allowed the touch. She extended its forefinger and guided it to the *wipe* button, back to the ship button again. It freed its hand and searched, the hand shaking violently as it passed above the keys. Figure Running, it keyed. Ship. Figure Running. Ship again. Hani. *Wipe.* It looked about at her.

"Yes," she said, recognizing the statement. Motioned for it to do more.

It turned again, made another search of the keys. Figure Supine, it stated. It found the pictorial for kif. That long-snouted gray face lit the screen beside the Figure Supine.

"Kif," Pyanfar said.

It understood. That was very clear. "Kif," it echoed. It had a voice full of vibrant sounds, like purring. It was strange to hear it articulate a familiar word . . . hard to pick that word out when the tongue managed neither the kif click nor the hani cough. And the look in its eyes now was more than apprehensive. Wild. Pyanfar put her claws out and demonstratively rested her hand over the image. Pushed *wipe*. She put the hani symbol back on, punched in voice-record; *hani,* the audio proclaimed, in hani mode. She picked up the cheap mike and spoke for the machine's study-tape, with the machine recording her voice. "Hani." She called up another image. "Stand." A third. "Walk."

It took a little repetition, but the Outsider began to involve itself in the process and not in its trembling hysteria over the kif image. It started with the first button . . . worked at the system, despite its physical weakness, recorded its own identification for all the simple symbols on the first row, soberly, with no joy in its discovery, but not sluggishly either. It began to go faster and faster, jabbed keys, spoke, one after the other, madly rapid, as if it were proving something. There were seventy-six keys on that unit and it ran through the lot, although toward the end its hand was hardly controllable.

Then it stopped and turned that same sullen look on them and reached for the seat it had left. It barely made it, sank down in the cushion and wrapped its blanket up about its shoulders, pale and sweating.

"It's gone its limit," Pyanfar said. "Get it some water."

Chur brought it from the dispenser. The Outsider accepted it one-handed, sniffed the paper cup, then drained it. It gave the empty cup back, pointed at itself, at the machine on the counter, looked at Pyanfar, correctly assessing who was in charge. It wanted, Pyanfar read the gestures, to continue.

"Hilfy," Pyanfar said, "the manual, on the counter. Give it here."

Hilfy handed it over. Pyanfar searched through the opening pages for the precise symbols of the module in the machine at present. "How many of those modules do we have?"

"Ten. Two manuals."

"That ought to carry us into abstracts. Good for Haral." She set the opened book into the Outsider's lap and pointed at the symbols it had just done, showed it how far the section went. Now it made the connection. It gathered the book against itself with both arms, intent on keeping it. "Yes," Pyanfar said, and nodded confirmation. Maybe nodding was a gesture they shared; it nodded in return, never looking happy, but there was less distress in its look. It clutched its book the tighter.

Pyanfar looked at Hilfy, at Geran and Chur, whose expressions were guarded. They well knew now what level of sentient they had aboard. How much they guessed of their difficulties with the kif was another matter: a lot, she reckoned—they picked up things out of the air, assembled them themselves without having to ask. "A passenger compartment," she said. "I think it might like clothes. Food and drink. Its book. Clean bedding and a bed to sleep in. *Civilized* facilities. That doesn't mean you shouldn't be careful with it. Let's move it, shall we, and let it rest."

It looked from Chur to Geran as the two closed in, grew distressed when Chur took its arm to get it on its feet. It pointed back at the machine . . . wanted that, its chance to communicate. Perhaps there was more it planned to say, in the symbols. Surely it expected to go back to the washroom corner. Pyanfar reached and touched its shoulder from the other side, touched the book it held and pressed its hand the tighter against it, indicating it should keep the book, the best promise she could think of that might tell it they were not done with talking. It calmed itself, at least, let itself be drawn to its feet and, once steadied, led out.

Pyanfar looked at the machine on the counter, walked over and turned it off. Hilfy was still standing there. "Move the whole rig," Pyanfar said. "We'll risk the equipment." She unplugged the keyboard module, which was no burden at all, but awkward. "Bring the screen."

"Aunt," said Hilfy, "what are we going to do with him?"

"That depends on what the kif had in mind to do with him. But we can hardly ask them, can we?" She followed after the Outsider and Chur and Geran, down the side corridor to one of the three rooms they kept for *The Pride*'s occasional paying passengers, up the curve into the area of the crew's private quarters. They were nicely appointed cabins. The one Chur and Geran had selected was in fresh greens with woven grass for the walls and with the bed and chairs in pale lime complement. Pyanfar counted the damage possible and winced, but they had suffered far worse in the cause than torn upholstery.

And the Outsider seemed to recognize a major change in its fortunes. It stood in the center of the room clutching its book and its blanket and staring about with a less sullen expression than before . . . seemed rather dazed by it all, if its narrow features were at all readable. "Better show it the sanitary facilities first," Pyanfar said. "I hope it understands."

Chur took it by the arm and drew it into the bath, carefully. Hilfy brought the screen in and Pyanfar added the module as she set it on the counter and plugged it into the auxiliary com/comp receptacle. From the bath there came briefly the sound of the shower working, then the toilet cycling. Chur brought the Outsider back into the main room, both looking embarrassed. Then the Outsider saw the translator hookup sitting on the counter, and its eyes flickered with interest.

Not joy. There was never that.

It said something. Two distinct words. For a moment it sounded as if it were speaking its own language. And then it sounded vaguely kif. Pyanfar's ears pricked up and she drew in a breath. "Say again," she urged it in kif, and made an encouraging motion toward her ear, standard dockside handsign.

"Kif . . . companion?"

"*No.*" She drew a deeper breath. "Bastard! You *do* understand." And again in kif: "Who are you? What kind are you?"

It shook its head, seeming helpless. Evidently *who* was not part of its repertoire. Pyanfar considered the anxious Outsider thoughtfully, reached and set her hand on Chur's convenient shoulder. "This is Chur," she said in kif. And in hani: "You do me a great favor, cousin, you sit with this Outsider on your watch. You keep him going on those identifications, change modules the minute you've got one fully identified, the audio track filled. Keep him at it while he will but don't force him. You know how to work it?"

"Yes," Chur said.

"You be careful. No knowing what it's thinking, what it's been through, and I don't put deviousness beyond its reach either. I want it communicative; don't be rough with it, don't frighten it. But don't put yourself in danger either. Geran, you stay outside, do your operations monitor by pager so long as Chur's inside, hear?"

Geran's ears—the right one was notched, marring what was otherwise a considerable beauty—flicked in distress, a winking of gold rings on the left. "Clearly understood," she said.

"Hilfy." Pyanfar motioned to her niece and started out the door. The Outsider started toward them, but Chur's outflung arm prevented it and it stopped, not willing to quarrel. Chur spoke to it quickly, gingerly touched its bare shoulder. It looked frightened, for the first time outright frightened.

"I think it wants *you*, aunt," Hilfy observed.

Pyanfar laid her ears back, abhorring the thought of fending off a grab at her person, walked out with Hilfy unhurried all the same. She looked back from the doorway. "Be careful with it," she told Chur and Geran again. "Ten times it may be gentle and agreeable . . . and go for your throat on the eleventh."

She walked off, the skin of her shoulders twitching with distaste. Hilfy trailed her, but Pyanfar jammed her hands into the back of her waistband and took no notice of her niece until they had gotten to the lift. Hilfy pressed the button to open the door and they got in. Pressed central; it brought them up and still without a word Pyanfar walked out into the bridgeward corridor.

"Aunt," Hilfy said.

Pyanfar looked back.

"What shall we do with it?"

"I'm sure I don't know," Pyanfar said tartly. Her ears were still back. She purposely put on a better face. "Not your fault, niece. This one is my own making."

"I'd take some of the slack; I'd help, if I knew what to do. With the cargo gone—"

Pyanfar frowned and the ears went down again. *You want to relieve me of worry?* she thought. *Then don't do anything stupid.* But there was that face, young and proud and wanting to do well. Most that Hilfy knew how to do on the ship had gone when cargo blew and scan shut down. "Youngster, I've gotten into a larger game than I planned, and there's no going home until we've gotten it straightened out. How we do that is another question, because the kif know our name. Have you got an idea you've been sitting on?"

"No, aunt—being ignorant about too much."

Pyanfar nodded. "So with myself, niece. Let it be a lesson to you. My situation precisely, when I took the Outsider in, instead of handing it right back to the kif."

"We couldn't have given him to them."

"No," Pyanfar agreed heavily. "But it would certainly have been more convenient." She shook her head. "Go rest, whelp, and this time I mean it. You were sick during jump; you'll be lagging when I do need you. And need you I will." She walked on, into the bridge, past the archway. Hilfy did not follow. Pyanfar sat down at her place, among all the dead instruments, listened to the sometime whisper of larger dust over the hull, called up all the record which had flowed in while she was gone, listening to that with one ear and the current comflow with the other.

Bad news. A second arrival in the system . . . more than one ship. It might be kif, might be someone else from the disaster at Meetpoint. In either case it was bad. The ones already here were on the hunt beyond question—kif were upset enough to have dumped cargo to get here from Meetpoint; no other ships had cause to hunt *The Pride,* or to call them thief. They were the same kif, beyond doubt, upset enough to have banded together in a hunt. Bad news all the way.

Urtur Station was into the comflow now . . . bluster, warning the kif of severe penalties and fines. That was very old chatter, from the beginning of the trouble, a wavefront just now reaching them. Threats from the kif—those were more current. The mahendo'sat ship . . . harassed, made its way stationward. The kif turned their attention to the new arrivals, to other things. They would begin to figure soon that the freighters last arrived had jumped behind *The Pride.* That *The Pride* had to have tricked them and gone elsewhere into stsho territories, or had to be here . . . doing precisely what they were doing; and very probably a nervous kif would play the surmise he had already staked his reputation on. They would start hunting shadows once they reached that conclusion, having questioned a few frightened *mahe.* They would fan out, prowl the system, stop minerships, ask close questions, probably commit small piracy at the same time, not to waste an opportunity. The Station could do nothing; a larger one might, but not Urtur, which was mostly manufacturing and scarcely defended. No mahendo'sat ship would be willing to be stopped—but there was no hope for them of outrunning that hyped kif ship, no chance, at least, which an ordinary mahendo'sat captain was equipped to take.

And there was no chance that one of those ships incoming from Meetpoint would turn out to be hani, and relieve them all of that guilt. *Handur's Voyager* was gone, beyond hope and help. Not even proximity to Meetpoint was likely to have saved anyone in that attack. The kif were nothing if not thorough: they practiced bloodfeud themselves, and left no survivors.

Kif had somehow missed killing one another off in their rise off their homeworld and into space. They had done it, hani had always suspected, in mutual distrust, in outright hatred. They had *contested* themselves into space, and hunted each other through it until they found easier pickings.

Not *The Pride,* she swore, and not Pyanfar Chanur.

That kif who was in command out there—she was certain beyond question that it was Akukkakk of *Hinukku,* who had come ahead to stake out Urtur and wait for them—once that kif knew they had gotten through, he would be checking all his backtime records, sniffing through everything hoping to catch some missed trace of *The Pride*'s arrival. They had left very little of a wavefront ghost to detect; but there might be something, some small missed flicker.

Running—now—had its hazards. As long as some of the kif shuttled the system at relatively high velocity, those ships could run down on them while they were trying to build theirs back from virtual dead stop. Their chances of breaking cover and running depended on the position of the kif ships, whether they had that critical time they might need to get their referent and to come up to position to jump. Blind as they had made themselves, the only way to find out where those ships were was to try something; and the only way to find out how many there were was to keep an ear to the kif chatter and see if they could pick out individual ships.

This Akukkakk would not be likely to be so careless. It was certain enough they were not outputting ID signal, which itself brought protests from the station; no ID signal and no locational signal from any of them. Only from miners and legitimate residents—if those signals were what they ought to be.

So, so, so. They were in a bottle, and it was too much to hope that the kif would not ultimately coerce mahendo'sat help in the hunt for them. Station and miners could be intimidated as the kif put the pressure on. What was more, hani ships came and went at Urtur, and those ships would be vulnerable to the kif, unsuspecting of atrocity such as the kif had committed at Meetpoint. They would come into confrontation with the kif having no idea of the stakes involved here. The kif might act against them without warning, to draw *The Pride* out. Such tactics were not hani practice; but she had been many years off Anuurn and among outsiders, and she knew well enough how to think like a kif, even if the process turned her stomach and bristled the hairs on her nape.

And then what do I do? she wondered to herself. *Do I come out meekly to die? Or let others?* Her crew had no more and no less right to life than the crew of any other hani ship which came straying into the trap. There were their lives involved. There was Hilfy's. And thereby—all of Chanur.

Next time home, she vowed, *I get that other gun battery moduled in, whatever it costs.*

Next time home.

She frowned, cut off the recording, which had come to the point at which she had come in. The present transmissions were few and terse. Someone should be up here directly and constantly monitoring the comflow and the rest. Hilfy was right on that score. But they were not a fighting ship and they had no personnel to spare for battle. Six of them, with ordinary duties and a prisoner to watch; there was course to plot, there were checks to be run after their jump under stress, systems they had to be sure of, and there was the chance that they might have to move, defend themselves and run at any moment, which meant three crew members had to be mentally and physically fit to take action at any instant, whatever the hour. The automations which ran *The Pride* in her normal workaday business had nothing to do with their situation now, systems overstressed from a jump the ship was never designed to make, makeshift security on an alien and possibly lunatic passenger. Gods. She double-checked the pager operation, which was transmission activated, advised the crew on watch that she was taking over monitor for a while, to give them rest from the responsibility.

"He's all right," Geran reported on the Outsider. "Resting a while."

It was good, she thought, that someone could.

She went finally to the galley, up the curve; she had no appetite in particular, but her limbs were weak from hunger. She heated up a meal from the freezer, forced it down against her stomach's earnest complaints, and tossed the dish into the sterilizer. Then she walked back to her private quarters to try to rest.

She fretted too much for sleep, paced the floor pointlessly, sorted the stack of charts into order and sat down and plotted and replotted possible alternatives, which she already guessed, against odds she already knew. At last she shoved all that work aside and used the console by her bed to link in on the Outsider's terminal, via main comp and access codes. It was active again; she heard the Outsider's voice as well as saw the symbols called up by the translator keys. He was using them one after the other, and when she keyed in on com as well, she could pick up Chur's voice in the room, quiet assistance—sounds which might go with pantomime. Occasionally there was a pairing of symbols the machine did not do—Chur's interference, perhaps, trying to get a point across. Pyanfar cut off com and the translator reception, stared at the dead screen. The chatter from Urtur system continued from the pager at her belt, subdued and depressing in content. Mahendo'sat ships were being advised by their own station not to run, to submit to search if singled out by the kif, to hug station if they were already there and hope for safety.

A hani voice objected a question.

Hani!

Pyanfar sprang from the bedside, the walls of her cabin immaterial before her vision of that station with a hani ship at dock; with kif able to move on it at will. The hani spoke . . . had spoken long ago, in the timelag. Whatever would happen . . . had long since taken place. Time as well as space lay between *The Pride* and that hani ship and the kif, and there was nothing she could do, blind, from a dead drift, to help it.

"*Gods!*" she spat, and hurled the desk chair forward on its track with a crash. It was a Faha vessel in port—*Faha's Starchaser* —and that was a house and a company allied to Chanur. Her brother Kohan's first wife was Huran Faha. Hilfy's mother, for the gods' sakes! There were bonds, compacts, agreements of alliance. . . .

And Hilfy.

The mahendo'sat at Urtur Station urged the hani ship to keep calm. The *mahe* had, they avowed, no intention of becoming involved in a kif quarrel, and they were not going to let a rash hani involve them.

The hani demanded information; kif hunted a Chanur ship. The Faha had been listening and fretting under restraint this long, and wanted answers. They knew this was going out over com, as the Station knew what the Faha were doing, making vocal trouble, making sure information got out into the dark where Chanur ears might pick it up.

O gods, o gods. There *was* an ally, doing the best for them that could be done at the moment . . . and they were both helpless to come at the enemy.

Pyanfar pulled the chair out again, sat down, lost in listening for a while. There was no further information. They had gotten that spurt on the station's longrange or on *Starchaser*'s . . . information like a beacon fired off into outsystem, deliberately. If they had it figured *The Pride* was here then so did the kif.

There were echoes, repetitions of the message; com was sorting them out, transmissions of differing degrees of clarity, and the hair prickled on Pyanfar's neck, with the sudden, grateful realization that ships all over the system had begun relaying that message, letting it off like multiple ripples in still water, massive defiance of the kif. And the kif had not ordered silence . . . on this timeline. They could not enforce such a demand, at the present limits of their aggression at Urtur, but those limits could change. The information was going out like a multiplied shout . . . had gone out, long ago, and was still traveling.

She found Hilfy for once where she was supposed to be, in her own quarters, asleep. She hesitated when the sleepy voice answered the doorcom hail, no more than hesitated. "Up," she said into the com. "I've somewhat to tell you."

Hilfy was quick to the door. It whipped open and Hilfy hung there, disheveled from bed and grimacing in the full light of the corridor. She had not paused for clothes.

Pyanfar walked in past her, waited while Hilfy brightened the interior lighting, and held up a restraining hand, that the brightening need not be permanent or full. It was a room Hilfy had made her own, a great deal of Chanur style in this cabin, more than in her own quarters, mementoes affixed to the walls, pictures of homeworld's mountains and the broad plains of the Chanur holdings, of the Holding itself, of gold stone, shaded with vines. Pyanfar looked about her, and looked at Hilfy. "Briefly," Pyanfar said, "I have to tell you a thing; and there's nothing can be done about it, I'll tell you that first. We've picked up a signal from a Faha ship docked at station. They're in the middle of the kif, and they fired a message off for station that I think they meant we should hear: noisy chatter. I think they know we're out here and in what kind of trouble. But there's the kif between us, and there's no way we can do much for each other. You understand?"

Hilfy's eyes had stopped flinching at the light. She stared, amber-rimmed about the black, and her ears flattened and pricked up again with effort. For a young woman and roused naked out of sleep, she acquired a quiet dignity in getting her wits collected. "Do you know which ship, aunt?"

"*Starchaser*. That's Lihan Faha in command."

Hilfy nodded. The ears flinched, ringless. Her face stayed composed. "They'll be in danger. Like *Voyager*. And they won't know it. No one would expect that kind of attack."

"Lihan's no tyro, imp, believe it. We don't play their hand; they don't interfere in ours. Can't. Nothing we can do out here."

"We could throw them a warning and run."

"I don't take that as an option at the moment. If we send it from distance the kif will have it before *Starchaser* has a chance. And that would constitute public defiance, involving *Starchaser* in our leaving, to which the kif would be obliged to react. For kif, revenge is part of their mindset. You have to calculate that into it. No. *Starchaser*'s riding her own luck. I don't plan to push it for her. So go back to bed, hear?"

Hilfy stood a moment without moving. Nodded after a moment, her dignity still about her.

"Good," Pyanfar said tightly, and walked out. She heard the door close after her, and walked the upcurving corridor which led from Hilfy's quarters to her own, across the main topside corridor and down a short distance.

So she might have cost Hilfy her sound sleep, and the meal she had eaten lay like lead at her own stomach, but Faha involvement in the hazard was not something for Hilfy to find out later, like a child, spared adult unpleasantnesses. Hilfy's face stayed before her; the pager unit at her hip kept up its static babble, dying echoes of the message, occasional spurts of closer transmission, but rarer and rarer. A stsho ship had come into the system. The kif disdained to harass it; it begged instructions of Urtur Station, anxious to scud in before the storm.

A lot of *mahe* in the system might have the same idea, for they would be miners who had already reckoned it time to head for port, getting themselves out of the way of the kif's hunt.

It was a vast system out there. Most of the ships in it were incapable of jump, insystem operators only. So far, everyone was keeping remarkably calm, even the hani at the eye of that storm.

Gods grant a great many ships pulled inward . . . and afforded the kif a harder target if they wanted to raid Station in search of one hani ship. That was one hope. Lihan Faha of *Starchaser* was too old, too wary to rush out to mismatched battle. Lihan would not expect stupidity of *The Pride*. The Faha would expect them to fend for themselves and above all not touch anything off prematurely. The Faha needed time. There was a chance that they could offload cargo and strip that ship down for speed, given time, shed mass without the need to lose a cargo. They would not expect any more help than that.

That was logic speaking.

But it hurt.

iv

She sat and listened a time in her cabin, finally contacted Geran belowdecks and turned over the monitoring to her. "Faha," was Geran's only comment.

"Hilfy knows," Pyanfar said.

"So," Geran murmured. And then: "I'm on. I've got it."

Pyanfar signed off and sighed heavily, sitting on the edge of her bed, arms on her knees—finally took a mild sedative and undressed and curled up in the bowlshaped bed for a precious while of oblivion, trying not to think of emergencies and contingencies and the horde of kif prowling about the system.

That did not work, but the sedative did. She went under like a stone into a pond and came out again startled by the alarm—but it was only the timer going off, and she lay in the bedclothes with her heart slowly stepping back down to normal.

"Any developments?" she asked lowerdeck op by com from her bedside. "Anything happened while I was off?"

"No, Captain." Haral's voice answered her. A shift change had occurred in her off time. "The situation seems to be temporary stalemate. Station is broadcasting only operational chatter now. We aren't getting much from the kif. Nothing alarming. We'd have waked you if there was news."

So their orders ran. Interpretations of emergency varied, but Haral was the wisest head in the crew, the canniest. Pyanfar lay there staring at the ceiling a moment and finally decided she might take her time. There was nowhere to rush. The rib muscles she had strained in *g* force had stiffened. "What about systems check? Has anyone had time to get to that?"

"We're still running the board, Captain, but it looks good all

the way. The blowout was absolutely clean and the recalibration
was right almost to the hair."

"Better luck than we deserve. What's the Outsider up to?"

"Back at work at the keyboard. Chur and Geran are off now,
and Tirun's on, but I didn't feel, by your leave, Captain, that
Tirun belonged in there with him in her condition, and I've had all
I can do with visual checks on the separation readouts—again by
your leave."

"You were right."

"He's slept a bit. He hasn't made any trouble. Gods, he worked
till he nearly dropped over, Chur said, and he's back at it again
this shift, shaky as he is. We fed him right away when he woke up,
and he ate it all and went back to his drills, polite as you please.
I've got his roomcom and his comp monitored from the op station,
so we've at least got an ear toward him."

"Huh." Pyanfar ran a hand through her mane and scowled up
at the brightening room light. The alarm had started the day cycle
in the room. "Let the Outsider work. If it falls over, then let it
rest. How's Tirun making it?"

"Limping, sore, and working with the leg propped up. She's still
white around the nose."

"I'm all right," Tirun's voice cut in.

"You go off," Pyanfar said, "anytime you feel you ought to.
We're dead drifting, and someone else can take up the slack if
those first checks are run. You see to it, Haral. Anything else I
should know?"

"That's the sum of it," Haral said. "We're all right so far."

"Huh," she said again, got out of the spring-held sheets and cut
the com off, pulled on her black trousers and put on her belt, her
bracelet, and her several earrings—shook the ear to settle them
and gave her mane and beard a quick comb into order. Vanity be
hanged. She left the cabin and paid a short visit to the galley, ate a
solitary breakfast, feeling somewhat better. She turned the pager
to the monitor channel in the meanwhile, listened to the chatter
which was reaching them and found it much what Haral had said,
a lull in events which in itself contained worrisome possibilities.
By now the kif had surely figured out what had happened, and by
now they would be hunting in stealth—hence the quiet. *The Pride*
had undergone a great deal of lateral drift from their entry point,
but if she were that kif captain, trying to reckon the arrival point
of a cargoless fugitive on a jump almost too much for the ship, she

would calculate a fringe area jump on a straight string from Meet-point's mass to that of Urtur. And that would narrow the hunting zone down considerably, from the vast tracts of Urtur's lenslike system to a specific zone on the fringe, and the direction of systemic drift, and certain places where a ship seeking cover might move. Time was the other factor; time defined the segment of space in which they might logically be drifting, two points-within-which, which then might be fined down tighter and tighter.

Time, time, and time.

They were running out of it.

She shut off the pager, went back to her cabin, spread out the charts of the last effort and picked up a comp link of her own, started as precise calculations as she could make on the options they had left.

From the hani ship—she interrupted herself to query Haral and Tirun on the point—there had been nothing during the past watch. No transmission at all. *Starchaser* would be feverishly busy at her own business, stripping down, not provoking anything at this juncture.

Waiting. All incoming transmission indicated that ships of all kinds were moving toward Urtur Station with all possible haste, a journey of days for some ships, and of weeks for others of the insystem operators . . . but even the gesture spoke to the kif, that the *mahe* would defend Urtur Station itself, abandoning other points to whatever the kif wished to do. The incoming jumpships had long since made it in, snugged close. They were armed ships, but one at least was stsho, and its arms were minor and its will to fight was virtually nonexistent.

Again, she reckoned, if she were that kif in command, those insystem ships would not go in unchallenged. For all those incoming from the suspect vector where a hani ship lay hidden, there would be closer scrutiny—to make sure a clever hani did not drift in disguised with the rest of the inbound traffic. ID transmission would be checked, identifications run through comp; ships might be boarded . . . all manner of unpleasantness. Most of them would pass visual inspection. There was precious little resemblance between a gut-blown jump freighter with its huge vanes, and a lumpy miner-processer whose propulsion was all insystem and hardly enough to move it along with its tow full.

Only the miners who might have had the bad luck to come in from the farthest edge of *The Pride*'s possible location might be stopped, have their records scanned, their comp stripped, their persons subjected to gross discomforts until they would volunteer information, if the kif were true to nature.

"Someone's jumped, Captain."

Tirun's voice, out of the com unit. Pyanfar instantly reached for the reply bar, twisting in her chair. "Who? Where?"

"Just got the characteristic ghost, that's all. I don't know. It was farside of system and long ago. No further data, but it fits within our timeline. That close."

"Give me the image."

Tirun passed it onto the screen. Nadir range and badly muddled pickup: there was too much debris in the way.

"Right," she said to Tirun. "No knowing."

"Out?" Tirun asked.

"Out," Pyanfar confirmed her, and keyed out the image as well, stared morosely at the charts and the figures which, no matter how twisted, kept coming up the same: that there was no way to singlejump beyond Urtur, however reduced in mass they were now.

That jump-ghost which had just arrived might have been someone successfully running for it. More ships than that one might have jumped from here, lost in the gas and debris of Urtur's environs.

But quite, quite likely that ship was kif, a surplus ship moving on to arrange ambush at the most logical jumppoint that they might use.

Rot Akukkakk. She recalled the flat black eyes, red-rimmed, the long gray face, the voice very different from the whining tone of lesser kif. A bitter taste came into her mouth.

How many of them? she wondered, and pulled the scattered charts toward her on the desk and again thought like a kif, wondering just where he might station his ships remaining at Urtur, having figured now, as he must have figured, what they were up to.

That inward flight which was making the station safer was also giving this Akukkakk a free field in which to operate. There were a finite number of opacities in the quadrant where the sweep of debris might be concealing *The Pride*. A diminishing number of other fugitives to confuse him . . . just them and him, finally, along with whatever other kif ships he had called in.

Four kif ships had been at Meetpoint. Some or all might have come with him. There might have been as many more at Urtur when *Hinukku* came in. Eight ships, say. Not beyond possibility.

She made her calculations again, pushed back from the desk and flicked her ears for the soothing sound of the rings.

Huh. So. She at least knew their options—or the lack of them. It was a thoroughly bad game to have gotten into. She levered her aching body out of the chair it had occupied too many hours, stretched again, calculating that they must be about due for Chur and Geran to come on again. And Hilfy; there had not been a word out of her. Possibly the imp had been late getting to sleep after the news which had broken in on her rest. If she had been sleeping, so much the better.

Pyanfar walked out into the corridor and down it, into the dim zone of the bridge, beyond the archway, where most of the lights were out and the dead screens made areas dark which should have been busy with lights. There was one unexpected bright spot, a counter alight in that ell nook of the bridge around the main comp bank. Someone had come back and left it on, she thought, walking up to turn it out; and came on Hilfy there, seated with her attention fixed on the translator, left hand propping her forehead and her right hand poised over the translator keyboard. The screen in front of her was alive with mahendo'sat symbols. Audio brought in a pathetic Outsider-voiced attempt at speech. Pyanfar frowned, walked closer, and Hilfy saw the movement and half turned, turned back in haste to close off the audio from the bridge. Pyanfar leaned on the back of her chair to observe the strings of symbols on the screen, and Hilfy got up in haste.

Go, the Outsider was trying to say. That was the symbol on the screen at the moment. *I go.*

"I thought you were supposed to be resting," Pyanfar said.

"I got tired of resting."

Pyanfar nodded toward the screen, where the Figure Walking was displayed. "How's it doing?"

"He."

"It, he, how's it doing?"

"Not so good on pronunciation."

"You've been cutting in on his lessons? Talking to him?"

"He doesn't know me from the machine." Hilfy had her ears flat, wary of reprimands. "You can't work the second manual without help: it's sentences. He has to have prompts. I've got more vocabulary filled in with him. We're well into abstracts and

I've been able to figure something about the way his own sentences are built from what he keeps doing wrong with ours."

"Huh. And have you perchance gotten a name out of him amid these mistakes? His species? An indication what he comes from? A location?"

"No."

"Well. I didn't expect. But well done, all the same. I'll check it out."

"Seven hundred fifty-three words. He ran the whole first manual. Chur demonstrated changing the keyboard and the cassette and he ran it all, just like that; and got into the second book, trying to do sentences. But he can't pronounce, aunt; it just comes out like that."

"Mouth shape is different. Can't say we can ever do much with his language either. It's like trying to talk to the tc'a or the knnn . . . maybe even a different hearing range, certainly not the same equipment to speak with—gods, no guaranteeing the same logic, but the latter I think we may have. Some things he does make half sense." She lowered herself into the vacated chair, reached and livened a second screen. "Go talk Tirun out of her work down in op, imp; she's been on duty and she shouldn't be. I'm going to try to run a translator tape on your seven hundred fifty-three words."

"I did that."

"Oh, did you?"

"While I was sitting here." Hilfy hastily reached for the counter, indicated the cassette in the slot of the translator input. "I pulled the basic pattern and sorted the words in. Sentence logic too. It's finished."

"Does it work?"

"I don't know, aunt. He hasn't given me a sentence in his own language. Just words. There's no one for him to talk his own to."

"Ah, well, so." Pyanfar was impressed. She ran some of the audio of the tape past, cut it, looked up at Hilfy, who looked uncommonly proud of herself. "You're sure of the tape."

"The master program seemed clear. I—learned the translator principles pretty thoroughly; father didn't connect that so much with spacing. I got to start that study from the first, but *I* knew what I wanted it for. Like comp. I'm good at that."

"Why don't we try it, then?"

Hilfy nodded, more and more self-pleased. Pyanfar rose and searched through the com board cabinets, pulled out the box of sanitary wrapped audio plugs and dropped a handful of those into Hilfy's palm, then located a spare pager from the same source. She sat down at main com and ran the double channels of the translator through bands two and three of the pagers. She took her own plug and inserted it in her ear, tested it out linked to the Outsider's room com for a moment, and got nothing back but bursts of white sound, which were mangled hani words that part of the schizoid translator mind refused to recognize as words. "We're two, he's three," she said to Hilfy, shutting the audio down for the moment. "Bring him up here."

"Here, aunt?"

"You and Haral. This Outsider who tries to impress us with his seven hundred fifty-three words . . . we find out once for all how his public manners are. Take no chances, imp. If the translator fails, don't. If he doesn't act stable, don't. Go."

"Yes, aunt." Hilfy stuffed the audio units and the other pager into her pockets, hastened out the archway in a paroxysm of importance.

"Huh," Pyanfar said after her, stood staring in that direction. Her ears flicked nervously, jangling the rings. The Outsider might do anything. It had chosen their ship to invade, out of a number of more convenient choices. It. *He.* Hilfy and the crew seemed unshakably convinced of the *he,* on analogy to hani structure; but that was still no guarantee. There were, after all, the stsho. Possibly it made the creature more tragic in their eyes.

Gods. Naked-hided, blunt-toothed and blunt-fingered. . . . It had had little chance in hand-to-hand argument with a clutch of kif. It should be grateful for its present situation.

No, she concluded. It should not. Everyone who got hands on it would have plans for this creature, of one kind and another, and perhaps it sensed that; hence its perpetually sullen and doleful look. She had her own plans, to be sure.

He, Hilfy insisted at every opportunity. Her first voyage, a tragic (and safely unavailable) alien prince. Adolescence.

Gods.

From the main section of the com board, outside transmission buzzed, whined, lapsed into a long convolute series of wails and spine-ruffling pipings. She jumped in spite of herself, sat down, keyed in the translator on com. *Knnn,* the screen informed her, which she already knew. *Song. No recognizable identity. No numerical content. Range: insufficient input.*

That kind frequented Urtur too, miners who worked without lifesupport in the methane hell of the moon Uroji and found it home. Odd folk in all senses, many-legged nests of hair, black and hating the light. They came to a station to dump ores and oddments, and to snatch furtively at whatever trade was in reach before scuttling back into the darknesses of their ships. Tc'a might understand them . . . and the chi, who were less rational . . . but no one had ever gotten a clear enough translation out of a tc'a to determine whether the tc'a in turn made any sense of the knnn. The knnn sang, irrationally, pleased with themselves, or lovelorn, or speaking a language. No one knew (but possibly the tc'a, and the tc'a never discussed any topic without wending off into a thousand other tangents before answering the central questions, proceeding in their thoughts as snake-fashioned as they did in their physical movements). No one had gotten the knnn to observe proper navigation: everyone else dodged them, having no other alternative. Generally they did give off numerical messages, which the mechanical translators had the capability to handle—but they were a code for specific situations . . . trade, or coming in, a blink code. There was nothing unusual in knnn presence here, a creature straying where it would, oblivious to oxygen-breather quarrels. There still came the occasional ping or clang of dust and rock against *The Pride*'s hull, the constant rumbling of the rotational core, the whisper of air in the ducts. The deadness of the instruments depressed her spirits. Screens stared back in the shadow of the bridge like so many blinded eyes.

And they were out here drifting with kif and rocks and a knnn who had no idea of the matters at issue.

"Captain," Tirun's voice broke in.

"Hearing you."

"Got a knnn out there."

"Hearing that too. What are Hilfy and Haral doing about the Outsider?"

"They've gone after him; I'm picking that up. He's not making any trouble."

"Understood. They're on their way up here. Keep your ear to the outside comflow; going to be busy up here."

"Yes, Captain."

The link broke off. Pyanfar dialed the pager to pick up the translator channel, received the white-sound of hani words. Everything seemed quiet. Eventually she heard the lift in operation, and heard steps in the corridor leading to the bridge.

He came like an apparition against the brighter corridor light beyond, tall and angular, with two hani shapes close behind him. He walked hesitantly into the dimness of the bridge itself, clear now to the eyes . . . startlingly pale mane and beard, pale skin mottled with bruises and the raking streaks of his wound, sealed with gel but angry red. Someone's blue work breeches, drawstring waisted and loose-kneed, accommodated his tall stature. He walked with his head a little bowed, under the bridge's lower overhead—not that he had to, but that the overhead might feel a little lower than he was accustomed to—he stopped, with Hilfy and Haral behind him on either side.

"Come ahead," Pyanfar urged him farther, and rose from her place to sit braced against the comp console, arms folded. The Outsider still had a sickly look, wobbly on his feet, but she reached back to key the lock on comp, which could only be coded free again, then looked back again at the Outsider . . . who was looking not at her, but about him at the bridge with an expression of longing, of—what feeling someone might have who had lately lost the freedom of such places.

He came from a ship, then, she thought. He must have.

Hilfy stood behind him. Haral moved to the other aisle, blocking retreat in that direction should he conceive some sudden impulse. They had him that way in a protective triangle, her, Hilfy, Haral; but he leaned unsteadily against the number-two cushion which was nearest him and showed no disposition to bolt. He wore the pager at his waist, had gotten the audio plug into his ear, however uncomfortable it might be for him. Pyanfar reached up and tightened her own, dialed the pager to receive, looked back at him from her perch against the counter. "All right?" she asked him, and his face turned toward her. "You do understand," she said. "That translator works both ways. You worked very hard on it. You knew well enough what you were doing, I'll reckon. So you've got what you worked to have. You understand us. You can speak and make us understand you. Do you want to sit down? Please do."

He felt after the bend of the cushion and sank down on the arm of it.

"Better," Pyanfar said. "What's your name, Outsider?"

Lips tautened. No answer.

"Listen to me," Pyanfar said evenly. "Since you came onto my ship, I've lost my cargo and hani have died—killed by the kif. Does that come through to you? I want to know who you are, where you came from, and why you ran to my ship when you could have gone to any other ship on the dock. So you tell me. Who are you? Where do you come from? What do you have to do with the kif and why my ship, Outsider?"

"You're not friends to the kif."

Loud and clear. Pyanfar drew in a breath, thrust her hands into her waistband before her and regarded the Outsider with a pursed-lip smile. "So. *Well.* No, we've said so. I'm not working for the kif and I'm no friend of theirs. Negative. Does the word stowaway come through? Illegal passenger? People who go on ships and don't pay?"

He thought that over, as much of it as did come through, but he had no answer for it. He breathed in deep breaths as if he were tired . . . jumped as a burst of knnn transmission came through the open com. He looked anxiously toward that bank, hands clenched on the cushion back.

"Just one of the neighbors," Pyanfar said. "I want an answer, Outsider. Why did you come to us and not to another ship?"

She had gotten his attention back. He looked at her with a thoughtful gnawing of a lip, a movement finally which might be a shrug. "You sit far from the kif ship. And you laugh."

"Laugh?"

He made a vague gesture back toward Hilfy and Haral. "Your crew work outside the ship, they laugh. They tell me go, go ####no weapons toward me. ### I come back ###."

"Into the rampway, you mean." Pyanfar frowned. "So. What did you plan to do in my ship? To steal? To take weapons? Is that what you wanted?"

"##### no ####."

"Slower. Speak slower for the translator. What did you want on the ship?"

He drew a deep breath, shut his eyes briefly as if trying to collect words or thoughts. Opened them again. "I don't ask weapons. I see the rampway . . . here with hani, small afraid."

"Less afraid of us, were you?" She was hardly flattered. "What's your name? *Name,* Outsider."

"Tully," he said. She heard it, like the occasional com sputter, from the other ear . . . a name like the natural flow of his language, which was purrs and moans combined with stranger sounds.

"Tully," she repeated back; he nodded, evidently recognizing the effort. She touched her own chest. "Pyanfar Chanur is my name. The translator can't do names for you. Py-an-far. Cha-nur."

He tried. Pyanfar was recognizable . . . at least that he purred the rhythm into his own tongue. "Good enough," she said. She sat more loosely, linked her hands in her lap. "Civilized. Civilized beings should deal with names. Tully. . . . Are you from a ship, Tully, or did the kif take you off some world?"

He thought about that. "Ship," he admitted finally.

"Did you shoot at them first? Did you shoot at the kif first, Tully?"

"*No*. No weapons. My ship have no weapons."

"Gods, that's no way to travel. What should I do with you? Take you back to what world, Tully?"

His hands tightened on the back of the cushion. He stared at her bleakly past it. "You want same they want. I don't say."

"You come onto my ship and you won't tell me. Hani are dead because of you, and you won't tell me."

"Dead."

"Kif hit a hani ship. They wanted you, Tully. They wanted you. Don't you think I should ask questions? This is my ship. You came to it. Don't you think you owe me some answers?"

He said nothing. Meant to say nothing, that was clear. His lips were clamped. Sweat had broken out on his face, glistening in the dim light.

"Gods rot this translator," Pyanfar said after a moment. "All right, so somebody treated you badly too. Is it better on this ship? Do we give you the right food? Have you enough clothes?"

He brushed at the trousers. Nodded unenthusiastically.

"You don't have to agree. Is there anything you want?"

"Want my door #."

"What, open?"

"Open."

"Huh."

His shoulders sagged. He had not expected agreement on that, it was evident. He made a vague motion of his hand about their surroundings. "Where are we? The sound. . . ."

The dust brushing past the hull. It had been background noise, a maddening whisper they lived with. Down in lowerdeck, he would have heard a lot of it. "We're drifting," she said. "Rocks and dust out there."

"We sit at a jumppoint?"

"Star system." She reached and cut on the telescope in the observation bubble, bringing the image onto the main screen. The scope tracked to Urtur itself, the inferno of energy in the center of the dusty lens-shaped system, a ringed star which flung out tendrils, the movement of which took centuries, ropy filaments dark against the blaze of the center. The image cast light on the Outsider's face, a moment of wonder: Urtur deserved that. She saw his face and rose to her feet, moved to the side of this shaggy-maned Outsider—a calculated move, because it was her art, to trade, to know the moment when a guard was down. "I tell you," she said, catching him by the arm—and he shivered, but he made no protest at being drawn to his feet. He towered above her as she pointed to the center of the image. "Telescope image, you see. A big system, a horde of planets and moons . . . the dark rings there, that's where the planets sweep the dust and rocks clear. There's a station in that widest band, orbiting a gas giant. The system is uninhabited except for mahendo'sat miners and a few knnn and tc'a who think the place is pleasant. Methane breathers. But a lot of miners, a lot of people of all kinds are in danger right now, in there, in that center. Urtur is the name of the star. And the kif are in there somewhere. They followed us when we jumped to this place, and now a lot of people are in danger because of you. Kif are there, you understand?"

"Authority." His skin was cold under her fingerpads, his muscles hard and shivering, whether from the relative coolness of the bridge's open spaces or from some other cause. "Authority of this system. Hani?"

"Mahendo'sat station. They don't like the kif much either. No one does, but it's not possible to get rid of them. Mahendo'sat, kif, hani, tc'a, stsho, knnn, chi . . . all trade here. We don't all like each other, but we keep our business to ourselves."

He listened, silent, for whatever he could understand of what she said. Com sputtered again, the whistles and wailing of the knnn.

"Some of them," Pyanfar said, "are stranger than you. But you don't know the names, do you? This whole region of space is strange to you."

"Far from my world," he said.

"Is it?"

That got a misgiving look from him. He pulled away from her hand, looked at her and at the others.

"Wherever it is," Pyanfar said in nonchalance. She looked back at Haral and Hilfy. "I think that's about enough. Our passenger's tired. He can go back to his quarters."

"I want talk you," Tully said. He took hold of the cushion nearest, resisting any attempt to move him. *"I want talk."*

"Do you?" Pyanfar asked. He reached toward her. She stood still with difficulty, but he did not touch. He drew the hand back. "What is it you want to talk about?"

He leaned, standing, against the cushion with both hands. His pale eyes were intent and wild, and whatever the precise emotion his face registered, it was distraught. "You #### me. Work, understand. I stay this ship and I work same crew. All you want. Where you go. # give me ###."

"Ah," she said. "You're offering to work for your passage."

"Work on this ship, yes."

"Huh." She would have looked down her nose at him, but it was a matter of looking up. "You make a deal, do you? You work for me, Outsider? You do what I say? All right. You rest now. You go back to your cabin and you learn your words and you think how to tell me what the kif want with you—because the kif still want this ship, you understand. They want you, and they'll come after this ship."

He thought about that a moment. He almost looked as if he might speak. His lips shaped a word and took it back again, and clamped shut. And something sealed in behind his eyes when he did that, a bleakness worse than had ever been there. It sent a prickle down her spine. *This creature is thinking of dying,* she thought. It was the look from against the wall, from the corner in the washroom, but colder still. "Hai," she said in her best dockside manner, and set her hand on his bowed shoulder, roughly but careful with the claws. Shook at him. "Tully. You aren't strong enough yet to work. Enough that you rest. You're safe. You understand me? Hani don't trade with kif."

There was a glimmering then, a sudden break in that seal. He reached out quite unexpectedly and seized her other hand, his blunt fingers both holding and exploring it, the furred web he lacked, the pads of the tips. Pressure hit the center of her hand and the claws came out, only slightly; she was careful, though her ears flattened in warning. To her further distress he set his other hand on her shoulder, then let go both holds and looked about at Haral and Hilfy, then back at her again. Crazy, she judged him; and then she thought about kif, and reckoned that he had license for a little strangeness. "I'll tell you something," she said, "for free. Kif followed you across the Meetpoint dock to my ship. They followed my ship here to Urtur, and right now we're sitting here, just trying to be quiet so the kif don't find us. Trying to decide how best to get out of here. There's one kif in particular, in command of a ship named *Hinukku*. Akukkakk. . . ."

"*Akukkakk*," he echoed, suddenly rigid. The sound came as names must, from the other ear, his own voice. His eyes were dilated.

"Ah. You do know."

"He want take me his ship. Big one. Authority."

"Very big. They have a word for his kind, do you know it? *Hakkikt*. That means he hunts and others pick up the scraps he leaves. I lost something at Meetpoint: a hani ship and my cargo. So did this great *hakkikt,* this great, this powerful kif. You escaped him. *You* ran from him. So it's more than profit that he wants out of this. He wants *you,* Tully, to settle accounts. It's his pride at stake, his reputation. For a kif, that's life itself. He's not going to give up. Do you know, he tried to buy you from me. He offered me gold, a lot of gold. He might even have kept the deal straight and not delayed for piracy afterward. He's that desperate."

Tully's eyes drifted from her to the others and back again. "You deal with him?"

"No. I want something for dead hani and lost cargo. I want this great *hakkikt*. You hear me, Tully?"

"Yes," Tully said suddenly. "*I* want same."

"Aunt," Hilfy protested in a faint voice.

"You want to work," Pyanfar said, ignoring her niece's disquiet. "There'll be the chance for that. But you wait, Tully. You rest. At shift change, I'll call you again. You come eat with us. Meal, understand? But you get some rest first, hear? You work on my ship, you take orders first. Follow instructions. Right?"

"Yes," he said.

"Go, then. Haral and Hilfy will take you back down. Go."

He nodded, delivered himself over to Haral and Hilfy together; not a backward look from either of them as they took him out. Or from him. She watched them go, found herself rubbing the hand that he had touched.

The knnn song wailed out again. Neighbors to the kif, the knnn. That bore remembering. That one was uncommonly talkative. No one was even sure what knnn senses were, or what motivated their migrations from star to star.

She turned to the com bank, pushed Record, and sent the song again to the translator. It gave her no more information than the last time. The song ceased, and there remained only the whisper of the dust. Urtur system everywhere had grown very still.

The translator still carried white sound, Haral's voice or Hilfy's. The Outsider was saying nothing while being taken back to his quarters. She was marginally uneasy about having him out of sight. Perhaps he was mad after all. Perhaps he would suicide and leave them with nothing to show for the encounter but a feud with the kif. Up to a point she could not prevent his killing himself, except by taking measures which would not encourage his good will.

But revenge was something of purpose, something to make life worthwhile. She had offered him that.

She thought of his face close at hand, lively, crazed eyes, a hand as cold as something an hour dead—a creature, she reminded herself, who had been fighting alone an enemy which would have turned a stsho to jelly.

She grinned somewhat, a drawing back of the lips and wrinkling of the nose, and stared thoughtfully toward the telescope image.

No disengagement possible. Not with this kif prince, this *hakkikt* Akukkakk, whose personal survival rode on this Outsider business. His own sycophants would turn on him if he lost face in this matter. He had lost this Outsider personally . . . perhaps by some small carelessness, the old kif game of tormenting victims with promises and threats and shreddings of the will. An old game . . . one which hani understood; irresistible to a kif who thrived on fear in his victims.

Akukkakk had to make up that embarrassment at Meetpoint. He would have been obliged to revenge if it were so much as a bauble stolen from him at dockside. But this Outsider Tully was far more than that. A communicative, spacefaring species, hitherto unknown, in a position to have come into kif hands without passing through more civilized regions. The kif had new neighbors.

Possible danger to them.

Possible expansion of kif hunting grounds . . . in directions which had nothing to do with hani and mahendo'sat. Those were high stakes, impossibly high stakes to be riding on one poor fugitive.

Urtur would swarm with kif, before all was said and done.

She delved into the com storage and started hunting components for a transmitter of some power, roused out Chur and sent her hunting through the darker areas of *The Pride*'s circumference for other supplies.

V

It was a monster, like Tully, this thing that they constructed in the spotlit, chill bowels of *The Pride*'s far rim. It had started out hani-shaped, a patched and hazardous eva-pod which they had stripped for parts and never succeeded in foisting off on another hani ship. Its limbs had just grown longer, sectioned off and spliced with tubing, and it was rigged with a wheezing lifesupport system.

"Get Tully," Pyanfar said, applying herself to the last of the welding which should get the system in order. "Rouse him out." And Chur went, bedraggled as herself with the dust and the grime of *The Pride*'s salvage storage.

Pyanfar worked, spliced and cursed when the system blew in another frustrating curl of smoke, unhitched that component and rummaged for a new one, sealed that in and congratulated herself when it worked, a vibration and a flicker of green lights on the belt and inside the helmet. She grinned, wiped her hands on the blue work breeches she had put on for this grimy task . . . a long time since she had practiced such things, a long time since she had worn blue roughspun and gotten blisters on her hands. In her youth, under another of *The Pride*'s captains, she had done such things, but only Haral and Tirun could recall those days. She licked a burn on her finger and squatted on the deck, content with the operation of the unit. Let it run a while, she decided, see if it would go on working. The suit stared back, stiff and gangling on its huge feet, reflecting her in distant miniature off its curved faceplate. It stood like some mahendo'sat demon, two limbs shy of that description, but ghastly enough in its exposed hoses and its malproportioned height, against the dark of the surrounding machine shop. A reek of blood mingled with the singed smell of the welding. A bucket on the deck caught the occasional drip from the skinned carcass which hung beyond it under the light. It was a little more than hani-sized, chained up to the hoist track above, long-faced head adroop on a longish neck, to thaw and drain. It had begun to reek under the lights. The long limbs were coming untucked, and the belly gaped. *Uruus.* Sweet meat and a fat one: the best steaks had already headed galleyward, in this raid on their private larder. It had wounds, this carcass, but that only lengthened the limbs, letting the haunches drop.

The door unsealed and sealed in the dark distance; steps whispered along the metal flooring. Pyanfar adjusted her translator and got nothing, but she could see the lights go on in the far dark expanse, illusionlike and high because of the upward curve of the deck in the vast storage chamber, picking out two figures, one gangling tall and pale. She sat and waited as the lights turned themselves on and off in sequence along the walkway, bringing the two nearer and nearer where she sat.

Tully and Chur, of course. The Outsider came willingly enough, but he stopped dead when he came close, and the light went out on him, leaving him and Chur in the dark outside the area where Pyanfar sat. She stood up, making him out clearly enough in the shadow. "Tully, it's safe. Come on. It's all right, Tully."

He did come, slowly, alien shadow in the rest of the strangeness, and Chur had hold of his arm in case. He looked at the vacant suit, and at the hanging carcass, and kept staring at it.

"Animal," Pyanfar said. "Tully. I want you to see what we're doing. I want you to understand. Hear?"

He turned toward her, eyes deep in their shadowed sockets, the angled light glancing off a pale mane and planes of feature decidedly un-hani. "You put me in this?"

"Put *that* in the suit," Pyanfar said cheerfully. "Transmitter sending signal hard as it can. We tell the kif that we're throwing you out and we give them *that,* you understand, Outsider? Make them chase that. And we run."

It began to get through to him. His eyes flickered over the business again, the vacant suit, the frozen carcass. "Their instruments see in it," he said.

"Their instruments will scan it, yes; and that's what they'll get."

He gestured toward the carcass. "This? This?"

"Food," she said. "Not a person, Tully. Animal. Food."

Of a sudden his face took on an alarming grin. His body heaved with a choking sound she recognized as laughter. He clapped Chur on the shoulder, turned that convulsed face toward her with moisture streaming from his eyes and still with that mahendo'sat grin. "You # the kif."

"Put that inside," she told him, motioning toward the carcass. "Bring it. You help, Tully."

He did, with Chur, his rangy body straining against the half-frozen weight, an occasional grimace of what might be disgust at the look or the feel of it. Pyanfar shut down the pod's lifesupport, opened up their work of art, and wrinkled her nose as the Outsider and Chur brought the reeking carcass over. There was trim work to do. She abandoned fastidiousness and did it herself, having some notion how it might fit. The head could be gotten into the helmet, a bit of the neck to stuff the vacant body cavity of the carcass, and a little scoring and breaking of the rib cage, a sectioning and straightening of stiff limbs.

"Going to smell good if that drifts a while with the heater on," Chur observed. Tully laughed his own choking laugh and wiped his face, smearing his mustache with the muck which coated his arms to the elbow. Pyanfar grinned, suddenly struck with the incongruity of things, squatting here in the dark with a crazed alien and a suit full of uruus carcass, the three of them in insane conspiracy. "Hold it," she ordered Chur, trying to get the belly seam fastened. Chur held the sides together at the bottom and Tully helped at the top, and there it was, sealed and Tully-shaped.

"Come," Pyanfar said, taking the feet, and Tully and Chur energetically got purchase on its shoulders, lumbering along with it as the lights recognized their presence and began to go on and off as they traveled.

"Cargo dump?" Chur asked.

"Airlock," Pyanfar said. "Should passengers leave a ship by any other route?"

It was no light weight. They staggered along the walk with the body of the pod dragging at this and that point, got it onto a cargo carrier at the next section and breathed sighs of relief as it lay corpselike on the carrier, mirrored faceplate staring up at the overhead. Tully was white and trembling from the exertion: sweat stood on his skin and he held onto the carrier's end rail, panting but bright-eyed.

"You're Pyanfar, right?" he asked between breaths. "Pyanfar?"

"Yes," she owned, wiped an itch on her nose with a dirty hand, reckoning she could get no dirtier, nodded at Chur and gave him Chur's name again.

"I #," he said, nodding affirmative. He pushed enthusiastically when they pushed, and they got the thing moving easily down the aisle through interior storage, past the hulking shadows of the tanks and the circulating machinery, out again into the normal lighted sections of belowdecks, under a lower ceiling, and through ordinary corridors to the lock.

"# he go #?" Tully asked, staggered as he helped them offload the pod, looked anxiously leftward as the lock's inner hatch opened. "Go quick out?"

"Ah, no," Pyanfar said. She carried the feet through and braced them as Chur and Tully got the upper body through and upright. "There, against the outer hatch. We blow that and he'll go right nicely." She set the feet down and added her weight as they heaved and braced it, stood back and surveyed her handiwork with a grin and a thought of the kif. She powered up the lifesupport with a touch of the buttons on the belt, and it stood a little stiffer, on minimum maintenance. She shut it down again, not to waste a good cylinder.

And for the moment Tully stood staring at it too, panting and sweating, arms at his sides, a haggard look suddenly replacing the laughter, an expression which held something of a shudder, as if after all he had begun to think about that thing and his situation, and to reckon questions he had not asked.

"Out," Pyanfar said, motioning Chur from the lock, including Tully with that sweep of her arm. He hesitated. She moved to take his arm in his seeming daze, and he suddenly hung his hand on her shoulder, one and then the other, and bowed his head against her cheek, brief gesture, quickly dropped, hands withdrawn as swiftly as her ears flattened. She caught herself short of a hiss, deliberately patted his hairless shoulder and brought him on through the lock into the corridor.

Thank you, that act seemed to signify. So. It had subtler understandings, this Tully. She flicked her ears, a look which got a quickly turned shoulder from Chur, and shoved the Outsider leftward in Chur's direction. "Go clean up," she said. "Get showered, hear? *Wash.*"

Chur took him, indicated to him that he should help her with the carrier, and they went trundling it past and down the corridor

to put that back where it belonged. Pyanfar blew a short breath
and closed the interior lock, then headed for the common washroom where she had left her better clothes—did a small shudder of
the skin where the Outsider's hand had rested on her shoulder.

But it had understood what they were doing, very well understood what they were up to with the decoy, and that in fact it was
not all a matter of humor.

Gods rot the kif.

And then she thought of the uruus' solemn long face, so be-
nignly stupid, and of the deadly pride of the great *hakkikt* of the
kif, and her nose wrinkled in laughter which had nothing to do
with humor.

Supper was on; a delicious aroma came from the galley topside,
Hilfy and Geran having stirred about for some time in that quarter
and in the larger facilities below. It was a real meal this time, one
of the delightful concoctions Geran was skilled at, the penultimate
contribution of the uruus to their comfort, prepared with all the
care they lavished on food on more ordinary voyages, when food
was an obsession, a precious variance in routine, an art they practiced to delight their occasional passengers and to amaze themselves.

Now dinner came with as great a welcome, aromatic courage
wafting the airflow from that corridor, and Pyanfar set her com
links to the bridge and did what was necessary to secure the place,
her hands all but trembling from hunger, and with an aching great
hollow in the middle of her. There had been nothing dire so far,
only nuisance coming over com, no indication of trouble more
than they already had; and the suited uruus waited in the lock,
melting and still—she checked the airlock vid—on its somewhat altered feet against the outer hatch. She cut that image and checked
the galley/commonroom link again, picked up Hilfy's voice and
shunted the flow the other way, vowed a great curse on any kif
who might interrupt the hour they had earned. But the link was
there if needed and the unit in the commonroom would carry any
business it had to. She got the word from Geran and passed it over
allship, finally left the bridge and walked on around to dinner,
clean again and full of anticipation.

She grinned inside and out at the sight, the table lengthened so
that it hardly gave them room to edge around it, the center spread
with fantastical culinary artistry, platters of meat, by the gods, no

stale freeze-dried chips and jerky and suchlike; gravies and sauces in which tidbits floated, garnished with herbs and crackling bits of fat. The sterile white commonroom was transformed, and Hilfy and Geran hastened about to lay cushions with bright patterns, Chanur heraldry, red and gold and blue.

"Wondrous," Pyanfar pronounced it, inhaling. Places for seven. She heard the lift and looked toward the corridor. In short order came Haral and Chur with Tully in tow, and Tirun limped along behind them, using her pipe-cane. "Sit, sit," Pyanfar bade them and Tully, and they sorted themselves and edged along as they had to in the narrow confines, took their places shoulder to shoulder. Pyanfar held the endmost seat bridgeward, Haral the endmost galleyward, and Tirun and Chur sandwiched Tully between them, while Hilfy and Geran took the other side. It presented a bizarre sight, this white-gold mane between two ruddy gold ones, hairless shoulders next to red-brown coated ones, and Tully hunching slightly to try to keep his gangling limbs out of his seatmates' way . . . Pyanfar chuckled in good humor and made the healthwish, which got the response of the others and startled Tully by its loudness. Then she poured gfi from her own flask by her cup; the whole company reached for theirs and did the same, Tully imitating them belatedly, and for a moment there was nothing but the clatter of knives and cups and plates as Geran's and Hilfy's monuments underwent swift demolition. Tully took snatches of this and that as the dishes rotated past him on the table's rotating center, small helpings at first, as if he were not sure what he had a right to, and larger ones as he darted furtive glances at what others took, and ladled on sauces and laid by small puddles of this and that in the evident case it might not come round a second time. No questions from him.

"Uruus," Chur said wickedly, crooking a claw onto his arm to catch his attention, gestured at the steaks. "Same thing, this, the animal we give the kif."

Tully looked momentarily uncertain, poked at the steak with his knife and looked up again at Chur's grin. "Same, this?"

"Same," Chur confirmed. Tully took on an odd look, then started eating, laughed to himself after a moment in a crazed fashion, shoulders bowed and attention turned wholly to the food, darting only occasional glances to their hands, trying to handle the utensils hani-style.

"Good?" Pyanfar broke the general silence. Tully looked up at once, darted looks at all of them, not knowing who had spoken. The translator speaking into his ear had no personality.

"I, Pyanfar. All right, Tully? This food's all right for you?"

"Yes," he said. "I'm hungry." *Hungry,* the translator said into her ear, dispassionately; but the look on his face for a moment put a great deal more into it. The bruises showed starkly clear in the commonroom's white light; the angularity of bones reached the surface on his shoulders and about his ribs.

"Says he's cold most of the time," Chur said. "He doesn't have our natural covering, after all. I tried a jacket on him, but he's too big. He still wants it, asks to cut it. Maybe better to start with something of Haral's in the first place."

"Still too small for those arms," Haral judged. "But I'll see what I can find."

"Cold," Tully said, in his limited understanding of the discussion.

"We're trying, Tully," Chur said. "I ask Haral, understand. Maybe find you something."

Tully nodded. "#" he said forlornly, and then with a brightened expression and a gesture at the meal: "Good. *Good.*"

"Not complaining, are you?" Pyanfar commented. "Don't— *gods.*"

The com broke in, a knnn-song, and Tully jumped. Everyone looked up reflexively toward the speaker, and Pyanfar drew a deep breath when knnn was all it turned out to be. Tully alone kept staring that way.

"That's nothing," Pyanfar said. "Knnn again. It'll shut up in a moment." She looked soberly at the others, now that business was on her mind. "Got ourselves a course laid, in case. It's in the comp when we need it. And we will. Got ourselves a decoy rigged too, Chur and Tully and I—a gift for the kif that's going to cost them critical speed if they want to pick it up; got it fixed so it'll look good to their sensors."

There was a moment's silence.

"All right to talk?" Hilfy asked.

Pyanfar nodded without comment.

"Where?" Hilfy asked. "If we're running—where? Meetpoint again?"

"No. I considered that, to be sure, throwing the kif off by that. But figuring it and refiguring—we came close enough not making it when we came in with all Urtur's mass to fix on; and there's not a prayer of doing it in reverse with only Meetpoint's little mass to bring us up. I've worked possible courses over and over again, and there's nothing for it—twojump, to Kirdu. It's a big station; and there's help possible there."

"The kif," said Geran, "will have it figured too. They'll intercept us at Kita."

"So we string the jumps," Pyanfar said, taking a sip of gfi. "No other way, Geran, absolutely no other."

"Gods," Chur muttered undiplomatically. Hilfy's expression was troubled. She quickly darted her eyes toward the others, who were more experienced. Tully had stopped eating again and looked up too, catching something of the conversation.

"Consecutive jump," Pyanfar said to Hilfy. "No delay for recovery time, no velocity dump in the interval and, gods know, a hazard where we're going: we're bound to boost some of this debris through with us. But the risk is still better than sitting here while the kif population increases. There's one jumppoint we have to make: Kita. Past Kita Point, the kif have to take three guesses where we went—Kura, Kirdu, Maing Tol. They might guess right after all, but they still might disperse some ships to cover other possibilities."

"We're going home," Hilfy surmised.

"Who said going home? We're going to sort this out, that's what. We're going to shake a few of them. Get ourselves a place where we can find some allies. That's what we're doing."

"Then the Faha—we could warn them."

"What, spill where we're bound? They'll figure too . . . the best hope's Kirdu. They'll probably go there."

"We could warn them. Here. Give them a chance to get out."

"They can take care of themselves."

"After we brought the trouble here—"

"My decision," Pyanfar said.

"I'm not saying that. I'm saying—"

"We can't help them by springing in their direction. Or how do you plan to get word to them? We'll make it worse for them, we can only make it worse. You hear me?"

"I hear." The ears went back, pricked up with a little effort. There was a silence at table, except for the knnn, who wailed on alone, rapt in whatever impulse moved knnn to sing.

And stopped. "Gods," Haral muttered irritably, shot a worried look the length of the table. Pyanfar returned it, past Hilfy, past the Outsider.

"Pyanfar." Tully spoke, sat holding his cup as if he had forgotten it, something obviously welling up in him which wanted saying, with a look close to panic. "I talk?" he asked. And when Pyanfar nodded: "What move make this ship?"

"Going closer to home territory, to hani space. We're going where kif won't follow us so easily, and where there's too much hani and mahendo'sat traffic to make it easy for them to move against us. Better place, you understand. Safer."

He set down the cup, made a vague gesture of a flat-nailed long-fingered hand. "Two jump."

"Yes."

"#. Need #, Captain. #."

He was sorely, urgently upset. Pyanfar drew in a breath, made a calming gesture. "Again, Tully. Say again. New way."

"*Sleep*. Need sleep in jump."

"Ah. Like the stsho. They have to, yes. I understand; you'll have your drugs, then, make you sleep, never fear."

He had started shaking. Of a sudden moisture broke from his eyes. He bowed his head and wiped at it, and was quiet for the moment. Everyone was, recognizing a profound distress. Perhaps he realized; he stirred in the silence and clumsily picked up his knife and jabbed at a bit of meat on his plate, carried it to his mouth and chewed, all without looking up.

"You need drugs to sleep," Pyanfar said, "and the kif took you through jump without them. That's what they did, was it?"

He looked up at her.

"Were you alone when you started, Tully? Were there others with you?"

"Dead," he said around the mouthful, and swallowed it with difficulty. "Dead."

"You know for sure."

"I'm sure."

"Did you talk to the kif? Did you tell them what they asked you?"

A shake of his head.

"No?"

"No," Tully said, looked down again and up under his pale brows. "We give wrong # to their translator."

"What, the wrong words?"

He still had the knife in his hand. It stayed there with its next morsel, the food forgotten.

"He fouled their translator," Tirun exclaimed in delight. "Gods!"

"And not ours?" Pyanfar observed.

Tully's eyes sought toward her.

"I thought you ran that board too quickly," Pyanfar said. "Clever Outsider. *We,* you said. Then there were more of you in the kif's hands at the start."

"The kif take four of us. They take us through jump with no medicine, awake, you understand; they give us no good food, not much water, make us work this translator keyboard same you have. We know what they want from us. We make slow work, make we don't understand the keyboard, don't understand the symbols, work all slow. They stand small time. They hit us, bad, push us, bad—make us work this machine, make quick. We work this machine all wrong, make. many wrong words, this word for that word, long, long tape—some right, most wrong. One day, two, three—all wrong." His face contorted. "They work the tape and we make mistake more. They understand what we do, they take one of us, kill her. Hit us all, much. They give us again same work, make a tape they want. We make number two tape wrong, different mistake. The kif kill second one my friends. I—man name Dick James—we two on the ship come to station. They make us know this Akukkakk; he come aboard ship see us. He—" Again a contortion of the face, a gesture. "He—take my friend arm, break it, break many time two arms, leg—I make fight him, do no good; he hit me—walk outside. And my friend—he ask—I kill him, you understand. I do it; I kill my friend, # kif no more hurt him."

The silence about the table was mortal. Pyanfar cleared her throat. Others' ears were back, eyes dilated.

"They come," Tully went on quietly. "Find my friend dead. They # angry, hit me, bring me out toward this second ship. Outside. Docks. I run. Run—long time. I come to your ship." He ducked his head, looked up again with a wan, mahendo'sat smile. "I make the keyboard right for you."

"That kif wants killing," Haral said.

"Tully," Pyanfar said. "I understand why you're careful about questions about where you come from. But I'll lay odds your space is near the kif—you just listen to me. I think your ship got among kif, and now they know there's a spacefaring species near their territories, either one they can take from—or one they're desperately afraid is a danger to them. I don't know which you are. But that's what the kif wanted with you, I'm betting—to know more about you. And you know that. And you're reluctant to talk to us either."

Tully sat unmoving for a moment. "My species is human." She caught the word from his own speech.

"Human."

"Yes, they try ask me. I don't say; make don't understand."

"Your ship—had no weapons. You don't carry them?"

No answer.

"You didn't know there was danger?"

"Don't know this space, no. Jump long. Two jump. # we hear transmission."

"Kif?"

He shook his head, his manner of no. "I hear—" He pointed to the com, which remained silent. "That. Make that sound."

"Knnn, for the gods' sake."

He touched his ear. "Say again. Don't understand."

"Knnn. A name. A species. Methane breather. You were in knnn territory. Worse and worse news, my friend. Knnn space is between stsho and kif."

"Captain," said Geran, "I'd lay bets with a chị the stsho had a finger in this too. Their station, after all . . . where the kif felt free to move him about the dock in public . . . I daresay the kif didn't get any questions at all from the stsho."

Pyanfar nodded thoughtfully, recalling the stsho official, the *change* in that office or that officer. A smiling welcome, impassive moonstone eyes and delicate lavender brows. A certain cold went up her back. "Stsho'd turn a blind eye to anything that looked like trouble, that's sure. . . . Imp," she said, seeing Hilfy's laidback ears and dilated eyes, "pay attention: this is the way of our friends and allies out here. Gods rot them. . . . Eat your dinner."

Tully stirred his plate about, turned his attention back to that, and Pyanfar chewed another bite, thoughtful.

Knnn, kif, stsho . . . gods, the whole pot had been stirred when this Outsider, this *human,* dropped into the middle of it. An uncomfortable feeling persisted at the back of her neck, like a cold wind of belated reason. The whole dock at Meetpoint, zealously trying not to hear or see anything amiss, with a fugitive on the loose and the kif on the hunt. . . .

There was no particular evil in the stsho—except the desire to avoid trouble. That had always been the way of them. But they were different. No hani read past the patterns. No hani understood them. And, gods, if the knnn were stirred up—along with the kif. . . .

She swallowed the dry mouthful and washed it down with a draught of gfi, poured herself another cupful. Tully ate with what looked like appetite. Food disappeared all around the table, and the plates rotated for second helpings.

"I'm going to put Tully on limited assignment," she said. "He can't read, sure enough. But some things he can do." He had looked up. "Niece," she said, "you're no longer juniormost on *The Pride,* this run. Ought to make you happy."

Hilfy's brown study evaporated into disquiet. *"He's* junior-most?"

"A willing worker," Pyanfar said with a wrinkling of her nose. "Your responsibility in part, now."

"Aunt, I—"

"I told you how it was, niece. Hear? You know what we're dealing with, and what stakes are involved?"

"I hear," Hilfy said in a faint voice. "No, I don't know. But I'm figuring it out."

"Kif," Geran spat. "They're different, when the odds go against them."

"Once . . ." Haral said, and winced. The knnn song was back again, shriller. "Rot that."

"Close," Pyanfar judged. It was exceedingly clear reception. She met Haral's eyes facing her down the length of the table, more and more uneasy. The song continued for a moment, too loud to talk above it, then wailed away, gibbering to itself into lower tones.

"Too rotted close," Haral said. "Captain—"

Pyanfar started to push herself back from table, surrendering to anxiety.

"Chanur Captain," com said far more faintly, a clicking voice speaking the hani tongue. *"Chanur Captain—don't trouble to acknowledge. Only listen. . . ."*

Pyanfar stiffened, looked toward com with a bristling at her nape and a lowering of her ears. Everyone was frozen in place.

"The bargain you refused at Meetpoint . . . is no longer available. Now I offer other terms, equal to the situation. A new bar-

gain. A safe departure from this system, for yourself and for the Faha ship now at dock. I guarantee things which properly interest you, in return for one which doesn't. Jettison the remnant of your cargo, hani thief. You know our ways. If you do the wise thing, we will not pursue you further. You know that we are the rightful owners of that merchandise. You know that we know your name and the names of your allies. We remember wrongs against us. All kif . . . remember crimes committed against us. But purge your name, Pyanfar Chanur. More, save lives which were not originally involved in your act of piracy. Give us only our property, Pyanfar Chanur, and we will take no further action against the Faha and yourself. That is my best offer. And you know now by experience that I make no empty threat. Is this matter worth your sure destruction and that of the Faha? Or if you think to run away again, deserting your ally, will you hope to run forever? That will not improve your trade, or make you welcome at stations who will learn the hazard of your company. Give it up, thief. It's small gain against your loss, this thing you've stolen."

"Akukkakk," Pyanfar said in a low voice when it had done. "So."

"Aunt," Hilfy said, carefully restrained. "They're going to go after *Starchaser*. First."

"Undoubtedly they are." The message began to repeat. Pyanfar thrust herself to her feet. "Gods rot that thing. Down it."

Chur was nearest. She sprang from her seat and turned down the volume of the wall unit. Others had started working themselves out of their places, Tully among them. Sweat had broken out on his skin, a fine, visible dew.

"Seal the galley," Pyanfar said. "Secure for jump. We're moving."

Hilfy turned a last, pleading look on her. Pyanfar glowered back. And with Geran urging him to move on, Tully delayed, putting out a hand to touch Pyanfar's shoulder. "Sleep," Tully pleaded, reminding her, panic large in his eyes.

"For the gods' sake put him out," Pyanfar snarled, turned and thrust her own plate and some of the nearer dishes into the disposal, shoved others into the hands of Haral and Tirun and Chur, who were throwing things in as fast as they could snatch them. Hilfy started to help. "Out," Pyanfar said to Chur. "That business in the airlock . . . get its lifesupport going. Move it!"

Chur scrambled over the top of the table and ran for the doorway in a scrabbling of claws. Pyanfar turned with fine economy and stalked out in her wake, toward controls. Tirun limped after her, but Pyanfar had no disposition to wait. Anxiety prickled up and down her gut, disturbing the meal she had just eaten, sudden distrust of all the choices she had made up till now, including the one that had a slightly crazed Outsider loose on the ship in a crisis; and knnn near them; and their eyes blinded and their ears deaf to the outside. . . .

She walked into the darkened bridge, slid into the well worn cushion which knew her body's dimensions, settled in and belted in, heard the stir of others about her, Tirun, Hilfy, Haral. The kif voice continued over com. Elsewhere she heard Tully pleading with Geran over something, trying to get something through the translator which he could only half say. She started running perfunctory clear checks, all internal, threw a look toward her companions. Haral and Tirun were settled and running personal checks on their posts, rough and solid and intent on business. Hilfy had her ears back, her hands visibly shaking in getting her boards ready. So. It was one thing to ride through kif fire at Meetpoint . . . quite another to face it after thinking about it.

"Please," a mahendo'sat voice came through, relayed suddenly from Hilfy's board to hers. *"Stand off from station. We appeal to all sides for calm. We suggest arbitration. . . ."*

They had thrown that out on longrange, plea to all the system, to all their unruly guests, this station full of innocents, where all who could in the system had taken refuge.

And among them, *Starchaser*.

"That had to antedate the other message," Pyanfar said morosely. "It's all old history at station." That for Hilfy, to get her mind straight. Tully was still talking; she took the translator plug from her ear, shutting down all communication from that quarter, trusting Geran's not inconsiderable right arm if all else failed.

"Captain." That was Chur on allship. "Lifesupport's on and the lock's sealed again."

"Understood, Chur," she muttered, plying the keyboard and calling up her course plottings. "Take station in lowerdeck op." She would rather Chur on the bridge; but there was Tully loose; there was a kif loose, and time running on them—it was getting late to risk someone moving about in the corridors. She spun half about, indecisive. Hilfy, the weak link, sat at com, scan backup. "What's the kif doing? Any pickup?"

"Negative," Hilfy said calmly enough. "Repeat of message. I'm getting a garble out of ships insystem, no sign yet of any disruption. The knnn. . . ."

That sound moaned through main com again, a transmission increasingly clear and distinct. Closer to them in this maelstrom of dust and debris. Pyanfar sucked in a breath. "Stand by to transmit, full sensors, all systems; I want a *look* out there, cousins." She started throwing switches. *The Pride*'s nervous system came alive again in flares of color and light, busy ripplings across the boards as systems recalibrated themselves. She hit propulsion and reoriented, reached for the main comp.

"Gods," Tirun muttered, throwing to her number-one screen the scan image which was coming in, a dusty soup pocked with rocks. "*Ship*," Haral said suddenly, number-one scan, and overrode with that sectorized image. Panic hit Pyanfar's gut. That was close to them, and moving.

"Resolution," she demanded. *The Pride* was accelerating, without her shields as yet. The whisper of dust over the hull became a shriek, a scream: they hit a rock and it shrilled along the hull; hit another and a screen erupted with static. "Gods, this muck!"

"Shields," Haral said.

"Not yet."

"No resolution," Tirun said. "Too much debris out there. We're still blind."

"Gods rot it." She hit the airlock control, blew it. "We lost something," Tirun said; "Beeper output," Hilfy said at once. "Loud and clear. Aunt, is that our decoy?"

Pyanfar ignored the questions, harried. "Longrange com to my board. Now."

It came through unquestioned, a light on her panel. She put the mike in. "This is Pyanfar Chanur, *Hinukku*. We've just put a pod out the lock. Call it enough, *hakkikt*. Leave off."

And breaking that contact, to Hilfy: "Get that on repeat, imp, twice over; and then cut all signal output and ID transmission and output the signal on translator channel five."

Half a second of paralysis: Hilfy reached for the board, froze and then punched something else over, static-ridden snarl, a hani voice. "*Chanur! Go! We're moving!*" It repeated, a rising shriek of urgency like that of the debris against the hull.

"It's not our timeline," Pyanfar snapped at Hilfy, but Hilfy was already moving again, outputting one transmission, then clearing, reaching with ears back and a panicked look after what recording she had been ordered, however insane.

"Prime course laid," Haral pronounced imperturbably. "Referent bracketed."

"Stand by." Their acceleration continued: the dust screamed over the hull. Another screen broke up and recovered.

"Aunt," Hilfy exclaimed, "we're outputting *knnn* signal."

"Right we are," Pyanfar said through her teeth. She angled *The Pride* for system zenith, where no outgoing ship belonged. A prickle of sweat chilled her nose, sickly cold, and the wail over the hull continued. "Readout behind us," Geran said, "confirmed knnn, that ship back there." Gods rot it, nothing was ever easy. Differential com was suddenly getting another signal in the sputter of dust. *"Chanur! Go. . . ."*

And a kif voice: *"Regrettable decision, Faha Captain."*

Pyanfar spat and gulped air against the drag of *g*, vision tunnelled with the stress and with anger. Hour old signal, that from the Faha; at least an hour old, maybe more than that.

"Second ship," Tirun said. "3/4 by 32 our referent."

"Get me *Starchaser*'s course," Pyanfar said.

"Been trying," Haral said. "Bearing nsr station, best guess uncertain." Figures leaped to the number-two screen, a schematic covering a quarter of Urtur's dust-barriered system, below them, system referent.

"Knnn ship," Hilfy said, "moving on the beeper.—Aunt, they're going to intercept it."

Pyanfar hesitated half a beat in turning, a glance at scan which flashed intercept probable on that ship trailing them. Knnn, by the gods, knnn were moving on the decoy, and they were not known for rescues. Something clenched on her heart, instinctive loathing, and in the next beat she flung her attention back toward the system schematic.

No way to help the Faha. None. *Starchaser* was on her own. Knnn had the decoy; kif were not going to like that. If there ever had been knnn. More than *The Pride* could play that dangerous game. The scream on the hull rose in pitch. . . . "Screens," she snapped at Haral. She reached for drive control, uncapped switches. "Stand by. Going to throw our navigation all to blazes; I'll keep Alijuun off our nose when we cycle back." She pulsed the jump drive, once, twice, three times, microsecond flarings of the vanes. Her stomach lurched, pulse quickened until the blood congested in her nose and behind her eyes, narrowing vision to a hazed pinpoint. They were blind a third time, instruments robbed of regained referents, velocity boosted in major increments. Dead, if Haral failed them now. But they were old hands at Urtur, knew the system, had a sense where they were even blinded, from a known start.

Down the throat of the kif's search pattern, from zenith . . . she pulsed the vanes again, another increment, swallowed hard against the dinner which was trying to come up again. Differential com got them a kif howl, and a mahendo'sat yammering distress. *That,* for whatever they had done against *Starchaser,* skinned their backsides for them, a streaking search for a target.

"*Ai!*" Haral yelped, and instruments flared, near collision. "*Chanur!*" she heard; the name would be infamy here as at Meetpoint. There were surges and flares all over the board. She pulsed out and in again and the instruments went manic. "Gods," Haral moaned, "I almost had it."

"Now, Haral! for the gods' sake find it!"

Instruments flickered and screens static-mad sorted themselves, manifoldly offended. An alien scream erupted from their own com. *Tully,* Pyanfar reckoned suddenly: his drugs were not quick enough. They had betrayed him like the kif.

Image appeared on her number-one screen: *Alijuun.* The star was sighted and bracketed and the ID was positive.

"*Hai!*" she yelled, purest relief, and hit the jump pulse for the long one. Her voice wound in and out in a dozen colors, coiled and recoiled through the lattices which opened for them, and the stomach-wrenching sensation of jump swallowed them down. . . .

vi

. . . and spat them up again, a dizzying percept of elsewhere. A shimmer before her eyes, that was the screen, and the automated instruments were searching. Keep conscious, don't go out, not now, keep the hand on controls. . . . "Working." Haral's low voice drifted to her out of infinity. "O gods." That was someone else. Hilfy? A star came into brackets on the screen and wobbled out again. "Check referent," Pyanfar said. Her blurring eyes sought instruments. A red light was on. "Got a problem," Haral said, sending cold chills along her back. "No positive ID on referent."

"Brace." She started aborting the proposed second jump, dumping speed sufficient for the scanning sensors to make their fix. There was a moan near her when the shift slammed in. Her hand shook over the controls, hovering over the button. "Gods, we've *missed*," Haral moaned; and then Tirun: *"Abort!* we're vectored massward!"

Dark mass was ahead of them, the mass which had pulled them in from jump, coming up in their faces. Sensors realized it; alarms went off, dinning through the ship. Pyanfar dumped again, hard, flinched as screens went static and one went dead. Something had given way.

"Turning," she warned the crew. *The Pride* veered in her next skip, and blood started in Pyanfar's nose, internal organs and joints and flesh hauled in independent motion. She spat and struggled with the muscles of her eyes to keep focused, fought a strained muscle to keep her hand at the controls. Scan showed hairbreadth miss now and she trimmed ship and let it ride, hurtling for a virtual skim of the obstacle.

A kif voice came in over com. "Identify: *urgent*." Someone was waiting in this place, stationed to guard, another of Akukkakk's long arms.

"Aunt," Hilfy's voice came weakly, bubbling liquid. "Kif . . ."

"Got it." Pyanfar sniffed blood or sweat, licked salt from her mouth, staring at the screens which showed the dark mass hoving up at them . . . tight skim, incredibly tight. Their own output was still knnn-song, wailing up and down the scale, tickings and whines . . . *that* had to put the kif off. Haral and Tirun talked frantically to each other, searching with the sensors for their way out.

"Got it!" Haral exclaimed suddenly. A star showed up in the bracket.

"Can't do it," Pyanfar said. The mass was too close. They had no choice now but to skim past and hope.

"Identify," the kif voice insisted.

Instruments flared suddenly, screens going static. "That was fire," Pyanfar said to Hilfy, "onto our former vector, thank the gods."

A second flaring: *The Pride* had returned a shot, automatic response. The alarms went again, crescendo of mechanical panic.

"Mass proximity," Pyanfar said into allship, for those riding it out below. "We're going to miss it."

The solidity was there, a sudden jump in every mass/drive instrument on the bridge, lights flaring red, a static washout on the number-four screen: Kita Point mass, a chunk of rock, a cinder radiating only the dimmest warmth into the dark, lightless, lonely and far, far too big for *The Pride* to drag with her into jump. . . .

Vid picked up flares of light, massive spots like the glow of a sun in that dark, illumining the surface of Kita mass. Rock boosted in their field out of Urtur had not changed vector. It hit the dark mass at near *c*, pyrotechnics which flowered the dark.

They passed in that flare of impact, slingshotted with a wrench which brought a new flood of blood to Pyanfar's throat . . . grayout . . .

. . . back again. *"Haral!"*

A frantic moment. *"There!"* Their referent was back in bracket. A kif voice clicked and chattered out of phase with what they should be getting: that was then a second ship, lying off Kita zenith.

Fire hit them.

Pyanfar slammed the drive back in, with the howl of the kif in her ears, the static spit of instruments trained on the chaos in their wake. She tried with all her wits to keep oriented, a slow reach of a sore arm while matter came undone about them, while they were naked to the between and time played games with the senses. No way that the kif could have followed. They had run the gauntlet. They were through the worst. After Kita it was one of three destinations and after the next, one of two more; and the choices multiplied, and the kif had harder and harder shift to bring numbers to bear against them. . . .

"We're fading," Haral said, words which stretched through infinity, emotion-dulled, nowhere; this was the way it went when ships lost themselves, when they jumped and failed to come out again . . . perhaps some mathematical limbo . . . or straight into mahendo'sat hell, where four-armed demons invented horrors . . . Pyanfar watched for another such wobble. Damage they had taken under fire could have done something to the vanes, robbed them of capacity, might lose them permanently. . . .

. . . second arrival, a blurring downdrop of the senses into here and when again. Pyanfar reached for the panel and ordered scan search. Differential com was already getting signal: it was the marker of Kirdu System, wondrous, beautiful mahendo'sat voice, the buoy of the jump range.

"We're in!" Hilfy cried. "We're *in*."

"Clear and in the range," Pyanfar said, smug. She hit the jump pulse to throw off velocity and the smugness evaporated somewhat; the pulse was queasy, less powerful than it ought to be.

"Captain?" Haral's voice.

"I feel it."

"Maintain knnn output?" Hilfy asked.

"Yes." Pyanfar kept her eyes on the readout, hit the pulse again. "Plot entry vector," she ordered Tirun. "We might have trailed some debris with us."

"Reckon we dumped most of the rocks on Kita," Tirun muttered. She started sending the schematic over, fired off a comp-signal warning for what good it would do a slow ship in the path of their debris-attended entry. The dump went on, sickly pulses which finally began to count.

"That's better," Pyanfar said, swallowing against the stress. "Hilfy, got a lag estimate?"

"Approximate," Hilfy said in a thin voice. "Thirty-minute round trip to station, estimate."

Close, by the gods, too close. Pyanfar kept the dump pulses going at the closest possible intervals, kept her eyes nowhere but the center screen now, the relayed scan from the station buoy which plotted the location of ships and planets and large objects in the system. Automation had added in the warning *The Pride* had sent out, a hazard zone in a cone headed transzenith of system.

"Getting refinement on course," Haral said as a schematic came up on number-two screen. It took only a little bending: *check velocity,* the warning kept flashing. Pyanfar coaxed another dump out of *The Pride* and made the slight correction, her senses swimming now with the prolonged strain of high-velocity reckonings, with stringing her mind along those distances and speeds which the ship's own comp handled in special conflict-dumping mode.

"Down the slot!" Tirun cried as the lines matched.

They were dead on at last, free and safe and headed down the approach path station had preassigned the next incomer in that area of the range. Pyanfar afforded herself a lighter breath, still with her eyes fixed on the scan, trying to figure how much more they could dump and how fast. Let one miner be where he ought not to be, let one skimmer go off for some private reason without advising station in advance, some idiot crossing the entry lanes, some mad knnn or chi, with whom there was never any reasoning, navigation hazards wherever they operated. . . .

Sweat ran, or blood. She sniffed and wiped at her nose, eyes still fixed and hand on the button. They rode the odds; they came in like a shot, counting on statistics and blind luck and traffic being exactly where it ought; one could do that a few times in a lifetime and not run out of luck.

"Acquiring station signal," Hilfy said. "That's tc'a talking now, I think. It's this knnn signal of ours. . . ."

"Cut the signal. Give station our proper ID. Relay pirate attack; damage and emergency, and probable accompanying debris."

"Got it," Hilfy said.

Pyanfar hit the dump again, forced them a little more toward a sane speed, and a board red-lighted. She cycled in a backup. Haral unbelted and leaned into the pit beside her console, frantic readjustments.

There might be kif in dock at Kirdu . . . gods, *would* be kif here, by all the odds, and just possibly one of them had come through from Urtur. But this was Kirdu: Mahendo'sat here, in their own territory, had teeth, and took no arguments from visitors. They would demand explanations for such an entry. Gods grant whatever remaining debris they had boosted through with them from Urtur found no mahendo'sat targets, or there would be more than an explanation due.

"Something's left station," Tirun said. The image showed up on the number-two screen. Ships were outbound, four of them, one after the other, moving on intercept, dopplering into their path. "Hilfy," Pyanfar said, "signal general alert, all hani ships in-system."

"Done," Hilfy said, moving to do it. Haral slid back into place, set to work in haste at the comp. The number-one screen started acquiring estimates, locational shifts on the oncomers and everything else in the system. That was station guard which had just put out, more than likely: *The Pride* had broken regulations from entry to this moment, heaps and piles of regulations. Some mangy *mahe* station official was no doubt elbow deep in the rule books this moment hunting penalties. Pyanfar's nose wrinkled at the thought of the fines, the levies, the arguments.

"Getting signal on the ships outcoming," Hilfy said. "They're mahendo'sat, all right."

"Huh." Pyanfar blew a sigh of relief. Worse had been possible, worse indeed. "Geran," she said over allship. "Chur. Are you getting this down there? We're all right; station's sending us an escort."

"Coming in clear, Captain."

"Is everything secure down there? How's Tully? Have you got a monitor on him?"

"He's here in op with us," Geran said. "Drugs are wearing off. He's muzzy but following what's going on."

"No more risks, rot you; who cleared that?—Take scan on number four for approach; give us some relief up here; and get him secure."

"*I friend.*" Tully's voice came back to her, hani words. And others, his own tongue, a flood of words. "Shut him down," Pyanfar hissed, and there was silence. "Working," Chur's voice reported, and Tirun paused in her frantic pace to take the chance for a drink from a plastic bottle from under-counter. She passed it to Hilfy and then to Tirun and then to Haral and Haral to Pyanfar. The remnant went down, a welcome cooling draught. Pyanfar took the chance to call up comp to locate the damage, gnawed her upper lip as the information came through incomplete. She looked right, at the others, at Hilfy, who was listening to something, with a bruised, exhausted look on her face. "Shunt that below when they get the Outsider settled," Pyanfar said to her, and looked at Haral, who was still doing updates. "Damage indeterminate," she said to Haral privately. "I don't feel any lag in the insystem responses, at least. It should be a normal dock, but we're going to have to get a hurryup on that repair and I don't know how by the gods we're going to finance the bribe."

"Aunt," Hilfy said, "station is on, wants to talk to you personally. I told them—"

"*Captain.*" Lowerdeck overrode, sent up an image on scan. Ship in the jump range, incoming, on their tail.

"*Gods,*" Pyanfar hissed. "Gods rot all kif. . . . Hilfy, ID, fast."

Hilfy hesitated half a breath; Tirun was already overreaching a long arm onto her territory. Wailing came through, and Pyanfar grimaced at the high-pitched squeal.

"Knnn," Tirun said. "Captain, it's that rotted knnn."

"We don't know it's *that* knnn," Pyanfar spat back, snatching the mike, waved it angrily at Hilfy. "Station. *Station,* and get your wits working, niece."

The ready light came on. "Go," Hilfy said, distraught and wild-eyed, and subdued the knnn pickup.

"*This is Kirdu Station,*" the machine-translated voice came through. "*We make urgent severe protest this entry. Go slow, hani captain incoming.*"

"This is *The Pride of Chanur,* Pyanfar Chanur speaking. We're incoming with an unidentified on our tail and with damage, but we have maneuverability. The ship behind us may pose a threat to station; I suggest your escort direct its attention to what's following us."

Com stayed dead, longer than lagtime dictated.

"Escort *is* passing turnover point," Geran's quiet voice came from the other op center. "Captain, they're going to pass us, going to go out and look that bastard over."

Pyanfar looked, saw, returned her attention to comp, where new estimate was coming up on the position of the incoming ship. It was close, moving hard, no dump of speed.

"Got a hani contact," said Hilfy. "Tahar."

"Gods and thunders." This was not a friendly house to Chanur. Pyanfar picked up the contact on her board. "Tahar ship, this is Pyanfar Chanur. Stand ready for trouble. Don't be caught at dock."

"Chanur, this is Dur Tahar. Is this your trouble?"

"It has no patent, Tahar, not so far. Stand out from station, I warn you. In case."

"Chanur," the translated voice of station broke in on them. *"Tahar Captain. Against regulation, this. Use station channel. And this station order stay. No moving out."*

"We're coming in, station. We advise you ships are destroyed and lives lost. If that ship back there is knnn, well; but if it isn't, Kirdu has trouble."

Another voice, clicking and harsh. Kif.

"That's from a docked ship," Hilfy said quickly. "Got it on station directional."

"Captain." That from Tirun. "Incomer's just begun dump. They're checking speed."

Pyanfar blinked, the suspicion of good news hitting dully on a dazed brain. She drew a whole breath. "Gods grant it *is* knnn," she muttered. "Station, you should be getting that now; we'll make a full explanation as soon as we get in and get our mechanical problems in order. We strongly urge you take full precautions and get a positive visual on that so-named knnn arrival. We have serious charges to lodge."

Silence from station. They were not, most likely, overjoyed.

Pyanfar broke the contact. "Bastards." She wiped her mouth. "Cowards." The escort passed and headed out to the incoming ship behind them. She settled back in her cushion and listened to the reports.

"Aunt," Hilfy said finally, "mahendo'sat report visual confirmation: it *is* a knnn ship."

"Thank the gods," Pyanfar muttered, and threw open the restraint on her cushion, leaned forward more comfortably. Station was coming up. A flurry of docking instructions was arriving on the number-three screen.

Not kif behind them, only a vastly confused knnn. She imagined the chagrin of the odd creatures, who had arrived to far more commotion than knnn were wont to stir under any circumstances. Coincidence, perhaps; ships came and went from everywhere—

gods, rare to have two ships come into a jump range that close, but not that rare. Kirdu had a great deal more traffic than that generated by *The Pride*. This was civilization, here at Kirdu, civilization, after all.

She drew a series of quieter breaths, watched the schematic which showed them the way toward docking. Tired. Indeed she was tired. She ached in her bones. It took a moral effort to settle in for docking maneuvers, to do it by manual because she wanted the feel of it, not to be surprised by some further malfunction under automatic.

She was already mentally sorting through possible arguments with the Tahar, a loan, anything to get *The Pride*'s repairs made and paid, to get out of this place: they needed no more damages than they had, and most of all they did not need prolonged residence here.

If they were very, very fortunate, the kif were sorting matters out with a certain knnn who had picked up a bit of salvage at Urtur; and that knnn might not be amused by a hani joke. The great *hakkikt* Akukkakk would be even less amused . . . but he would have a hard time negotiating with the knnn for a look at its prize; and a harder time with his fellow kif . . . indeed he would. She felt, in all, *satisfied*.

But a knnn had happened through jump with them; had happened to crowd them. Gods . . . did they have apparatus which made tracking possible?

Its voice was back, distant and eerie, like that which she had duplicated at Urtur, to use a knnn voice as shield and disguise.

Gods knew what message they had been transmitting to knnn hearing: *follow me? Help me?* Something far less friendly?

Tc'a might know; but there was no querying that side of Kirdu Station.

They came up on dock, moving in next to the Tahar ship. Kirdu wanted its hani problems collected, apparently, giving them berths next each other. In some part that was good, because it gave them private access to talk without witnesses; and in another part it was not, because it made them one single target.

"Where are the kif?" she asked station bluntly, stalling on the approach. "I'm not putting my nose into station until I know what berths they have."

"Number twenty and twenty-one," station informed her. *"Mahe* and stsho in the between numbers, no trouble, no trouble, hani Captain. You make easy dock, please."

She wrinkled her nose and committed them, not without contrary thoughts.

vii

The Pride's nose went gently into dock, the grapples clanged to and accesses thumped open, and Pyanfar thrust back from the panel with a sudden watery feeling about the joints. Station chattered at them, requests for routine cooperations. "Shut down," she said curtly, waved a weary signal at Haral and pushed the cushion around the slight bit it could go. "Hilfy, tell station offices. Tell them we've got some shakeup. I'll talk with them when we get internal business settled."

"Aye," Hilfy murmured, and relayed the message, with much flicking of the ears in talking with the official and a final flattening of them. Pyanfar shortened her focus, on Tirun, who was running her last few checks. Her hands made small uncertain movements; her ears were drooping. "Tirun," Pyanfar said, and Tirun's face when she looked around showed the strain. "Out," Pyanfar said. "Now."

Tirun stared at her half a moment, and ordinarily Tirun would have mustered argument. She looked only numb, and tried a faltering effort which got her to her feet and a reach which got her to the next console. They all scrambled for her, but Hilfy was quickest, flung an arm about her. "She goes to quarters," Pyanfar said. "Aye," Haral said, and took charge from Hilfy, replacing Tirun's support on that side.

Hilfy stood a moment. Pyanfar looked on her back, on the backs of Tirun and Haral as Tirun limped away trying not to limp; and Hilfy straightened her shoulders and looked back.

"I'll stay on the com," Hilfy offered.

"Leave it. Let station wonder. Clean up."

Hilfy nodded stiffly, turned and walked out, quite, quite without swagger, with a hand to steady her against the curvature-feeling of the deck when they were docked. It occurred to Pyanfar then that Hilfy had not been sick, not this time. Pyanfar drew a deep breath, let it go, turned and leaned over the com. "Lowerdeck, who's at station?"

"Geran," the voice came back. "All stable below."

"Clean up. Above all get Tully straightened up and presentable."

"Understood."

Pyanfar broke the connection. There was another call coming over com.

"*Chanur, this is* Tahar's Moon Rising. *Private conference.*"

"Tahar, this is Pyanfar Chanur: we have a medical situation in progress. Stand by that conference."

"*Do you require assistance,* Pride of Chanur?"

There was, infinitesimal in the tone, satisfaction in that possibility. Pyanfar sweetened her voice with prodigious effort. "Hardly, *Moon Rising.* I'll return the call at the earliest possible. Chanur's respects, Tahar. Out."

She broke off with abruptness, pushed back and strode off, without swagger in her stride either. All her joints seemed rearranged, her head sitting precariously throbbing on a body which complained of abuses. Her nape bristled, not at kif presence, but at an enemy who sat much closer to home.

Gods. Beg of the Tahar?

Of a house which had presented formidable threat to Chanur during Kohan's holding? The satisfaction in the Tahar whelp's voice hardly surprised her. It was a spectacle, *The Pride* with her gut missing and her tail singed. There would be hissing laughter in Tahar, the vid image carried home for the edification of Kahi Tahar and his mates and daughters.

And from Tahar it would go out over Anuurn, so that it would be sure to come to Kohan. There would be challenges over this, beyond doubt there would be challenges. Some Tahar whelp would get his neck broken before the dust settled, indeed he would; young males were always optimists, always ready to set off at the smell of advantage, even with the least edge it might afford them.

They would try. So. They had done that before.

That was what Dur Tahar had wind of.

"She's well enough," Haral reported at the door of the crew's quarters on the lower deck. Pyanfar looked beyond and saw Tirun snugged down in bed and oblivious to it all. "Leg swelled a bit under the stress, but no worry."

Pyanfar frowned. "Good medical facilities here onstation. But it might be we'd have to pull out abruptly; I don't want to risk leaving any of us behind for a layover, not . . . under the circumstances."

"No," Haral agreed. "No need for that. But we're wearing thin, Captain."

"I know," she said.

"You too, begging your leave."

"Huh." She laid her hand on Haral's shoulder. Walked away to the lift, paused there and listened in the direction of Chur and Geran's post. She walked back that way and leaned in at the door of op, where Geran sat watch, washed and in clean blue trousers, but looking on the world with the dull look someone ought to have who had gone from one on-shift to the next without sleep. "Right," Pyanfar said simply, recalling that she had given them orders they were following, and leaned an arm against the doorframe. "Tully made it all right down here, did he?"

"No trouble from him."

"I'm going to have to take him up on that work offer. You and Chur trade off with him, one on and one off. Tirun's ailing."

"Bad?"

"G stress didn't favor that leg. We'll rest here as much as we can. I'm going to see what charity I can get out of Tahar. Need to find out what damage we've got, first off."

"Got a remote on it," Geran said, turned about and called it up on the nearest screen. Pyanfar came into the room, looked at the exterior camera image, which was from the observation blister, and suffered a physical pang at the sight. Number-one vane had a mooring line snaking loose, drifting about under station's rotation, and there were panels missing, dark spots on the long silver bar. "That was our fade," Pyanfar said with a belated chill. "Gods. Could have lost it all coming in with that loose. Going to take a skimmer crew to get that linked back up, no way the six of us can do it."

"Money," Geran said dismally. "Might have to sell one of us to the kif after all."

"Bad joke," Pyanfar said, and walked out.

Tully, she had thought, with an impulse of which she was heartily ashamed.

But she kept thinking of it, all the way up to her own quarters.

She stripped and showered, shed a mass of fur into the drain; dried and combed and arranged her mane and beard. It was the red silk breeches this time, the gold armlet, the pendant pearl. She surveyed herself with a satisfaction that lifted her spirits. Appearances meant something, after all. The mahendo'sat were sensitive to the matter, quite as much as the stsho.

Offended prosperity, that was the tack to take with them. They knew *The Pride.* As long as it seemed that Chanur's fortunes were intact and that Chanur was still a power to reckon with among hani, that long they might hold some hope of mahendo'sat eagerness to serve.

And there was, she reckoned, smiling coldy at the splendid hani captain in the mirror, there was deadly earnest in this haste.

There was Akukkakk.

Gods rot it all.

Possibly she had embarrassed him enough so that his own would turn on him. That would take time to know. A long time out from homeport, keeping her ear alert for rumor.

Get rid of the Outsider Tully . . . would that the disentanglement were that easy.

She stared into her own eyes, ears flat, and meditated on the villainy that any trader seeing the Outsider would think of, and after a little thinking her lips pursed in a grimly smug smile.

So, so, so, Pyanfar Chanur. There was a way to settle more than one problem. Probably Tully would not like it, but an Outsider who came begging passage could take what he could get, and it was not in her mind to beg from Tahar.

She checked com, found the expected clutter of messages awaiting attention. "Nothing really urgent," Geran said. "Station's still upset, that's the sum of them."

"Chur's got Tully, has she, cleaning him up?"

"A little problem there."

"Don't tell me problem. I've got problems. What problem?"

"He has his own ideas, our Tully does. He wants to be shaved."

"Gods and thunders. Washroom?"

"Here, now."

"I'm coming down there."

She started for the door, went back and picked up the audio plug for the translator and headed down in haste. *Shaved*. Her ears flattened, pricked again in a forced reckoning that customs were customs.

But appearances, by the gods. . . .

She arrived in op in deliberate haste, found the trio there, Geran, Chur, Tully, all cleanly and haggard and drowning their miseries in a round of gfi. They looked up, Tully most anxious of all, still possessed, thank the gods, of all his mane and beard and decent-looking in a fresh pair of trousers.

"Pyanfar," he said, rising.

"Captain," she corrected him sternly. "You want what, Tully? What problem?"

"Wants the clippers," Chur said. "I trimmed him up a bit." She had. It was a good job. "He wants the beard off."

"Huh. *No,* Tully. Wrong."

Tully sank down again, the cup of gfi in his two hands, looked chagrined. "Wrong."

Pyanfar heaved a sigh. "That's reasonable. You do what I say, Tully. You have to look right for the mahendo'sat. You look good. Fine."

"Same # hani."

"Like hani, yes."

"Mahendo'sat. Here."

"You're safe. It's all right. Friendly folk."

Tully's mouth tightened thoughtfully. He nodded peaceably enough. Then he reached a hand behind his head and knotted the pale mane back in his fingers. "Right, that?"

"No," Pyanfar said. The hand dropped.

"I do all you say."

Pyanfar flicked her ears, thrust her hands into her waistband. "Do all?" She felt pricklish in the area of her honor, and the Outsider's pale eyes gazed up at her with disturbing confidence. "It might frighten you, what I want. I might ask too much."

Some of that got through. The confidence visibly diminished.

"I make you afraid, Tully?" She gestured wide, toward the bow. "There's a station out there, Kirdu Station. Mahendo'sat species is the authority in this place. There's a hani ship docked next to us. Stsho species too, down the dock."

"Kif?"

"Two kif ships, not the same ones. Not Akukkakk's, not likely.

Traders. They're trouble if we linger here too long, but they won't make any sudden move. I want you to go outside, Tully. I want you to come with me, out in the open, on station dock, and meet the mahendo'sat."

He did understand. A muscle jerked in his jaw. "I'm crew of this ship," he said. It seemed a question.

"Yes. I won't leave you here. You stay with me."

"I come," he said.

That simply. She stared at him a moment, deliberately held out her hand toward the cup in his. He looked perplexed for a moment, then surrendered it to her. She drank, subduing a certain shudder, handed it back to him.

He drank as well, glanced at her, measuring her reaction by that look, finished the cup. No prejudices. No squeamishness about other species. She nodded approval.

"Go with you, Captain," Chur offered.

"Come on, then," Pyanfar said. "Geran, you stay; can't leave the ship with no one watching things, and the others are off. We're going just to station offices and back, and it shouldn't be trouble. I don't expect it, at least."

"Right," Geran said, not without a worried look.

Pyanfar put a hand on Tully's shoulder, realized the chill of his skin, the perpetually hunched posture when he was sitting. He stood up, shivered a bit. "Tully. The translator won't work outside the ship, understand. Once out the rampway, we can't understand each other. So I tell you here: you stay with me; you don't leave me; you do all that I say."

"Go to the offices."

"Offices, right." She pressed one sharp-clawed fingertip against his chest. "I'll try to get it through to you, my friend. If we go about with you aboard in secret, if we leave mahendo'sat territory with you and go on to Anuurn, to our own world—that could be trouble. Mahendo'sat might think we kept something they should have known about. So we make you public, let them all have a look at you, mahendo'sat, stsho, yes, even the kif. You wear clothes, you talk some hani words, you get yourself registered, proper papers, all the things a good civilized being needs to be a legal entity in the Compact. I'll get it all arranged for you. There's no way after you have those papers that anyone can claim you're not a sapient. I'll register you as part of my crew. I'll give you a paper and where I tell you, you put your name on it. And you

don't give me any trouble. Does enough of that get through? It's
the last thing I can tell you."

"Don't understand all. You ask. I do it."

She impatiently waved her hand at Chur. "Come on."

Chur came. Tully did, blindly trusting, at which she scowled
and walked along in front of them both to the lock, wondering
whether station offices had detectors and whether they could get
away with a concealed weapon, going where they were going. She
decided against it, whatever the other risks.

A watcher stood by the rampway outside, a *mahe* dock-worker
who scampered off quickly enough when they showed outside, and
who probably made a call to his superiors . . . the mahendo'sat
were discreetly perturbed, polite in their surveillance. But they
were there. Pyanfar saw it, and Chur did; and Tully turned a
frightened look toward the sudden movement. He talked at them,
but the translator was helpless now, outside the range of the inship
pickup, and Pyanfar laid a reassuring hand on his shoulder and
kept him moving. "Just a precaution," she said quietly, and
looked beyond to the rampway access of *Moon Rising,* where
a far more hazardous watcher stood, a hani crewwoman.

"Better take care of that business," Pyanfar said to Chur, and
diverted her course diagonally among the canister-carriers toward
Moon Rising.

Another hani showed up outside, on the run: second crewwoman, doubled reflection of the other, same wide stance and
steady stare. At a certain distance Pyanfar stopped, and waited,
and made a subtle sign to Chur, who strode forward to meet the
others.

There was an exchange too quiet for her ears . . . no friendliness in the postures, but no overt unpleasantness. Chur came
back, not in haste, not delaying any either, ears flat.

"Their captain's asleep," Chur reported. "She proposes to come
aboard *The Pride* when her nap's done. Answer, Captain?"

"Why should I? I wasn't advised. But I may let her come. It
suits me." She turned without a glance at the others, put a hand on
Tully's hairless back and steered him away with them.

And if the Tahar captain was in fact sleeping, she would not be
by the time those two rag-ears got back inside, to report the
Chanur captain had a companion of unknown species, headed for
station offices. The Tahar had gotten caught in their own arro-

gance, and Chanur failed to rise to the insult, simply walked off. Pyanfar threw a little swagger into the departure, for the Tahar and for the gaping *mahe* dock-workers, some of whom fled in haste to report to superiors or to gather comrades, a dark-furred and scantly clad crowd.

"They noticed," Chur said.

"That they have." Pyanfar locked her hands behind her and they strolled along in company, one tall hani captain in scarlet, one smallish hani crewwoman in roughspun blue, and improbably between them, a towering wide-shouldered Outsider with naked skin and a beautiful golden mane, excruciatingly conspicuous. Pyanfar suffered an irrepressible rush of the blood, a tightening of the lips as a crowd began to gather, far more people than those who worked the docks. Mahendo'sat, dockers and merchanters and miners and gods knew what else; and a scatter of stsho, pale and pastel among the crowd, their whitish eyes round as moons, holding each others' hands and chattering together in shock. Of the kif . . . no sign as yet, but the rumor would draw them, she was sure of that, and wished that she had that gun she had thought of taking.

They reached the lift, pushed the button, *mahe* giving way about them and crowding back again at every opportunity, a roar of crowd noise about them. "Captain," someone asked, one of the mahendo'sat, "what is this being?"

She turned about with a grin which lacked all patience, and mahendo'sat who knew hani backed up, but there was humor in it too, satisfaction at the turmoil. The lift arrived, and a half dozen startled *mahe* decided to vacate it, whether or not they had planned on getting out on this level. They edged out the door in haste and Pyanfar seized Tully by the arm and put him inside. Chur delayed while she stepped in, and came last, facing the crowd. The door delayed, time enough for anyone else who thought they wanted to ride up with them, but no one entered.

The door closed, and the lift shot upward. Pyanfar let go of Tully's arm and put her hand on his back, ready to indicate to him to move out. He was sweating despite the chill in the air. On the other side of him Chur patted his arm. The lift stopped once. Those waiting decided against entering, eyes wide; and the lift went on up.

"Friend," Tully said nervously, out of his scant hani repertoire.

"Mahendo'sat and stsho," Pyanfar said. "Friend. Yes."

The car stopped a second time, a quieter corridor in the office complex. Tully walked with them, out and down the hall, startling other *mahe* workers.

And stopped abruptly. A kif came from the offices ahead, stopped and stared, anonymous in gray robes and doleful kifish face. Pyanfar seized Tully's arm, pulled the claws in when he winced, but the sting got him moving. They passed the kif and the kif turned; Pyanfar did not react to it, but Chur, crew unburdened with captaincy, faced about with ears flat and a snarl on her face. The kif kept staring. Pyanfar whisked Tully through the welcome office doors ahead and only then turned to cast a look back; but the kif was on its way, robes aswirl in its haste, and Chur, ears still flat, joined them inside the registry office. Tully smelled of sweat. Veins stood out in his arms. Pyanfar patted his shoulder and looked around the gaudy colored room at a frozen officeful of mahendo'sat, most standing.

"I'm Pyanfar Chanur. You requested an interview."

There was a general flutter, the foremost of the officials dithering about letting them through the general registry area to the more secluded complex behind the doors, with a dozen looks at Tully in the process.

"Come along," Pyanfar urged him softly, keeping a hand on his elbow, and now she sweated, reckoning the shocks Tully had endured thus far, a kif in the hall, close spaces . . . one irrational moment and he could bolt; or strike at someone. "Friend," she said, and he stayed by her.

The official let them through into a luxurious waiting area, thick carpet and pillowlike couches in bright colors, hastened about providing them refreshment as they settled on a facing group of couches. "Sit, sit," Pyanfar said, providing Tully the example, legs tucked and ankles crossed, and Chur waited until Tully had settled nervously on the facing couch. Chur sank down in relief.

The official set the welcoming tray on a portable table in their midst. His dark *mahe* eyes were alive with curiosity. "Beg understanding, hani captain . . . this is . . . passenger?"

"Crew," Pyanfar said with a prim pursing of the lips. She accepted the glass the squatting *mahe* filled, two-handed, *mahe* style in her holding of it; and saw to her satisfaction that the *mahe* had in fact provided three glasses. He filled the second and gave it to Chur, whose manners were impeccable, and with some diffidence, offered to Tully.

Tully took his after the same fashion, keen mimic. Pyanfar smiled to herself and smothered the smile in a sip of mahendo'sat liquor. The official pattered out with effusive and anxious bows, leaving them alone; and whatever Tully thought of the liquor he had the self-possession not to flinch from it.

"Friend," Tully said again, looking worried. Chur, beside him, put a hand on his knee and he seemed to take reassurance from that. Panic, not quite, but his skin glistened with sweat, his muscles were taut. Steps sounded just outside the door at the side of the room and he would have looked around, but Chur patted his knee and he refrained.

The door opened. A handful of mahendo'sat, important with elaborate bright kilts and collars, came in on them, one of them attended by a small brown and white fluff which scurried about the floor at its feet and bristled at the scent of hani. It hissed and had to be scooped up in the official's arms; and Pyanfar kept a wary eye on it all the same. Chur and Tully followed her lead, and she bowed and suffered the mahendo'sat's frankly appraising stare at Tully. They chattered among themselves, no little disturbed, and some of that she caught, exclamations of curiosity. The fluff growled, and its owner—an elderly *mahe* whose dark fur was graying and whose flat face had all the other attributes of age—looked toward her with a lowering of the ears.

"Chanur Captain?"

"The same. Have I the honor to know you?"

"Ahe Stasteburana-to, I."

The stationmaster in person. She made another bow, and the stationmaster did the same, keeping the equilibrium of the pampered creature in his arms, soothing its growls unsuccessfully as he straightened again. And with apparent distraction Stasteburana strolled off, while another of the company made a stiffer bow and launched into them. "You pay, Chanur Captain, fines for reckless approach. Fines for bring debris boosted through, danger to all innocent. Fines for reckless haste near station. For bring hazardous situation."

"I spit at your charges. I dumped the debris at Kita and warned you only in the remote chance there was still some with me, dumped it, I might add, and sustained damage protecting your worthless station from injury. As for fines, you're brigands, bloodsuckers, to prey off a friendly ship with a long-standing account at this station, when for the preservation of our lives and the protection of the Compact we had to come in for shelter against piracy. A hani, a hani, mind, asks shelter, and when have we ever done such a thing? Are you blind and deaf as well as greedy?"

"We have outrage. We have knnn act crazy out there. We have report—"

The Personage Stasteburana held up his aged and manicured hand. His Voice silenced herself and broke off with a bow, while Stasteburana strolled back, stroking his ball of fluff, which had never ceased to growl. "You make large commotion, honorable Chanur, great hani captain, yes, we know you—long time absent; maybe trade our rival Ajir, but we know you. Good friend, we. Maybe make deal on fines. But serious matter. Where come from?"

"Meetpoint and Urtur via Kita, wise *mahe*."

"With *this*?" An ears-flat look at Tully.

"An unfortunate. A being of great sensitivity, wise and gentle *mahe*. His ship was wrecked, his companions gone . . . he cast himself on my charity and proves of considerable value."

"Value, hani Captain?"

"He needs papers, wise *mahe*, and my ship needs repairs."

Again Stasteburana walked away, aloof from the Voice. "Your ship got no cargo," the Voice spat. "You come empty hand, make big trouble here. You near ask credit, hani Captain; what credit? We make you fines, you send Anuurn get cargo, maybe two, three hani ship pay off damages. You got us knnn. You got us kif. We know this. You go talk hani at next berth, ask she pay your fines."

"Trivial. I have cargo, better than *Moon Rising*. I make you a deal, indeed I shall, in spite of your uncivilized behavior. I make a deal all mahendo'sat will want."

The Voice looked at Tully, and the Personage turned about, moved in with a leisurely grace, handed the small noisy animal to the Voice, and frowned. Stasteburana made a further sign to his other three companions, and one of them called to someone in the hall.

It was not easy to make distinctions of mahendo'sat of the same age and sex and build; but about the large and relatively plain fellow who answered that summons . . . there was an instant and queasy familiarity—particularly when he flashed a broad gilt-edged smile. Pyanfar sucked in her breath and tucked her hands behind her, pulling the claws back in.

"Captain Ana Ismehanan-min of the freighter *Mahijiru*," Stas-teburana said softly. "Acquaintance to you, yes."

"Indeed," Pyanfar said, and bowed, which gesture Goldtooth returned with a flourish.

"This kif business," said Stasteburana, folding his wrinkled hands at his middle. "Explain, hani Captain."

"Who am I to know what a kif thinks? They let this unfortu-nate being slip through their fingers and expected me to sell him back, plainly illegal. Then they attacked a hani ship which was completely ignorant of the matter. A Handur ship was completely destroyed unless the captain of *Mahijiru* has better news."

"No good news," Goldtooth agreed sadly. "All lost, hani Cap-tain. All. I get away quick, come here tell story my port."

The Personage turned and tapped Goldtooth on the shoulder, spoke to him in one of those obscure *mahen* languages outside her reckoning. Goldtooth bowed profoundly and backed aside, and Pyanfar looked warily at the Personage. "You know," she said, to recover the initiative, "*What* the kif wanted; and you know that there's no chance of hiding such a prize, not here, not on Anuurn either. No good hiding it at all."

"I make you. . . ." There was a beep from someone's pager. A voice followed, and one of the attendants came forward in con-sternation, offered the instrument to the hand of the Personage Stasteburana. There was talk of knnn: that much past the local di-alect; and the Personage's dark eyes grew wider. "*Where* is it?" Pyanfar caught that much of the conversation, and saw distress among the others. "You *come*," said Stasteburana himself, not using his Voice for instruction, and swept a gesture to the door-way from which the mahendo'sat had come into the room.

"Come," Pyanfar echoed to Chur and Tully, and walked along amid the *mahe,* the attendants and the Voice and the cap-tain of *Mahijiru,* all in the wake of the Personage, who was has-tening with some evident alarm.

The corridor debouched on an operations center. Technicians in the aisles melted aside for the Personage and his entourage. The Voice hissed orders, and the fluff hissed too, in general menace. On the air a tc'a spoke, a sound like static bursts and clicking.

"Screen," Stasteburana ordered in his own tongue.

The main screen livened in front of them, meters wide and showing a dimly lit dockside. Blues and violets, a horrid light, like nightmare, and a scuttling shape like a snarl of hair possessed of an indefinite number of thin black legs. It darted this way and that, dragging with it, clutched in jaws—appendages under the hair?—something which glittered with metal and had the look of a long-limbed hani body.

With a sinking feeling Pyanfar recognized it. It was a good bet that Chur and Tully did, who had conspired in its construction.

"That's a knnn," Pyanfar said to Tully. He said something back, short and unhappy. On the screen the creature scurried this way and that with its burden, eluding the attempts of writhing shapes in the shadows which tried to deal with it: those were tc'a. Something stiltlike joined the commotion, darted at the flitting knnn and tugged at the prize, skittered off again. *Chi,* by the gods, those manic beggars; the limbs glowed phosphorescent yellow, left confusing trails on the screen in its haste.

Suddenly a pair of tc'a writhed into the knnn's way, physically dispossessed the knnn of its burden; and the knnn darted about the harder, wailing with rage or distress or simply trying to communicate. The scene was complete chaos; and suddenly more knnn poured in. The solitary chi fled, a blur of yellow-glowing sticks; and in the mahendo'sat control center, technicians who had been seated stood up to watch what had become riot. Hisses and clicks and wails came from the audio. The knnn began to give ground, a phalanx of hairy snarled masses.

Suddenly one darted forward, seized one of the leathery, serpent-shaped tc'a and dragged it off into their retreating line. There was a frantic hissing and clicking from the mass of tc'a, but apart from a milling about, a writhing and twining of dozens of serpentine bodies like so many fingers lacing and unlacing in distress . . . nothing. Not the least attempt at counterattack or rescue. Pyanfar watched the kidnapping with her ears laid back.

So the knnn had traded, after its fashion, darted onto station and laid down its offered goods—made off with something it took for fair; and now another species had descended to trading in sapients.

"What is it?" a *mahe* asked distressedly, and fell silent. The main body of the tc'a managed to drag the knnn's trade goods along, a grotesque flailing of suited arms and legs. A communication came through, and a technician approached the Personage Stasteburana. "Hani-make eva-pod," that one said, and Stasteburana turned a disturbed glance on Pyanfar, who lifted her ears and assumed her most careless expression.

"I shouldn't want to disturb you," Pyanfar said. "All you'll find in that suit, wise *mahe,* is a very spoiled lot of meat from our locker; I'd advise you take decontamination precautions before taking that pod helmet off."

"What you do?" Stasteburana spoke in anger without his Voice, and waved his Voice off when she attempted to intervene. "What you do, Chanur Captain?"

"The knnn seems to have intercepted a gift of mine meant for the kif. It's confused, I'm sure. Probably it'll return the tc'a. . . . It was, at the time, a matter of necessity, revered *mahe.*"

"Necessity!"

"Only spoiled food, I assure you. Nothing more. . . . We were on the point of discussing repairs to my ship . . . which are urgent. You'll not want me sitting at your dock any longer than you have to. Ask the honest captain of *Mahijiru.*"

"Outrage!" the Voice proclaimed. "Extortion!"

"Shall we discuss the matter?"

The fluffball suffered another transfer, to the nearest of the dignitaries, and the Voice looked to be preparing for verbal combat; but the Personage lifted a placid and silencing hand, motioned the group back down the corridor, delaying to give an instruction regarding the tc'a. Then the Personage led the way back into the comfortable room down the corridor.

"Profit," Pyanfar said quickly and soothingly when the elder *mahe* and his entourage turned to face her and hers.

"Trouble first with kif and now with knnn and with tc'a. Deceptions and hazards to this station."

"A new species, revered *mahe.* That's the prize that has the kif disturbed. They see the hope of profit the like of which they've not known before; and I have the sole surviving member of his company, a spacefaring people, communicative, *civilized,* wise *mahe,* and fit to tilt the balance of the Compact. This was the prize at Meetpoint. This was the reason of the loss of the Handur ship, and this was the part of my cargo I refused to jettison. Surely we agree, revered *mahe,* what the kif meant to do if they had gotten this information first. Shall I tell you more of my suspicions . . . that the stsho knew something about what was going on? That kif meant to annex a large portion of adjacent space . . . having intimidated the stsho? That having done so, they would then be in a position to expand their operations and rearrange the map of the Compact to suit themselves—an acquisition from which the other members of the Compact would be positionally excluded; only the stsho . . . who would lick the kif's feet. And what future for the Compact then? What of this Compact which holds all of our very profitable trade together? What of the balance of things? But I shall tell you what I have: a tape, a tape, my good, my great and farsighted *mahe* elder, for a symbol translator . . . a tape which the kif spent sapient lives to obtain and failed to get. We aren't selfish; I make this tape available to mahendo'sat as freely as hani, in the interests of spreading this knowledge as far as possible among like-minded people. But I want my ship repaired, the fines forgotten, the assurance that Chanur will continue in the friendship of this great and powerful station."

The Personage laid his ears back, his eyes dilated. He turned away, leaving his Voice to face the matter. "Where come this creature? How we know sapient? How we know friendly?"

"Tully," Pyanfar said, and put a hand on his arm and drew him forward. "Tully, this is the Voice of the stationmaster . . . friend, Tully."

For a terrible moment that arm was tense, as if Tully might bolt. "Friend," he said then obediently. The Voice frowned, peered this way and that at Tully's face . . . on a level with the *mahe*'s own. "Speak hani?" the Voice asked.

"I go on Pyanfar ship. Friend."

Gods. A sentence. Pyanfar squeezed the arm and put him protectively behind her. The Voice frowned; and behind the Voice the Personage had turned back with interest. "You bring this trouble to us," Stasteburana said. "And knnn . . . why knnn?"

"A resident of Urtur. I claim no understanding of knnn. It's become disturbed . . . but not of *my* doing, noble *mahe*. The safest thing for Kirdu Station in all events is to have me safely on my way . . . and to have that, I fear, there's a matter of certain essential repairs—"

The elder flared his nostrils and puffed breaths back and forth. He consulted with his Voice, who spoke to him rapidly involving kif and knnn. The Personage turned back yet again. "This tape deal—"

"—key to another species, revered *mahe*. Mahendo'sat will have access to this development; meet ships of this kind—assured peaceful meeting, full communication. And mind, you deal with no stranger, no one who will cheat you and be gone. Chanur expects to be back at Kirdu in the future, expects—may I speak to you in confidence—to *develop* this new find."

Stasteburana cast a nervous glance at Tully. "And what you find, a? Find trouble. Make trouble."

"Are you willing to have the kif do the moving and the growing and the getting? They assuredly will, good *mahe,* if we don't."

The Personage made nervous moves of his hands, walked to the one of his companions who held the angry ball of fluff and took it back, stroking it and talking to it softly. He looked up. "Repairs begin," Stasteburana said, and walked near Tully, who stood his ground despite the growling creature in the *mahe*'s arms. The growling grew louder. The *mahe* stood and stared a long moment, gave a visible twitch of the skin of his shoulders and lifted a hand from his pet to sign to his Voice. "Make papers this sapient being. Make repairs. All hani go. Go away." He looked suddenly at Pyanfar. "But you give tape. We say nothing to kif."

"Wise *mahe,*" Pyanfar said with all her grace, and bowed. The Personage waggled fingers and dismissed them in the company of the Voice, and the fluff growled at their backs.

So, Pyanfar thought, as they delayed at the desks outside, as nervous mahendo'sat officials went through the mechanics of identifications with Tully. So they had promises. She kept her ears up, her expression pleasant, and smiled with extraordinary goodwill at the desk-dwellers. Chur kept her hand hovering near Tully's arm, at his back, constantly reassuring him at this and that step, answering for him, keeping him calm when they wanted his picture, urging him to sign where appropriate. Pyanfar craned forward, got a glimpse of a signature of intricate regularity which could not be an illiterate's mark in anyone's eyes.

"Good," she said, patted Tully on the shoulder as the document went back into the hands of mahendo'sat officials—looked about again, nose wrinkling to a scent of perfume, for two stsho had just come into the offices. They stood there with their jeweled pallor looking out of place in mahendo'sat massive architecture, the huge blocky desks and the garish colors. Moonstone eyes stared unabashedly at Tully and at them. Capacious stsho brains stored up a wealth of detail for gossip, which stsho traded like other commodities. Pyanfar bared her teeth at them and they wisely came no closer.

The papers came back, plasticized and permanent, with Tully's face staring back from them, species handwritten, classification general spacer semiskilled, sex male, and most of the other circles unfilled. The official gave the folder to Pyanfar. She gave it to Tully, clapped him on the shoulder, faced him about and headed him for the door, past the gawking stsho.

Elsewhere, she trusted, orders were being passed which would get a repair skimmer prioritied for *The Pride*. The mahendo'sat's prime concern had become getting rid of them at utmost speed; she did not doubt it.

There would be a *mahe* official demanding that tape before all was done. That was beyond doubt too. There would be some little quibble which came first, repairs or tape; repairs, she was determined. The *mahe* had little choice.

They walked the corridor to the right from the office doorway, toward the lift, the three of them, past occasional mahendo'sat office workers and business folk who either found reason to duck back into their doorways or anxiously tried to ignore them.

But the three who waited before them at the lift . . . Pyanfar stopped half a step, made it a wider one. "You," she said, striding forward, and the foremost *mahe* stood out from his two companions, gilt teeth hidden in a black scowl.

"Bring trouble, you," said the captain of *Mahijiru*.

"How you live, *mahe*? A? Sell information every port you touch?"

"My port, Kirdu. You make trouble."

"Huh. Trouble found me. Got crew shot getting you your rotted welders to keep our deal. Do I say anything about pearls you owe me? No. I give you a gift, brave *mahe*. I ask no return."

Goldtooth frowned the more, looked at Chur and walked closer to Tully, tilted his round chin and looked Tully up and down, but kept his hands off him. Then he threw a glance at Pyanfar. "This you pick up on the dock."

"You ask questions for the Personage? Same you gather information at Meetpoint?"

For the first time the *mahe* flashed that sharp-edged gold grin. "You clever, hani Captain."

"You *know* this Akukkakk."

The grin died, leaving deadly seriousness. "Maybe."

"You really merchant, *mahe* Captain?"

"Long time, honest hani. *Mahijiru* longtime merchant ship, me, my crew, longtime merchanter, sons and daughters merchanters. But we know this *Hinukku,* yes. Longtime bad trouble."

Pyanfar looked into that broad dark face and wrinkled her nose. "Swear to you, *mahe* Captain, I didn't think to bring trouble down on you. I give you the trade goods, make no claim for return. You saved our hides, put us onto that kif bastard. Owe you plenty for that."

The *mahe* frowned. "Deal, hani. They make you repair, you get quick leave . . . danger. Tell you that free."

"*Mahijiru* took no damage getting out of Meetpoint?"

"Small damage. You take advice, hani."

"I take it." She pressed the lift button, took a second look, to remember the face of this *mahe* beyond doubt. "Come," she said as the lift arrived empty. She shepherded Chur and Tully through the door and turned once inside. Goldtooth/Ismehanan and his companions showed no inclination to go with them. The door closed between and the lift started down. She looked back, at Tully and at Chur, and gathered Tully by the elbow as the car, unstopped this time by other passengers, made the whole trip down and let them out on the docks.

The crowd had dispersed somewhat, thank the gods, but not enough. It gathered quickly enough as they crossed the dock, and Pyanfar watched on all sides, flicking quick glances this way and that, reckoning that by now trouble had time to have organized itself.

And it was there. Kif—by the gantries, watching. That presence did not at all surprise her. Tully failed to spot them, seeming dazed in the swirl of bodies, none of which pressed too closely on them, but stayed about them.

The rampway access gaped ahead. A group of mahendo'sat law enforcement stood there, sticks in hand, and the crowd went no farther. Pyanfar thrust her companions through that line, with her own legs trembling under her—want of sleep, gods, want of rest. Chur was in the same condition, surely, and Tully was hardly steady on his feet, unfit mentally and physically for this kind of turmoil. She sighted on the rampway and went, hard-breathing.

But among the gantries beside them . . . hani shadows. *Moon Rising*'s folk, none of her own, had spilled over from the next berth, behind the security line. "Come on," she said to Chur and Tully. "Ignore them."

She headed into the rampway's ribbed and lighted gullet, had led the two of them up the curving course almost to the security of their own airlock when she heard someone coming behind. *"In,"* she said to her companions, and turned to bar the intruder who appeared around the curve. Her ears were flat; she reached instinctively for the weapon she had left behind—but the figure was hani, silk-breeched and jeweled, striding boldly right up the rampway.

"Tahar," she spat, waved a dismissing hand. "Gods, do we need complications?"

"I've done napping." The Tahar captain stopped just short of her, took her stance, hands at her waist, a large figure, with a torn left ear beringed with prosperity. Broad-faced . . . a black scar crossed her mustache, making it scant on the left side, and giving Dur Tahar no pleasant expression. Her beard was crisply rippled and so was her mane, characteristic of the southerners, dark bronze. Two of her crew showed up behind her, like a set of clones.

"We've managed," Pyanfar said, "without troubling your rest."

Dur Tahar ignored her, looked beyond her shoulder—at what sight, Pyanfar had no trouble guessing. "What's that thing, Chanur? What creature is that?"

"That's a problem we've got settled, thank you."

"By the gods, settled! We've just been ordered off the station, and it's all over the dock about this passenger of yours. About hani involved with the kif. About a deal you've made—by the gods, I'll reckon you've settled things. What are you, trading in live bodies now? You've found yourself something special, haven't you? That fracas that sent you kiting in here with your tail singed —involved with *that?*"

"That's enough." Her claws came out. She was tired, gods, shaking on her feet, and she stared at Dur Tahar with a dark tunnel closing about her vision. "If you want to talk about this, you ask me by com. Not now."

"Ah. You *don't* need our help. Are you planning to stay here in dock with your tail hanging . . . or did you and the mahendo'sat come up with a deal? What kind of game are you proposing, Chanur?"

"I'll make it clear enough. Later. Get clear of my airlock."

"What species is it? Where from? The rumor flying the dock says kif space. Or knnn. Says there's a knnn ship here that dropped a hani body."

"I'll tell it to you once, Tahar: we got this item at Meetpoint and the kif took out *Handur's Voyager* for spite, no survivors. Caught them sitting at dock, and they and we hadn't even been in communication. We dumped cargo and ran for Urtur, and the kif who followed us struck at *Faha's Starchaser* with no better reason. Whether *Starchaser* got away or not I don't know, but they at least had a run at it. The kif want this fellow badly. And it's gotten beyond simple profit and loss with them. There's a *hakkikt* involved, and there's no stopping this thing till we've got him. Maybe we did, at Urtur. He looked bad, and that may settle it. But if you want to make yourself useful, you're welcome to run our course."

"Suppose you make yourself generous. Give this thing into my hands. I'll see it gets safe to Anuurn."

"No, thanks."

"I'll bet not. You can deal with the mahendo'sat, after all, but not with a rival. Well, Chanur's not going to sit on this one, I'll promise you that, Pyanfar Chanur. And if this turns out to be the fiasco it promises to be, I'll be on your heels. That brother of yours is getting soft. Back home, they know it. This should do it, shouldn't it?"

"Out!"

"Give me the information you traded the mahendo'sat. And we may view things in a better light."

"If you were *mahe* I'd trust you more. Look him over, Dur Tahar. But anything else you want to know . . . I'll decide on when I've got this straightened out. Never fear; you'll get the same data I gave the mahendo'sat. But if you leave this in our laps, then by the gods, we'll settle it our way without your help."

Dur Tahar laid her ears back and started to go, lingered for one poisonous look beyond, toward the airlock, and a focus snapped back on center. "I'll ask you at Anuurn, then. And you'll have answers, gods rot you. You'll come up with them."

"Nothing personal, Tahar. You always did lack vision."

"When you beg my help—I *might* give it."

"Out."

Dur Tahar had made her offer. Perhaps she expected a different answer. She flinched, managed a lazy indifference, smoothed her rippled beard, turned and looked back toward the airlock a last time, slowly, before she stalked out, gathering her two crewwomen as she went.

"Gods," Pyanfar muttered through her teeth, put a hand wearily to the rampway wall and turned about to the airlock, feeling suddenly older. *That* was muffed. She should have been quicker on her mental feet, slower of temper. The Tahar might have been talked into it. Maybe wanted to be talked into it. If a Tahar could be trusted at their backs. She hated the whole of it, *mahe,* Tahar, Outsider, all of it—winced under Chur's stare. Not a word from Chur the whole way back, regarding the business she had conducted, this tape-selling, trust-selling.

And Tully's face . . . suddenly he jerked away from Chur's grip and went into the airlock, Chur hastening to stop him. Pyanfar broke into a run into the hatchway, but Chur had got him. Tully had stopped against the inside wall, his back against it, his eyes full of anger.

"Captain," Chur said, "the translator was working."

Pyanfar reached into her pocket and thrust her audio plug into her ear, faced Tully, who looked steadily toward her. "Tully. That was *not* a friend. What did you hear? What?"

"You're same like kif. Want the same, maybe. What deal with the mahendo'sat?"

"I saved your miserable hide. What do you think? That you can travel through Compact territory without everyone who sees you having the same thoughts? You didn't want to deal with the kif— good sense; but by the gods, you haven't got a choice but us or the kif, my friend Tully. All right. I traded them the tape you made— but not that I couldn't have gotten the ship repaired without that: they're anxious to get rid of us; they'd have come round tape or no tape, you can bet they would. But now everyone's going to know about your kind; gods, let the mahendo'sat make copies of it; let them sell it in the standard kit. It's the best deal you can get. I'm not selling *you,* you rag-eared bastard; can I make you understand that? And maybe if your ships meet our ships . . . there'll be a tape in the translators that may keep us from shooting at each other. We meet and trade. Understand? Better deal than the kif give you."

A tremor passed over his face, expressions she could not read. The eyes spilled water, and he made a move of his arm, jerked at Chur's grip on it and Chur cautiously let him go.

"You understand me?" Pyanfar asked. "Do I make myself understood?"

No response.

"You're free," Pyanfar said. "Those papers let you go anywhere. You want to walk out the rampway, onto the dock? You want to go back to station offices and stay with the *mahe?*"

He shook his head.

"That's no."

"No. Pyanfar. I #."

"Say again."

He reached to his waist and drew out the papers, offered them to her.

"*Your* papers," Pyanfar said. "All in order. Go anywhere you like."

He might have understood. He pointed toward the door. "This hani—want me go with him."

"Her. Dur Tahar. No friend of mine. Or to this ship. Nothing that concerns you."

He stood a moment, seeming to think it over. Finally he pointed back toward the inner hatch. "I go sit down," he said, shoulders slumping. "I go sit. Right?"

"Go," she said. "It's all right, Tully. You're all right."

"Friend," he said, and touched her arm in leaving, walked out with his head down and exhaustion in his posture. "Follow him?" Chur asked.

"Not conspicuously. Docking's got his quarters out of commission. Get a proper cot for the washroom."

"We could take him into crew quarters."

"No. I don't want that. There's nothing wrong with the washroom, for the gods' sake. Just get him a sedative. I think he's had enough."

"He's scared, Captain. I don't much blame him."

"He's got sense. Go. Tell Geran if she doesn't hear something about that repair crew within half an hour, come get me."

"Aye," Chur murmured, and hastened off in Tully's wake.

So. Done, for good or ill. Pyanfar leaned against the wall, aching in all her bones, her vision fuzzing. After a moment she walked out, down the vacant corridor toward the lifts, hoping to all the gods Geran could find no incident to put between her and bed.

No one stopped her. She rode the lift up, walked a sleep-drunken course down the central corridor to her own door.

"Aunt," Hilfy's voice pursued her. She stopped with her hand against the lockplate and looked about with a sour and forbidding stare.

"Repair crew's on its way," Hilfy said ever so quietly. "I thought you'd want to know. Message just came."

"You've been sitting watch topside?"

"Got a little rest. I thought—"

"If Geran's on, it's waste to duplicate effort. Get yourself back to quarters and stay there. Sleep, gods rot you; am I supposed to coddle you later? Take something if you can't. Don't come complaining to me later."

"Captain," Hilfy murmured, ears back, and bowed.

Pyanfar hit the bar and opened the door, walked in and punched it closed before the automatic could function. Belatedly the look on Hilfy's face occurred to her; and the long duty Hilfy had spent at com through transit, and that she had intended to say something approving of that, and had not.

Gods rot it. She sat down on the side of the bed and dropped her head into her hands. Gods, that she had staggered through the requisite interview with the mahendo'sat, bargained with them, offended the Tahar—and Tully. . . . She had traded off what three of his shipmates had died to keep to themselves.

In such a condition she gambled, with Chanur and Tully's whole species on the board.

She dropped her hands between her knees, finally reached for the bedside drawer where she kept a boxful of pills. She shook one into her hand and put it into her mouth—spat it out in sudden revulsion and flung the open boxful across the cabin. Pills rattled and circled and lay still. She lay down on the bed as she was, drew the coverlet over herself, tucked her arms about her head and shut her eyes, flinging herself into an extended calculation about their routing out of here and refusing to let her mind off that technical problem. She built the numbers in front of her eyes and fended off the recollection of Tully's face or Hilfy's, or the scuttling figure of the knnn with its prize, or the kif which skulked and whispered together out on the docks.

viii

"*Aunt.*"

It was not com; it was Hilfy in person, leaning over her bed, shaking at her. "*Aunt.*" Pyanfar came out of sleep with a wild reach to get her elbow under her, shook herself, stared into Hilfy's dilated eyes. "It's *Starchaser*," Hilfy said. "They've come through. They're in trouble. They can't get dumped. The word just came in—"

"O gods." Pyanfar kicked the coverlet off, scrambled out, dressed as she was, and seized Hilfy by the arm on her way out of the room. "Talk, imp: has anyone scrambled?"

"Station's called miners in the path . . . some mention of an outbound freighter being able to change course. . . ." Hilfy let herself be pulled through the doorway into the corridor and loped along keeping up with her on the way to the bridge. "They're twenty minutes lag out, crossing Lijahan track zenith."

"Twenty now?"

"About."

Haral was on the bridge, standing by scan, with the area-light on her face, and her expression was grim when she looked around at their arrival. "They've got to get to the pod," Haral said. "No way anyone can get to her in time. No way any rescue can haul that mass down, even if she's stripped."

"What's our status?"

"We can't get there," Hilfy objected, plain logic.

"Not for rescue," Pyanfar said quietly.

"Repairs underway," Haral said. "Vane's unsecured. If they're running ahead of company—we're in trouble."

Tirun came limping in, loping haste, and there was a query

from lowerdeck. "You're getting all we've got," Haral relayed to Geran and Chur below. "Can't tell anything yet."

"Come on," Pyanfar muttered to the blip on systemic image. "*Do* it, Faha. Get out of there." She sank down into the com cushion, an eye still toward the screen, and punched through the station op code. "This is *The Pride of Chanur*. Urgent relay the stationmaster, Pyanfar Chanur speaking: warn you of possible hostile pursuit on tail of incoming emergency. Repeat: warn you of possible hostile pursuit of incoming emergency."

"*This message receive clear,* Pride of Chanur. Mahen *ships answer emergency. Please stand by.*"

She watched scan, rested a knuckle against her teeth and hissed a breath. Ships showed in the schematic, traffic at dead standstill compared to the incoming streak that was *Starchaser,* motion slowed enough to see only because of system-wide scale. Everything was history, the images on the scope, the voices from the zone of emergency. Unable to dump velocity, *Starchaser* would streak helplessly across the system and lose herself on an unaimed voyage to infinity. It was a long way to die.

"Lost the transmission," Haral said. Hilfy edged in, looking desperate, tried the switches herself past Haral's side. Pyanfar gnawed the underside of a claw and shook her head. The business of getting a jump-mazed crew on their feet and headed to the escape pod—in *Starchaser*'s type, high up on the frame—and get it away, all this within the minutes they had left . . .

Then they could only hope, if they could make it that far, that the pod's engines could hammer down the velocity, give some jumpship the chance to match velocities and lock onto the pod's small, manageable mass, so that they could be dumped down. That freighter out there was the best chance the crew had, if only they could get loose.

"Pod's away!" Haral exclaimed, and Tirun and Hilfy were pounding each other on the back. Pyanfar clenched her two hands together in front of her mouth and stared flat-eared at the scan, where a new schematic indicated the probable course of the pod which had now parted company with doomed *Starchaser.* Both dots advanced along the track, but a gap developed, the pod's deceleration far from sufficient to rid itself of a jumpship's velocity before it gave out, but doing what it could. The crew would probably black out in the stress: that was a mercy. Now it was a race to see if the freighter could overhaul the pod or whether the pod would leave the system.

"*Mahe* freighter?" Pyanfar asked.

Haral nodded.

The Pride was on station-fed transmission; and station had to be using the feed from ships farther out, the Lijahan mines, whatever was in a position to have data, and relative time was hard to calculate now. The freighter came up by major increments while the minutes passed, boosting itself on its jump field. The gap still narrowed with agonizing sluggishness, as scan shifted, keeping up with events which were now long decided.

Com sputtered, a wailing transmission. Knnn. "Gods," Tirun said. "A knnn's out there in it."

Station command responded, a tc'a voice. There were other transmissions, knnn voices, more than one, a dissonance of wails.

"*Chanur,*" said a hani voice, clear and close at hand. "*Is this also your doing?*"

Pyanfar reached for it, punched in the contact, retracted the claw with a moral effort. "Tahar, is that a question or a complaint?"

"*This is Dur Tahar. It's a question, Chanur. What do you know about this?*"

"I told you. Let's keep it off com, Tahar."

Silence. The Tahar were no allies of the Faha crew. It was a Chanur partisan in trouble, but if any ship at station could have moved in time, *Moon Rising* would have tried: she did not doubt it. It was a painful thing to watch, what was happening on scan. Close to her, Tirun had settled, and Hilfy, simply watching the screen while her Faha kinswomen and the wreckage that had been a Faha ship hurtled closer and closer to the boundaries of the pickup. After such a point insystem scan could not follow them. Station was getting transmission now from a different source, from the merchanter *Hasatso,* the freighter tracking *Starchaser,* the only ship in range. The blip that was *Starchaser* itself finally went off the screen.

"Chanur ship," station sent. "Tahar ship. Advise you merchanter *Hasatso* have make cargo dump; do all possible."

"Chanur and Faha will compensate," Pyanfar replied, and hard upon that *Moon Rising* sent thanks to *Hasatso* via station. "Gods look on them," Haral muttered—a cargo dumped, to close the gap, to close on an emergency not of their species.

Knnn wailed. Elsewhere there was silence. For a long while there seemed only one rhythm of breaths on *The Pride,* above and below.

"They're nearly on it," Hilfy breathed.

"They've got them," said Tirun. "No way they can miss now." It went slowly. The transmissions from *Hasatso* became more and more encouraging; and at long last they reported capture. "Hani signal," *Hasatso* told Kirdu Station, "in pod. Live."

Pyanfar breathed out the breath she had been holding. Grinned, reached and squeezed Hilfy's arm. Hilfy looked drained. "Tahar," Pyanfar sent then, "did you receive that report?"

"Received," Tahar said curtly.

Pyanfar broke it off, sat a moment with hands clasped on the board in front of her. A ship lost; a tradition; that deserved its own mourning. Home and life to the Faha crew, and that was gone. "Station," she sent after a moment, "advise the Faha crew that Chanur sends its profound sorrow, and that *ker* Hilfy Chanur *par* Faha will offer the resources of *The Pride of Chanur,* such as they are."

"Advise them," another voice sent directly, *"that Dur Tahar of* Tahar's Moon Rising *also offers her assistance."*

That was courtesy. Pyanfar leaned back in the cushion, finally turned and rose with a stretch of her shoulders. "What can be done's done. Go fetch something to drink, Hilfy; if I'm roused out, someone owes me that. Drink for all that want it. Breakfast. I'll hear reports less urgent during.—Haral, who's supposed to be on duty?"

"I am."

"So. Then close down lowerdeck. Tirun, back you go."

"Aye," Tirun muttered, and levered herself up stiffly and limped off in Hilfy's wake. Pyanfar settled against the com post counter and looked at Haral, seated at the number two spot.

"That knnn's fallen into pattern about Lijahan," Haral said, paying attention to the screens. "Still making commotion. A wonder they don't try for the cargo salvage out there."

"Huh. Only grant they all stay put."

"Skimmer's still working out there at our tail. They've got a crew outside working the connectors. The cable's ready to secure. But fourteen panels were missing and six loose, and they estimate another twenty hours working shift on shift to get the new ones hooked up."

"Gods." Pyanfar ran a hand over her brow and into her mane, thinking of kif—of attack which had chewed *Starchaser* to scrap. There were others besides the knnn who might be expected to rush to that salvage out there; there were the onstation kif . . . who showed no sign of moving. That was unnatural. No one was moving, except maybe a few miners out there with ambition. No one from station. Word was out; rumor . . . had a wind up everyone's back.

"The Tahar," Haral said further, after a moment, "appealed that order to put out with an appeal to finish cargo operations. It was allowed."

"Helpful. At least they're here."

"Helpful as the Tahar in general. Begging your pardon."

"I'll talk to them."

"You think Tahar'd move to guard our tail?"

"No," she said. "I don't. Not unless they see profit in it. What are they doing? Not taking cargo."

"Offloading. Stripping to run. Canisters pouring out like maggots."

Pyanfar nodded. "Station wants that cargo safe then; and Tahar's going to dump that out fast down to the bit she uses to stall with. The Personage has backed down, that's what; got a few of his onstation companies wailing about losses, and Tahar'll stay here as long as she likes. That'll give me time."

"Gods, the bill on this."

"Expensive, our Outsider. In all senses." She looked about as Hilfy came through the archway with a large tray, two cups and two breakfasts. "Thanks," Pyanfar said, taking plate and cup . . . paused to look at Hilfy, who had stopped to look at the situation on the screen. They were still getting transmission relayed from *Hasatso,* with occasional breakup which indicated velocity dump. "Going to be a while," Pyanfar said. "Unless they've got a medical emergency I doubt they'll boost up again after turnover, just ride it slow in. Hours from now. Go on back to quarters. I mean it."

A few ports ago Hilfy might have argued, might have laid her ears back and sulked. She nodded now and went. Pyanfar glanced at Haral, who stared after the retreating youngster and then nodded once, thoughtfully.

"Huh," Pyanfar said, digging into the breakfast, and for some little time she and Haral sat and watched the scan and ate. "Tell you, cousin," Pyanfar said finally, "you go offwatch and I'll take it."

"Not needful, Captain."

"Don't be noble. I've got some things to do. One thing you can do for me. When you go down, look in on Tully. Make sure he's all right."

"Right," Haral said. She stood up and gathered the dishes onto the tray. "But he's all right, Captain. Chur's bedded down to keep an eye on him."

Pyanfar had been finishing her last sip of gfi, to surrender the cup. She banged it down on the tray. "Gods blast—Did I or did I not order him separate?"

Haral's ears dropped in dismay. "Chur said he was upset, Captain; made herself a pallet in the washroom so's he wouldn't wake up by himself. She said—your pardon, Captain—sedated, he looked so bad. You were in bed, Captain. It was my discretion."

Pyanfar exhaled shortly. "So. Well. Depressed, Chur says."

Haral nodded. "We'd take him," Haral said.

"Chur said."

"Um." Haral figured that train of things suddenly and her mustache hairs drew down. "Sorry, Captain."

"*Him,* for the gods' sake."

"Not as if he was hani, Captain."

"Not as if," Pyanfar said after a moment. "All right. Put him where you want; that's crew business, none of mine. Work him. He claims to be a scan tech. Let him sit watch. Who's on next?"

"*Ker* Hilfy."

"With someone of the experienced crew. Someone who's made their mistakes."

Haral grinned and rubbed the black scar which crossed her nose. "Aye. One of us will sort him out."

"Off with you."

Haral went. Pyanfar slid down off the counter and transferred the activity to her own board, sat down in her own deeply padded cushion and ran the incoming messages of hours past. There was nothing there but what Haral had said, Tahar's argument about staying and the beginnings of *Starchaser*'s crisis. Sporadic information still came in: *Hasatso* sent word of four survivors. . . .

Four. A cold depression settled over her.

Four out of seven crew on that ship. It was more than the phys-

ical body of *Starchaser* lost out there, more even than a life or two
in a crew kin-close. Four out of seven was too heavy casualties for
a group to recover itself—not the way it had once been. Gods, to
start over, having lost that heavily—

"Station," she sent, "this is Pyanfar Chanur: confirm that transmission from *Hasatso*. Names of survivors."

"*Pride of Chanur*," station sent back to her, "Hasatso *transmit
four survivors good condition. No more information. We relay
query.*"

She thanked station absently, sat staring at the screen a moment. There was lagtime to contend with on that request, nothing
to do but wait. She bestirred herself to run checks with the ships at
repair on their own damages, to contact station market and to arrange a few purchases and deliveries via dockside courier services.
There was delay on the communications: everyone at station
seemed muddle-witted in the confusion, down to the jobbers in
commodities.

"Station, what's keeping that answer?" she sent main op.

"*Crew refuse reply,*" the answer came back. Communication
failure there too. Nerves. Possibly shaken-up hani and *mahe* res-
cuers were at odds. Ship lost, cargoes lost, lives lost. An ugly
business.

And one of the knnn had put out from station, putting out wailing transmission and wallowing uncertainly about station's pe-
ripheries like a globe of marshfire, touching off ticking objections/
accusations/pleas? from the tc'a control.

Gods. The oxygen-breather command went silent for the moment. Tc'a chattered and hissed. Pyanfar reached for translation
output, but it failed: tc'a translated best when it was simple docking instruction or operations which were common to all ships. This
was something else, gods rot them.

There was silence finally, even from the tc'a. The knnn moved
out farther and stayed there. *Hasatso* continued its slow inward
progress. At last the mahendo'sat side of station came on again,
quiet operational directions for the incoming freighter, nothing in-
formational.

Pyanfar sent them no questions. No one did.

The news came when *Hasatso* entered final approach: four survivors, a fifth dead in the stress of the pod eject, of wounds, and
allowed to go with the pod when *Hasatso* released it, not a hani

choice, but *mahe* honor. Two went with *Starchaser,* dead in the attack or unable to get to the pod—the information was not clear. There was a name: first officer Hilan Faha, survivor; and another: Lihan Faha—the captain, the third casualty.

"Aunt," Hilfy said, when Pyanfar called her to the bridge and told her, "I'd like to go down to the dock where they are. I know it's dangerous. But I'd like to go. By your leave."

Pyanfar set her hand on Hilfy's shoulder. Nodded. "I'll go with you," she said, at which Hilfy looked both relieved and pleased. "Geran," she said, turning to lean over the com board, putting it through on allship. "Geran."

The acknowledgment came back.

"Geran, take watch again, lowerdeck op. New word's come in. *Starchaser* captain is lost, and two of the crew. Hilfy and I are going to meet the rescue ship; we'll bring the Faha back aboard if they're so inclined. No sense them having to put up with *mahe* questions and forms."

There was a moment's delay, a sorrowful acknowledgment.

"Come," Pyanfar said to Hilfy then, and they walked out toward the lift. Hilfy's bearing was straight enough, her face composed . . . not good news, when she had gone to sleep thinking that things were better than they were; but they had something, at least, of the Faha crew, something saved; and that was still more than they had once hoped.

Another matter to the kif account, when it came to reckonings. But if there were kif out there now—and there might be, hovering at the system's edges, the same game that they themselves had played at Urtur—then they were waiting some moment of advantage, some moment when there were not five armed mahendo'sat patrol ships cruising a pattern out there.

Allship had waked more than Geran. Tirun was up, sitting in op when they came down toward the lock; and Geran, who had been assigned the duty; and Chur was standing about with Tully, who looked vaguely distressed in this disturbance he failed to comprehend. Haral showed up in haste from further down the corridor. "Going with you, by your leave," Haral said, and Pyanfar nodded, not sorry of it. "Kif out there," Pyanfar said. "I'm not getting caught twice the same way."

"Take care," Tirun wished them as they went, and in the airlock, while Haral opened the outer hatch, Pyanfar delayed so she could take the pistol from its secure place in the locker by com and to slip it into her pocket.

"No detectors to pass," Pyanfar said. "Come on."

The hatchway stayed open behind them; they walked out the ribbed rampway and down onto the dockside. Engines whined on their left: *Moon Rising* was still about her offloading, and canisters were coming off into the hands of mahendo'sat dock-workers, not hani crew.

"They may have gone to meet the Faha too," Pyanfar judged, marking the total absence of a hani supervisor outside. It was a courtesy to be expected, politics aside in a hani ship's misfortune.

"Not much stirring," Haral said.

That was so. Where normally the vast docks would have had a busy pedestrian traffic up and down the vast curve, there was a dearth of casual strollers, and the activity about *Moon Rising* was the only activity of any measure in sight. Dock-workers, service workers, *mahe* with specific business underway paused to stare at them and after them as they walked. Stsho huddled near their accesses and whispered together. The kif were out about, predictably, clustered together near the accessway of one of the ships, a mass of black robes, seven, eight of them, who lounged near their canisters and clicked insults after them.

And at one of those insults Pyanfar's ears flicked, and she stopped the impulse in mid-twitch, trying to make believe she had not heard or understood. *He knows, hani thief. How many more hani ships will you kill?*

"Captain—" Haral murmured, and Hilfy started to turn around. "Front, gods—" Pyanfar hissed and seized Hilfy by the arm. "What do you want to start, at what odds?"

"What do we do?" Hilfy asked, walking obediently between them. "*How* can he know?"

"Because one of those kif ships is his, imp; came in here from Kita; and now Akukkakk's enlisted other ships to help him. They'll scatter out of here like spores when we go, and gods help us, we're stuck till we get that repair done."

"They as good as hit *Starchaser* themselves. I'd like to—"

"We'd all like to, but we have better sense. Come on."

"If they catch us on the dock—"

"All the more reason we get the survivors aboard and get off the docks. Afraid you're not going to get that station liberty here either, imp."

"Think I can do without," Hilfy muttered.

They kept walking, down among the gantries, past idle crews, as far as number fifty-two berth, where a surplus of bystanders gathered, a dark crowd of mahendo'sat, sleek-furred, tall bodies which made it difficult to see anything. Medical personnel were among them; and station officials, conspicuous by their collars and kilts.

And hani, to be sure. Elbowing through the gathering, Pyanfar caught sight of bronze manes and a glitter of jewels on a hani ear, and she made for that group with Haral and Hilfy behind her.

"It's high time you showed up," Dur Tahar said when she arrived.

"Mind yourself," Pyanfar said. "My niece behind me is Faha."

Dur Tahar slid a glance in that direction without comment. *"Hasatso's* due to touch any moment," she said.

"We've got some kif getting together down the dock. I'd watch that if I were you."

"Your problem."

"A warning, that's all."

"If you start something, Chanur, don't look for our help."

"Gods rot you, you give me no encouragement to be civil."

"I don't need your civility."

"A mutual hazard, Tahar."

"What, are you asking favors?"

The claws twitched. "Asking sense, rot you."

"I'll think on it."

Hasatso touched, a crashing of locks and grapples. Gantries slid up and crews opened station ports one after another in response to the ship, connected lines, started the rampway out to meet the lock. It was an agonizingly slow process from the spectator ranks, and only the mahendo'sat found occasion to chatter.

And finally a distant whine and thump announced the breaching of the freighter's hatch, first in procedure: station reciprocated, and the *mahe* crew escorted off four hani, exhausted hani, one with an arm bandaged and bound to her chest, all of them looking as if they were doing well to be walking at all. Necessarily the mahendo'sat officials moved in: there was signing of papers, *mahe* and hani; and Pyanfar took Hilfy by the shoulder, worked forward with her. Hilfy went the last on her own and offered an embrace to the refugees, an embrace wearily returned by the Faha, one after the other.

"My Captain," Hilfy said then, "my aunt Pyanfar Chanur; my crewmate Haral Araun *par* Chanur."

There were embraces down the line. "Our ship is open to you," Pyanfar told the first officer, whose haggard face and dazed eyes took her in and seemed at the moment to have too much to take in, with the *mahe* offering medical assistance, station wanting immediate statements. Pyanfar left the Faha momentarily to Hilfy and to the Tahar who had moved up to offer their own condolences, and herself took the hands of the *mahe* rescue crew one after the other, and those of the apparent captain, a tall hulking fellow who looked as bruised and bewildered as the Faha, who was probably at the moment reckoning his lost cargo and the wrath of companies and what comfort all this gratitude was going to win him when the shouting died down and the bills came in.

"You're captain, *mahe?*" Pyanfar asked.

A sign of the head.

"I'm Pyanfar Chanur; Chanur has filed a report in your behalf at Kirdu; Chanur company will give you hani status at Anuurn: you come there, understand? Make runs to Anuurn. No tax."

Dark *mahe* eyes brightened somewhat. "Good," he said, "good," and squeezed both her hands in a crushing grip, turned and chattered at his own folk—likely one of those *mahe* who could scarcely understand the pidgin, and *good* might be about half his speaking vocabulary. He seemed to make it clear to the others, who broke out in grins, and Pyanfar escaped through the crush toward Hilfy and the others, got her arm about Hilfy and got the whole hani group moving through the pressure of tall mahendo'sat bodies. The Tahar made a wedge with them, and they broke into the clear.

"This way," Pyanfar said, and first officer Hilan Faha took the other elbow of her injured companion and made sure of the other two, and they started walking, escaping the officials who called after them about forms—Chanur, Faha, and Tahar in one group up the dock, toward the upcurved horizon where *The Pride* and *Moon Rising* were docked.

"How far?" the Faha officer asked in a shaking voice.

"Close enough," Hilfy assured her. "Take your time."

The way back seemed far longer, slower with the Faha's pace; Pyanfar scanned the dark places along their route, not the only one watching, she was sure. Inevitably there were the kif ships; and the kif were there, ten of them now . . . calling out in mocking clicks their insults and their invitation to come and ship with them. "We take you to your port," they howled. "We see you get your reward, hani thieves."

A wild look came into Hilan Faha's eyes. She stopped dead and turned that stare on them. "No," Pyanfar said at once. "We're here on station's tolerance. This isn't our territory. Not on the docks."

The kif howled and chirred their abuse. But the Faha moved, and they made their way farther with the kif voices fading in the distance, past the stsho, who stared with large, pale eyes, up past a comforting number of mahendo'sat vessels, and virtual silence, dock crews and passersby standing quietly and watching with respectful sympathy.

"Not so much farther," Pyanfar said.

The Faha had not the breath to answer, only kept walking beside them, and finally, at long last, they had reached the area of *The Pride*'s berth. "Faha," Dur Tahar said then, "*Moon Rising* has no damage, and *The Pride* does. We offer you passage that's assuredly more direct and quicker home."

"We'll accept," Hilan Faha said, to Pyanfar's consternation.

"Cousin," Hilfy said in a voice carefully modulated. "Cousin, *The Pride* will put out quickly enough; and we need the help. We need you, cousins. You might find common cause in the company."

"Tamun's had all she can stand," Hilan Faha said, with a protective move of her hand on her injured comrade's shoulder. She looked toward the Tahar. "We'll board, by your leave."

"Come," Dur Tahar said, and the Tahar fell about the four and escorted them across to their own access. Hilfy took a couple of steps forward, ears flat, stood there, hands fallen to her sides, and took a good long moment before she turned about again, with her kinswomen disappearing upward into the rampway of *Moon Rising*. Mortification was in every line of her stance, a youngster's humiliation, that set her down as well as set her aside, and Pyanfar thrust hands into her waistband to keep them from awkwardness— no reaching out to the imp as if she were a child, no comfort to be offered. It was Hilfy's affair, to take it how she would. "They've had a shock," Hilfy said after a moment. "I'm sorry, aunt."

"Come on," Pyanfar said, nodding toward their rampway. There was a red wash about her own vision, a slow seething. She was bound to take the matter as it fell for Hilfy's sake, but it rankled, all the same. She walked up first and Haral last, leaving Hilfy her silence and her dignity.

Cowards, Pyanfar thought, and swallowed that thought too for Hilfy's sake. They desperately needed the added hands: that thought also gnawed at her, less worthy. They needed the Faha. But the Faha had had enough of kif.

And there were kif ships out there, waiting. She was increasingly certain of it—if not actually on the fringes of Kirdu System, which they might be, at least scattered all about, waiting the moment. More and more kif ships, a gathering swarm of them, unprecedented in their cooperation with each other.

She passed the airlock into the corridor, and Chur and Tirun who had turned out with the evident intention of welcoming their Faha guests—stopped in their exit from the op room, simply stopped.

"Our friends changed their minds," Pyanfar said curtly. "They decided to take passage with Tahar. Something about an injury one of them suffered, and the Tahar promised them a more direct route home."

That put at least an acceptable face on matters for Hilfy's sake. They retreated as Pyanfar walked into the op room, looked at Geran and Tully who sat there, Geran having well understood and Tully looking disturbed, catching the temper in the air, no doubt, but not understanding it. "Nothing to do with you," Pyanfar said absently, settling into a chair at the far counter, looking at the system-image which Geran had been monitoring. Hilfy and Haral came in together, and there was a strained silence in the op room, all of them gathered there and Hilfy trying to keep a good face on.

"Well, good luck to them," Tirun muttered. "Gods know they've seen enough."

"There are kif out there on the dock," Pyanfar said, "who know too much. Getting cheeky about it. They've come in from Kita ahead of us, part of the bunch from Meetpoint or Urtur—Urtur, I'll reckon, since I checked names and they weren't the same as there. Just passing the message from one kif to the next. It's getting tight here."

"There'll be more soon," Haral said. "I'll bet there's some outsystem. Captain, think we can talk the *mahe* to run us escort to our jumppoint? Surely we've got leverage enough for that."

"That story will go from station to station," Pyanfar said bitterly. "Gods, but I don't think we've got much choice. Get them to shepherd us out of here."

"When we can get our tail put together again," Tirun said glumly.

There was a noise from down the hall, a footstep in the airlock. Every head turned for the doorway and Pyanfar reached for the gun in her pocket and thrust her way past Tirun getting to the op room door and the corridor, clicking the safety off the gun.

It was hani—Hilan Faha, who flung up a startled hand and stopped at the sight of her. Pyanfar punched the safety back on with a clawtip and thrust the weapon back into her pocket, aware of others of her crew now behind her.

"Changed your mind suddenly?" she asked the Faha.

"Need to talk to you. To my young cousin."

"To your cousin, rot you; and to me. Come on inside. Neither she nor I'll talk out here like dockside peddlers."

"*Ker* Pyanfar," the Faha murmured, manners which in no way mollified her temper. Pyanfar waved the lot of them back into the op room—only then recalled Tully, who was trapped there in the corner, but there was nothing of secret in his presence on the ship, and no cause to send him slinking out past them all. Let the Faha talk in front of him; let her deliver her excuses under an Outsider's stare—served her right.

And Hilan Faha stopped in the doorway at the sight of Tully, this naked-skinned creature hani-styled and hani-dressed sitting at the counter among the crew; and Hilan's ears went flat. "This," she said, rounding on Pyanfar, "this is that item the kif wanted—isn't it?"

"His *name* is Tully."

Hilan's mouth tightened, an ominous furrowing of the nose. "A live item. By the greater gods, where have you been, Chanur, and what's going on with this business?"

"If you were traveling on this ship you might ask and I might answer. As things are, you can learn when the Tahar do."

"Rot you, *Starchaser* died in your cause, for this—" She spat, swallowed down a surplus of words when Pyanfar stared at her sullenly. "It was the captain's decision: we offloaded everything at Urtur and tried to run to give you a break for it. But where were you then? Where was *our* help?"

"Blind, Hilan Faha—off in the dust and stark blind. We tried, believe that; but at the last we had to jump for it or risk collision; we hoped you could get off in what confusion we created."

Hilan drew a quieter breath. "The captain's decision, not mine. I'd not have budged out of dock: know that. I'd have sat there and let you sort it out with the kif, this so-named theft of yours. . . ."

"You take kif word above mine?"

"If you have an explanation I'll be glad to hear it. My cousins are dead. We're broken. We'll not get another ship, not so likely. Great Chanur makes plans, but the likes of us—we'll go on other Faha ships, wherever we can get a berth. I'll reckon you know where the profit's to be found, and, gods rot your conniving hide, you've stirred up what a lot of ships are going to bleed for. What a lot of small companies are going to go under for. They gave me a message to give you, Pyanfar Chanur—the kif gave me this to tell you: that what you've done is too much to ignore and too great to let pass. That they'll come after you wherever you are in whatever numbers it takes—*even to Anuurn*. That they'll make it clear to all hani that this prize of yours is no profit to you. This from their *hakkikt*. Akukkakk. Him from Urtur. His words."

"Kif threats. I'd thought you had more nerve."

"No empty threats," Hilan said, eyes dilated, her nostrils flared and sweat-glistening. "Tell all hani, this Akukkakk says—desert this Pyanfar Chanur or see desolation . . . even to Anuurn space."

"And where did you hear all this? From a scattering of ships and a kif who never caught us—who failed to catch *you*, Hilan Faha; and if we'd gotten together at Urtur—"

"No.—No. You don't understand. They *did* catch us, Chanur. Did overhaul us. Killed two of my cousins doing it. At Kita. And they let us go . . . but we broke down in the jump. They let us go to deliver that message."

The Faha's shame was intense. There was a silence in the room, no one seeming to breathe.

"So," said Pyanfar, "do you believe all your enemies say?"

"I see *this*," Hilan said, gesturing at Tully. "And all of a sudden the game looks a lot larger than before. All of a sudden I see reason that the kif might gather, and why they might not stop. Chanur's ambition—has gone too far this time. Whatever you're into, I don't want part of it. My sister's alive; and two of my cousins; and we're going home.—Cousin," she said, looking at Hilfy, "to you—I apologize."

Hilfy said nothing, only stared with hurt in her eyes.

"Hilfy can leave with you if she likes," Pyanfar said. "Without my blame. It might be a prudent thing to do . . . as you point out."

"I'd be pleased to take her," Hilan said.

"I stay with my ship," Hilfy said, and Pyanfar folded her arms over a stomach moiling with wishes one way and the other at once. And pride—that too.

"So," Pyanfar said, "I wish you safe journey. Best we should travel together, but I'm sure that's not in the Tahar's mind now."

"No. It's not." The Faha looked down, and up again, in Tully's direction, a darkening of the eyes. "If you considered your relations to others, you wouldn't have done this thing. You've taken on too much this time. And others will think so."

"What I took on myself, arrived on our ship without a by your leave or my knowledge it existed. What would you do with a refugee who ran onto your ship? Hand him over to the kif at their asking? I don't sell lives."

"But you don't mind losing them."

"You throw away what they did," Hilfy said suddenly, "with your smallness."

The Faha's ears flattened. "What are *you* to judge? Talk to me when you've got some years on you, cousin. *This—*" She came dangerously near Tully, and Chur who had been sitting on a counter slid down to plant both feet, barring the way. Tully got out of his chair and stood as far back in the bend of the counter as he could get. The Faha shrugged, a careless gesture throwing away her intent. "I've another word," the Faha said, looking straight at Pyanfar. "Whether or not you intended what you've involved yourself in—it just may be the finish. Your allies might have stood by you, but it's all gotten too tangled. It's gotten too risky. How long since you've been home?"

"Some few months." Pyanfar drew in a breath and thrust her hands into her belt, with the taste of something bad coming—that ill feeling of a house at its height, in which any breath of change was trouble; and suddenly she disliked that look on the Faha's face, that truculence which melted into something of discomfort, a decent shame. "Maybe more than that," Pyanfar said, "if you count that I didn't go downworld last call. What is it, Faha? What is it you're bursting to tell me?"

"A son of yours—has taken Mahn from Khym Mahn. He's neighbor to Chanur now. He has ambitions. The old Mahn is in exile, and Kohan Chanur is finding sudden need of all his allies." Hilan Faha shrugged, down-eared and white about the nose and looking altogether as if she would wish to be elsewhere at the moment, instead of bringing such news to a Chanur ship. "My captain would have backed you; but what are we now, with one of our ships gone, one out of the three Faha owns; and what do we think when you take on something like this when you already have as much as Chanur can handle? You've lost your cargo; you've gotten yourself a feud with the kif, and kif threatening to go into Anuurn zones, for the gods' sake—how can Chanur hold onto its other allies when that starts? I've lost my ship, my captain, some of my cousins—and I have to think of my family. I *can't* involve myself with you, not now: I can't make Faha part of this and get our ships a feud with the kif. You're about to lose everything. Others will decide the same, and Chanur won't be there even *if* you get back. I'm going home, *ker* Pyanfar, on the Tahar ship because I have to, because I'm not tangling what's left of us in Chanur fortunes."

"You're young," Pyanfar said, looking down her nose. "The young always worry. You're right, your captain would have backed me. She had the nerve for it. But go your way, Hilan Faha. I'll pay your debts because I promised; Chanur will reward the *mahe* who pulled you out. And when I've settled with that whelp Kara I'll be in better humor, so I may even forget this. So you won't worry how to meet me in future—don't fear too much. I'll not regard you too badly . . . the young do grow; but by the gods I'll never regard you the way I did your captain. You're not Lihan, Hilan Faha, and maybe you never will be."

The Faha fairly shook with anger. "To be paid the way you paid her—"

"She'd curse me to a *mahe* hell if she were here, but she'd not do what you've done. She'd not run out on a friend. Go on, Hilan Faha, leave my deck. A safe voyage to you and a quick one."

For a moment the Faha might have struck out; but she was worn thin and hopeless and the moment and the courage went. *"Her* curse on you then," she said, and turned and stalked out, not so straight in the shoulders, not so high of head as she had come in. Pyanfar scowled and looked at Hilfy, and Hilfy herself was virtually shaking.

"Kohan never said anything about this Mahn business in his letter," Pyanfar said. "What do *you* know, niece?"

"I don't," Hilfy said. "I won't believe it. I think the Faha's been listening to rumors."

"How much *did* you know about the estates when you were at home? Where was your head then, but on *The Pride?* Is it possible something was brewing and you didn't hear?"

"There was always talk; Kara Mahn was always hanging about the district. He and Tahy. There—was some calling back and forth; I think *na* Khym talked to father direct."

"Rot his hide. Kohan could have said something in that letter."

"He sent me," Hilfy said in a small, stricken voice. "When *The Pride* turned up in system I asked to go, and he said he'd never permit it; and then—the next night he gave me the letter and put me in the plane and gods, I was off to the port like that. Hardly a chance to pack. Said I had to hurry or *The Pride* would leave port and I'd miss my chance. Like that, at night; but I thought—I thought it was because ships don't calculate day and night, and that shuttle was going up anyway."

"O gods," Pyanfar groaned, and sat down against the counter, looked up at all the ring of anxious faces. "Not yet that son of mine doesn't. Gods blight the kif; we'll settle them, but we're going to take care of that small business at home; that's first."

Ears pricked. "We're with you," Haral said. "Gods, yes, *home*. Going to shake me some scruffs when I get there."

"Hai!" Geran agreed, and Tirun; and Tully visibly flinched, calmed again as Chur patted his shoulder. He settled and Hilfy sat down beside him, put her hand on his other shoulder, two disconsolate souls who shared not much at all but their misery.

"We'll straighten it out," Pyanfar said to Hilfy. "We'll do it on our terms. Agreed, niece?"

"He got me out of there," Hilfy said. "I could have helped, and he saw it coming and he moved me out."

"Huh. You're not old enough to know your father from my view, with all respect for your own. He *thinks,* some time before a problem comes on him—not much meditation during, gods know, but he sets things up like pieces on a board. Too rotted proud to call me downworld, ah, yes; too rotted smart to have young Hilfy Chanur at hand to get herself in a tangle with her Mahn cousins and to pitchfork that temper of Kohan's into it . . . don't get your ears down at me, imp; we're family here. The sun rises and sets on your shoulder so far as your father's concerned, and that blasted son of mine would go right for the greatest irritance he could give your father if he wanted to take on Chanur—your precious inexperienced self. No, Kohan just cleared the deck, that's all. Chances are he was wrong; he's not immune to that either. I'd sooner have had you there; I think you'd have handled young Kara right enough; and Tahy with him. But if *Moon Rising*'s going home, it's to carry the kind of news the Tahar have gotten here; it's going to make trouble, no thanks to the Faha; and there's a time past which Kohan's going to be hard put. He's got—what mates in residence? Your mother and who?"

"Akify and Lilun."

"Hope your mother stands by him," Pyanfar said heavily; the Kihan and the Garas were ornaments. She walked over to the counter and stared at the scan a moment. "No matter. Whatever's going on, we'll put it in order."

"Pyanfar—"

Tully's strange voice. She turned about and looked at him, recalled the pager and turned it on broadcast, not bothering with the plug.

"Question," Tully said, and made a vague gesture toward the door where the Faha had left. "He fight."

"She," Pyanfar said impatiently. "All she." Tully bit his lip and looked confused. "It's nothing to do with you," Pyanfar said. "Nothing you'd understand."

"I go," he offered, starting to slide from his place on the counter, but Chur held his shoulder. "No," Chur said. "It's all right, Tully. No one's angry at you."

"You're not the cause," Pyanfar said. "Not of this." She walked to the door, looked back at the crew. "We'll settle it," she said to the crew, and turned and walked out, down the corridor and alone toward the lift.

Khym overthrown. Dead, maybe. At the least in exile. The loss of her mate oppressed her to a surprising degree. Mahn in young Kara's hands would not be what it had been in Khym's. Khym's style had been easygoing and gracious and admittedly lazy: he was a comfortable sort of fellow to come back to, who liked fine things and loved to sit in the shade of his garden and listen to the tales she could spin of far ports he would never see. Boundless curiosity, gentle curiosity. That was Khym Mahn. And the son he had indulged and pardoned had come back and taken his garden and his house and his name, while poor Khym—gods knew where he was, or in what misery.

She rode the lift up to main level and entered her own quarters, shut the door and sat down at the desk . . . forbore for a long time to pull out the few mementoes she bothered to keep, keeping home more in her mind than in objects. Finally she looked at what she had, a picture, a smooth gray stone—odd how pleasant a bit of stone felt, and how alien in this steel world; stone that conjured the Kahin Hills, the look and the sound of grass in the wind, and the warmth of the sun and the slick cold of the rain on the rocks which thrust up out of the grassy hillsides.

Her son . . . cast Khym out; moved in next to Chanur to threaten Kohan himself, to break apart all that she had done and built and all that Kohan held. Small wonder Kohan had wanted Hilfy out of harm's way—out of a situation in which tempers could be triggered and reason lost.

Put some experience on her, Kohan had asked. And: Take care of her.

She put the things away, and sat thinking, because while repairs proceeded, there was little else she could do. They sat here locked into station's embrace and hoping that the kif stayed off their vulnerable backside. Sat here while their enemies had time to do what they liked.

Strike at Anuurn itself—Akukkakk could not be so rash. He had not that many ships, that he could do such a thing. It was bluster, of the sort the kif always used, hyperbole . . . of the sort they always flung out, hoping for more gains from an enemy's panic than force could win. Unless the *hakkikt* was mad . . . a definition which, between species, lacked precision. Unless the *hakkikt* commanded followers more interested in damage than in gain.

No *hakkikt* on record had ever stirred as wide a distance, involving so many ships. No one had ever done what this one had done, attacking a stsho station, harassing and threatening an entire star system and all its traffic as he had done at Urtur.

She sat and gnawed at her lip and reckoned that the threat might have substance to it after all. She checked scan finally, on her own terminal. Nothing showed but the expected. The knnn still hovered off from station: when she searched audio the singing came back, placid now and wavering over three discordant tones.

The tc'a were silent, but one, which babbled static in tones as slow as the knnn's. The prisoner? she wondered. Lamenting its fate? Beyond those voices there was only normal station noise, and the close-in chatter of the skimmer crews who had never ceased their work on *The Pride*'s damage. Normally some of these jump freighters would have put out: *Hasatso*'s venture out only to meet emergency had frozen everything. Not even the miners were stirring out from their berths with the orehaulers and those were snugged into orbit about Mala or Kilaunan.

She patched a call through to station services, complained about the late delivery on ordered goods: the courier service issued promises after the time-honored fashion, and she took them, reckoning on the usual carrier arriving about the time the rampway was about to close down.

Stasteburana-to used sense, at least; and the patrols stayed out, shuttling the system, alert against trouble. The *mahe* kept faith.

She expected less of the Tahar.

ix

Moon Rising pulled out in the offshift, a departure without word to them, in Pyanfar's night. She ignored it, snarling an incoherency from out the bedclothes to the com at bedside when she was advised, and pulling the cover back over herself; it was not worth getting up to see, and she had no courtesies to pay the Tahar, who deserted another hani to strangers, crippled as they still sat. She was hardly surprised. Watch had their standing orders, and there was no need to wake up and deal with it. Hilfy slept: there was no need to rouse her out for what Hilfy also expected. Pyanfar burrowed into sleep again and shed the matter from her mind . . . no getting her adrenalin up to rob herself of rest, no thinking about here, or home, or anything in particular, only maybe the repairs which were still proceeding, which ought to be virtually finished by the time she waked, all the panels in place now, and *mahe* working out on their tail checking all the sorry little connections on which their lives relied.

The dark took her back. She snugged down with a feeling of rare luxury.

"Captain. Captain, hate to disturb you, but we're getting some movement out of the knnn."

She thrust an arm about, felt for the time switch. An hour and a half from wakeup. She kept moving, swinging her feet out.

"Captain." That was Tirun on watch. "Urgent."

"I'm with you. Feed it here. What's happening?"

The screen lit in the darkened cabin. Pyanfar blinked and rubbed her eyes and focused on the schematic. Ship markers were blinking in hazard warning, too close to each other for safety.

"Every knnn at dock," Tirun said. "They're breaking dock and the general direction—"

"After *Moon Rising?* Query station. What's going on with them?"

"Did, Captain; official no comment."

"Rot their hides. Put me through."

It took a moment. Pyanfar rummaged in the halflight from the screen after her breeches, pulled them on and jerked the ties.

"Station's still refusing contact, Captain: they insist communication by courier only."

Pyanfar tied the knot and swallowed down a rush of temper. "My regards to them. What are the kif doing?"

"Sitting still. If they're talking to each other it's by runner or by line."

"Just keep watching it. I'm awake." She went to the bath, turned on the lights and washed, walked out again and took a look at the situation on the screen. Ten ships out of dock now, all chasing out after *Moon Rising,* as if that same rotted knnn had gotten utterly muddled which hani was which and convinced all the others—ludicrous, absolutely ludicrous; but humor failed her—there had been misunderstandings in the old days, before stsho had gotten the idea of the Compact across to the tc'a, and the tc'a in turn had gotten the knnn and chi to comprehend Compact civilization . . . enough to come and go in it without trouble; to trade with it; to avoid collisions and provocations and sometimes to cooperate. The methane-breathers were dangerous when stirred. She frowned over the image, combed, cut off the com and headed out down the corridor for the lift.

"No change?" she asked when she walked in on Tirun in op.

"No change," Tirun said. Her injured leg was not propped, through thrust out at an angle as she leaned to tap the screen. "They're all in a string, all ten of them, all after the Tahar."

"Gods," Pyanfar muttered. "A mess."

"They've got ID signals—they have to know that's not us."

Pyanfar shrugged helplessly. She walked back to the door. "I'm going to get the others. About time for you to go off, isn't it?"

"Half an hour."

"Who's up next?"

"Haral."

"So we start early." Pyanfar walked out and down the corridor toward the large cabin that was in-dock crew quarters, pushed the bar to open the door and inside, the one that started dawn-cycle on the lights. "Up. Got a little disturbance. Knnn have gone berserk. I don't want us abed if they come this way."

There was a general stirring of blanketed bodies in the halflight, on a row of bunks under the protective netting of the overhead; bunks and cots—Tully was at the left, curtained off, but not from her vantage, a tousled head and bewildered stare from among the blankets—and Hilfy . . . Hilfy was on the other side of the room, stirring out with the rest, naked as the rest, as Tully, who was getting out of bed on his side of the curtain. Gods. Anger coursed her nerves, a distaste for this upset in order which had swept *The Pride*. They voyaged celibate. In her mind she could hear Tahar gossip—something else that would be told on Anuurn. And gods, she could see the look in Kohan's eyes. She scowled. "Hilfy. Breakfast on watch, half an hour. Move!"

"Aunt." Hilfy stood up and jerked up her breeches with dispatch.

Pyanfar stalked out, headed back to the op room, shook off her distaste in self-reproach. So Hilfy had resigned the privilege of guest quarters and snugged in with the crew; she guessed why— with the parting of ways with the Faha. And the crew had invited: that was territory in which the invitation came from inside and she did not intervene. In their eyes, then, Hilfy belonged.

As they had taken Tully in.

Gods. Her nape prickled.

"Breakfast and relief is coming," she told Tirun as she arrived.

"No change," Tirun said. "Same courses, all involved. Not a move from the kif, not a word."

"Huh." Pyanfar sat down sideways on the counter. "Confused likewise. I hope."

"They couldn't be in communication with them." Tirun turned a disquieted stare toward her.

"I'm out of the assumption market."

The rout progressed, *Moon Rising* proceeding outsystem with a *mahe* escort at great distance and a manic flood of knnn behind.

"They're mad," Tirun said.

Pyanfar sat and watched, glaring at the screen.

Haral arrived, with Hilfy and breakfast; the others showed up hard on their heels, a procession, Geran and Chur and Tully carrying their own trays. "What's going on out there?" Haral asked.

"Tahar," Tirun said, "leading every scatter-witted knnn at the station—"

The screen had changed, the dots parting on the scan, that which was Tahar going on, the knnn. . . .

"They're stopping," Hilfy said.

"Wonderful," Pyanfar muttered, took up her cup of gfi and sipped it, watching as the gap widened. Turnover eventually, she reckoned; the knnn developed other plans. Tully spoke, a flood of alien babble, but she had left the pager in her cabin. Chur turned hers to broadcast. "Enemy ship," it rendered.

"Knnn," Haral said. "Not an enemy. Neutral. But trouble. That's *Moon Rising*. The knnn followed them; now they've quit."

"Why?"

"Don't know, Tully."

Moon Rising made jump, a sudden wink off station scan—knnnless. "Gods," Hilfy exclaimed, as the knnn bent a turn.

"Knnn maneuver," Tirun said. "The bastards are showing off. They can jump boost and turn like that. It'd kill a hani. Any oxygen breather. Can't outmaneuver them. Gods forbid, if we should have to shoot at one—comp plotting can't hit one: not programmed for their moves."

"They don't shoot at us. They aren't armed."

"In the old days," Haral said, "they never caught the knnn shooting either. But ships turned up gutted. Before my time. But I heard they'd swarm a ship, jump it elsewhere—haul its mass off where they'd open it at their leisure—"

"Haul it between them?" Hilfy's face mirrored disbelief.

"Among them. A dozen. All synched. So I heard. Hani ships'd tear each other to junk; but knnn can synch like that."

"Huh," Pyanfar said. It was an old bunk yarn, like ghost ships. Like aliens outside the Compact. She stared at Tully and thought about that. Ate her dried chips and washed it down with gfi. On com, station sent instructions to its patrol to stay out of the way of the knnn. A tc'a went on, presumably talking to the knnn.

And a message light blinked on their own board, something directed at them.

Revise estimate, the letters crept across the screen when Tirun keyed it. *15 hours repair additional. Regret. Make more worker this job. Two team. Repeat . . .*

"Gods help us." Pyanfar snatched the mike and punched in station op. "What kind of trouble this? *What* fifteen hours? Fifteen *more* hours?"

Station routed the complaint, one to the next, to the almost incomprehensible *mahe* skimmer supervisor. "All skimmer station work," was the answer, three times repeated, in rising volume, as if loudness improved communication. "Thanks," Pyanfar muttered. "Out." She ran a hand through her mane, put the mike down, looked around at staring eyes and managed a better face.

"Well," Haral said in a quiet voice, "at least they found it before they sent us out with it."

"I'll go out the aft lock," Geran said, "and check them out on it."

"No," Pyanfar said. "I don't doubt you'll find damage. Longshot it from the observation dome. And by the gods, if there's something new I want to know about it." She composed herself a moment. "No, gods rot them, the *mahe*'d gouge us on fines and charges, but if I've got the measure of that foreman she's not the type. Still . . . Do the check anyhow."

"Right." Geran snatched up the tray and headed out, down the corridor for the bubble access, a cold trip to the frame. Pyanfar thought of going herself, delayed to finish her breakfast and watched the knnn, who had stopped again, hovering off in utter violation of lanes and regulations. Station operations reported a ship coming in, a mahendo'sat freighter arriving in the zenith range: they had their own problems. So did the *mahen* freighter, coming in to what should be a safe haven and finding traffic snugged down and knnn gone berserk.

"I'm going to main," she said finally. "Go off down here. Rest. Haral, I'll take it, up there. I'll key you."

"Captain—" Haral started to object, swallowed it, having a sense about such things. "Right."

Pyanfar walked out, hitched up the trousers which had gotten too loose in recent days, headed for the lift. Go in person to station offices and take the place apart? It tempted. At the moment she wanted something breakable within reach. But it would hardly mend matters. Fifteen hours. It was hardly surprising; repairs for all of time and to all ends of the Compact ran behind schedule and over estimate. And then it was sixteen and seventeen and another twenty—

She took the lift up, ensconced herself in her cushion on the bridge and sent rapid inquiry through all appropriate channels.

Defect vane yoke, the answer came back from the station office, and hard upon that, from Geran: "Got closeup; they've swarmed in on the vane collar, but I can't tell much." The image came through, two skimmers and three workers in eva-pods grappled onto the afflicted vane where it attached to the strut, cables and vane and strut strung with red hazard lights to prevent accidents in shadow. It was a plausible repair, gods—nothing cheap; the damage that had blown the panels loose could have stressed it . . . one of those systems for which there was no bypass, through which a third of the power of the jump drive passed. "Yoke," Pyanfar sent to Geran, who was likely shivering her teeth loose in the bubble. "Come on inship; there's no more we can do."

It was a fifteen-hour job. A gnawing suspicion worked at her gut. The defect should have shown up on the board: there were reasons why it might not—that it had blown as they came in . . . something *had* red-lighted, so many things had red-lighted at one instant and gone back to normal status . . . possibly, possibly it was real. Possibly too it was one of those demon touches, the mahendo'sat called them, that lost ships, something loose that contacted in stresses and killed. It was five to five they owed the mahendo'sat crew profound thanks; or they were being stalled, conned, set up. Check it now and it was bound to red-light: the casing was off. She sat staring at the vid screen with her blood pressure up and a smoldering rage with nowhere to send it.

"Haral," she said into com.

"Captain?"

"That problem you fixed as we were coming in. *Was* the number-one yoke involved? Could you tell?"

A long moment of silence. "Captain, we were losing the input; I put in a new board and we got it cleared. But that fade had stressed everything; the whole board was fouled. I couldn't say beyond doubt. It was everywhere. I thought it was the panels. I'm sorry, Captain."

There was misery in Haral's voice. Haral was not accustomed to be wrong. Ever. "It's one of those things," Pyanfar said, "that would red-light if the panels were overloaded; I'm not so sure you were wrong, Haral. I'm not at all sure you were wrong."

"I'll go out there," Haral said.

"And do what? They've got it in a mess it takes skimmers to put back. *Mahen* skimmers. No. We sit it out."

"Supplies arriving," Chur informed her eventually via com from belowdecks. That was frozen fish off Kirdu II's onworld ponds; and some stsho goods for Tully and some more translator tapes. She checked the time; *after* their originally scheduled departure. The courier service had been informed of the delay as quickly as they had been, which insolence sent her blood pressure up another several points. "Captain?" Chur asked. "Noted," Pyanfar said coldly, and Chur broke the contact.

Another hour. The vid showed continual activity about the vane. Pyanfar diverted herself into board maintenance, burrowed into under-console spaces, checked and rechecked, surfaced now and again to dart a jaundiced look at the vid or to listen to some communication coming in. The station was getting back to normal; only the knnn . . . stayed out, fell into systemic drift, wailing still to each other.

The lift down the corridor hummed and opened doors: Pyanfar heard that and worked her way out of a finished job, stood up and wiped her hands and straightened her mane—soft quick footfalls in the corridor. "Aunt?"

She sat down on the armrest of her own cushion, scowled at her niece. Hilfy stood in the archway with a paper in her hand, came and offered it. "Just came. Couriered. Security seal."

Pyanfar snatched it, hooked a claw in it, ripped it open, nose wrinkling. Stasteburana's signature. Greetings, respects, and the assurance all possible was being done. "The stationmaster's compliments," Pyanfar translated sourly. "We get escort to our jumppoint when we go; departure's firm for that fifteenth hour. Rot them, they knew about this, or they'd have been here asking for that tape. They want it, to be sure—before the job's sealed off. Is the courier waiting?"

"No."

"Rot them all."

"Tully's tape, you mean."

She looked up at Hilfy, whose adolescent-bearded face held a hint of a frown. "Is that a comment?"

"No, aunt."

"I told the Outsider why."

"Tully, aunt."

Pyanfar sucked in a breath. *"Tully,* if you please. I told him why. Did I get through?"

"He—talked to Chur about it."

"What did he say?"

"That he understood."

"And the rest of you?"

Hilfy tucked her hands behind her, looked down and up under her brow. "He senses . . . how much trouble's going on. Last offshift, he tried to talk to all of us, gods, how he tried. Finally—" Her ears went down, a second glance at the deck. "Finally he put his arms around Chur and then he went from one to the next of us all and did the same, not—male-female, not like that. Just like he had something to say and he didn't have any other way to say it."

Pyanfar said nothing, jaw set.

"He's started another tape," Hilfy said. "The new manual."

"Is he?"

"We gave it to him; he sat down with it in op and he's feeding the words in as fast as he can go."

Pyanfar frowned, taken aback.

"He liked the stsho shirts you came up with too. *Warm,* he says, never mind the fancywork."

"Huh." Pyanfar thrust herself to her feet, poked an extended claw at Hilfy. "Nice fellow, this Tully, so understanding and grateful and all. I've been back and forth this route a few voyages, imp, and I've seen my share of con artists. In the first place, since we bring it up, I don't like the Outsider bedding down with the lot of you. I permitted it in a moment of soft-headedness, because I didn't like his moping about and I didn't want himself killing himself the way, mark you, imp, the way he admits to killing a companion of his—for friendship's sake."

"It's not fair to say that. It was brave, what he did."

"Granted. And maybe he's got a few more brave notions. The crew's used to alien ways and I figured they'd keep their judgment, but I don't like you down there. Gods know you've earned the right to *be* down there—that's where I'd rather you were, all things equal, but they aren't; there's that rotted Outsider in the company, and he makes me nervous, niece, the way things make me nervous that just may blow up without warning. I don't like you near him."

Hilfy's ears were plastered flat to her skull. "Pardon, aunt. If you order me to go back to my quarters, I will."

"No," Pyanfar said. "I'll do you one worse. I'll rely on your sense. I'll just tell you to think what gets blown to ruin if some triviality sets our guest off at the wrong moment. Chanur, niece. You understand that?"

The ears came up. Hilfy's nose wrinkled all the same, the shot gone home. "I know I want to get back to Anuurn, aunt; but I know too that I want to be proud of *one* side of the family when I get there."

Pyanfar raised her hand—got that far with it, and stopped the blow and turned it into a gesture of dismissal. "Out, imp. Out."

Hilfy turned on her heel and went. Pyanfar slid into the cushion and crumpled the stationmaster's message with the other hand, punched claws through it. Gods rot it, to have leaned on the youngster in *that* matter . . . and to no point, to no point; underway, they would be back to wider spaces, to—gods knew what they would be up against.

She reached and keyed through the translator channel, heard Tully's steady input, jabbed it out again.

After a moment she shook her head, smoothed out the paper and filed it in fax. Punched the translator key on again and listened to Tully, a quiet, familiar voice, putting word after word into memory.

Six hours; nine; twelve; thirteen. The day passed in meals-at-station, in checks and counterchecks; in enforced rest and secure-for-jump procedures and most of all in monitoring scan and com. Pyanfar reached the stage of pacing and fretting by the twelfth hour, fed and napped beyond endurance—wore off claw-tips on the flooring and disguised the anxiety when any of the crew came near on errands.

But Hilfy managed not to come. Stayed below, in what frame of mind or what understanding Pyanfar could not find a way to ask.

"Courier's here." Chur's voice cracked out of the silence on the bridge, com from lowerdeck. "Asking the tape, Captain."

"Ask the courier," Pyanfar said, "the finish time on the repair." A delay.

"The courier says within the hour, Captain."

"Understood." Pyanfar caught her breath, looked left where she had laid the tape she had prepared, reached and pocketed the cassette and headed out for the lift, in such a fever that it was not till she had started the lift downward that she had thought again what it was she went down to trade: away from this place was all the thought; and the tape was a means to get free; and the shedding of the whole ugly necessity something she was only too glad to have done, to get *The Pride* free of mahendo'sat and loose and on her way.

But Hilfy was down there. That recollection hit her. The lift stopped, the door opened, and she hesitated half a heartbeat in walking out, sucked up a breath she wanted all too much to spend on the *mahe* for the delay, and strode out quite bereft of the breath and the anger she wanted to loose.

Tully. Ye gods, Tully was in op too, off the corridor where any visitor to the ship not confined to the airlock would be brought as a matter of course.

She rounded the corner and found a gathering indeed—a dignified-looking *mahe* in a jeweled collar and kilt; a *mahe* attendant; Haral, Tirun, and Hilfy. She walked into the group suddenly conscious of her own informal attire, scowled and drew herself up to all her stature—none too tall in mahendo'sat reckoning.

"Bad mess," the ranking *mahe* spat at her. "Big trouble you cause, hani. All same we fix ship."

The Voice of the stationmaster, primed with accusations and bluster. The Voice looked her up and down, with grand hauteur. Jeweled and perfumed. Pyanfar flexed her claws, pointedly and with grander coolness turned her shoulder and looked toward her own. "Tully. Where's Tully? Is he still in op?"

"You endanger the station," the Voice railed on her dutifully. "Big trouble with tc'a; knnn bastard kidnap and extortion. You want take with you the eva-pod the knnn bring for trade for good tc'a citizen, hah? Got your name on it, hani. *Pride of Chanur,* clear letters."

"*Tully!* Get your rotted self out here. Now!"

"They don't come into station now, the knnn, no, make navigation hazard all this system. All disturb. Mining stop. Trade stop. All business stand dead still. You use knnn signal, a? Upset the knnn; take kif property, upset the kif; get tc'a kidnap, tc'a upset; get fight stsho station, stsho make charge; hani don't speak to you —what for we deal with you, hani, a?"

Tully came out of the op room, Chur attending him. He had on his new stsho-made shirt, white silk and blue borders—looked immaculately civilized and no little upset at the shouting. "The papers, Tully," Pyanfar said. "Show them to this kind *mahe*."

He fished in his pocket for the folder, pale eyes anxious.

"I got no need cursed papers," the Voice snapped. Tully had

them all the same, held them open in front of the *mahe,* who
waved them aside.

"You issued them," Pyanfar said. *"Property* of the kif. *Property* of the kif, you say. You look at this fine, this honest, this
documented member of an intelligent and civilized spacefaring
species and you talk about him with words like *property of the
kif?* I call down shame on you; I ask you to explain to him, you,
in your own words, explain this *property.*"

The Voice flattened her ears, looked aside at her attendant, who
proffered a scent bottle. In elaborate indirection the Voice unstopped it and inhaled, recollecting herself in retreat. Her face
when next she looked down at them was tolerably mild.

"The tapes," the Voice said. "The tapes you make deal cover
some damage."

"All the damages. No fines. No charges. No complaints."

"Starchaser rescue."

"A separate matter. Chanur and Faha together will stand good
for it when we reach home. As for the captain of the rescue ship,
he has my guarantee, which is worth more than his losses. It's
settled."

The Voice considered a moment, nodded. "The tape," she said,
holding out her hand. "This give, repair finish. Give you safe escort. Fair deal, Chanur."

Pyanfar took it from her pocket, an uncommon warmth about
her ears—looked aside at Tully. She thrust it at him. *"You* give it.
Yours."

Hilfy opened her mouth to say something, and shut it. Tully
looked down at the cassette, looked up at the Voice and hesitantly
handed the tape toward her. "Friend," he said in the hani tongue.
"Friend to *mahe.*"

The dark-furred hand closed on the cassette. The Voice laid
back her ears and pursed her mouth in thoughtful consideration.
Tully still had his hand out—his own kind of gesture, who was always touching—kept it out. Slowly the *mahe* reached out, alien
protocol being her calling, and gamely suffered Tully to clasp her
hand, took it back without visible flinching . . . but with a subdued quiet unlike herself. She bowed her head that slightest degree
of courtesy. "I carry your word," she said.

And with a scowl and a glance at Pyanfar: "Undock one hour,
firm. Kirdu Station give you all possible help. Urge you give us lo-

cation of this good fellow homeworld—danger to lose you, him, all, this trip."

"Beyond the kif is the location we presently suspect. Haven't had the time to learn, honorable."

"Stupid," the Voice said with her professional license.

"Our unfortunate friend was dragged through miserable circumstances with the kif; hurt; not stupid—too wise to talk without understanding. Now there's too little time. You help us get out of here and we'll settle the kif sooner or later."

"This *hakkikt*. . . . Akukkakk. We *know* this one. Bad trouble, Chanur Captain."

"What do you know?" Pyanfar asked, suddenly and not for the first time suspicious of every *mahe* at Kirdu. "What do you know about this kif?"

"You undock one hour. Skimmers go now. You make good quick voyage, Chanur Captain."

"What do you know about the kif?"

"Good voyage," the Voice pronounced, and bowed once and generally, collected her attendant and walked for the airlock.

"Hai," Pyanfar said in vexation, and with a wave of her hand sent Haral striding after the Voice and her companion. She looked about at Hilfy, whose ears were somewhat down; and at Tirun and Chur and Tully. Tully looked disquieted. "Good," Pyanfar said to him, clapping him on the arm. "Good touch, that 'friend.' You laid the burden on her, you know that? That's the Voice that speaks to and for the Personage himself, the stationmaster of Kirdu; and by the gods you did it, my clever, my mannerly Outsider, you threw that one right in the stationmaster's lap."

Tully glanced down, made a small shrug, no less troubled-looking. She was not wearing the translator plug. "An hour, hear?" she said to the others, to Tirun and Hilfy and Chur—and Geran, who would be keeping watch in the op room with strangers running in and out of the ship: no way it was unattended. "An hour and we're underway, out of here. *Home.*"

"How are we doing it?" Geran called from out of the room. "Stringing the jumps like before?"

"Close as we can cut it," Pyanfar said, and looked left as movement caught her eye, Haral's return from the lock, as far as the beginning of the corridor.

"Seal us up, Captain?" Haral shouted down the corridor.

"Seal us up," Pyanfar confirmed, and stopped in midwave as a tall dark figure appeared in the corridor behind Haral. *"Ware!"*

Mahendo'sat. Haral had already spun about, and the lanky, dark-furred *mahe* walked on in as if he belonged, flashing a gilt-edged grin.

"Ismehanan—" Pyanfar shouted. "—*Goldtooth,* gods rot you, slinking into my corridors without a by your leave—Who let you in?"

The grin in no way diminished. The *mahe* gave a sweeping bow and straightened as she strode up to him. "Got sudden business, Chanur, maybe same you course."

"Whose business?"

"Maybe same you business."

She swelled up with a breath and looked up at him. "Maybe you talk straight, Captain. Once."

"Where you go?"

"Maybe I should broadcast it on the dock. For the kif."

"Home, maybe? Ajir route?"

"Guess as you like."

"Got *Mahijiru* weapons first rate; friend mine make port today, also got number-one rig. Wait over, Chanur."

"Bastard!"

He stepped back, held a hand up, blunt-nailed; hers, lifted, was not. He grinned with the fending gesture. "Necessity, time *mahe* shed cargo."

"You egg-sucking liars. Where I'm going has nothing to do with you; hani business, you hear that? Private business. You want a quarrel with the kif you go find your own."

"Go home, do you?"

"Private business, I'm telling you."

"Warn you," Goldtooth said. "Once. Maybe now go make deal hani port; lots trade. You talk for your good friend there, yes?"

"Goldtooth, what game are you playing?"

He grinned and turned on his heel, walked off toward the lock, where Haral stood in scowling indignation.

"Goldtooth!"

He paused to wave. *"Mahijiru* you escort, Captain. You got number-one best."

"Rot your hide, I'm not playing decoy in some *mahen* game with the kif!"

He was gone while the echoes were still ringing. Haral, lacking orders, looked back at her, and Pyanfar slung her arms to her sides, not reckoning on giving any. It was the *mahe*'s terms and there was nothing they could do to stop him from following. "Seal that lock," she said. "Gods know what else might get in." Haral went on the run. Pyanfar looked about at the others, at Tully, and Chur and Hilfy and Tirun; and Geran, who had stepped out of op.

"*Mahijiru*'s on," Geran said. "Someone's just hooked up a shielded line and we're getting transmission. They claim they've got orders and they're asking data."

"We're going home," Pyanfar said shortly. "Home, by the gods. They've cost us time. If Stasteburana's got notions of using us, rot him, two can play that game. I'll give them our course; I'll give them a lead-in inside the Anuurn perimeter."

"Chanur—" Tirun objected quietly.

"More than Chanur's got a stake in this. Maybe Anuurn needs to see that. We've got ourselves trouble. Widespread trouble. We don't know how far it stretches. There ought to be hani here, do you mark that? Lots of hani ships coming and going here, not just Tahar. Here we are at one of the prime stops on our rivals' route . . . and no hani ships but that one. Homebound. I'll lay you odds, cousins, they've been staying home when they've come to port. That's what's vacated the track we've been on. *Starchaser* knew; word's been passing, at every port, every contact."

"Aye," Chur murmured. "Aye. Gods. Six months they could have had at this—"

"I'm going to the bridge. Bridge crew this passage—Haral, Geran, Chur. The rest of you take op station; and get Tully his sedative, now, before someone forgets."

"Aunt!" Hilfy called after her. Pyanfar stopped and turned. "Captain," Hilfy said in a quieter voice.

"Question?" Pyanfar asked, scowling. Hilfy's chin went up. "No, Captain," Hilfy said quite steadily. Pyanfar nodded, with a small tightening of the mouth, looked satisfaction into Hilfy's clear eyes, then turned again and strode off to the lift.

Down the corridor, the lock boomed shut. *The Pride* had begun her separation.

X

"Getting pickup on the companion," Chur said, snugged in com station. "They swear it's a secure line."

"Huh." Pyanfar finished up the checks and reached for the contact flashing on her com module. "Chanur here."

"Introduce you," Goldtooth's voice came back to her. "Captain Pyanfar Chanur, got link to *Aja Jin*. Captain Nomesteturjai."

"Chanur," a voice rumbled back. "Name *Jik,* here."

"Number-one fellow, Jik," Goldtooth said. "Honest same you, Pyanfar Chanur."

"Honest like stall me off; like delay me. Chanur's fighting for its life, you rag-eared bastard, does that get through your head? *Challenge,* and I'm not there. In your spying about, do you know what that means?"

"Ah," Goldtooth said. "Know this trouble. Yes."

Pyanfar said nothing, forced the claws back in.

"Know where this Akukkakk too," Goldtooth said. "Interested, hani Captain?"

"After I've settled my own business."

"Same place."

"*Anuurn?*"

"Keep you alive, hani. We make slow maybe, but you make deal we want. More big than pearls and welders, a, hani?"

"You follow, rot you." She keyed through the course and the graph on comp. "There's the way."

A *mahen* hiss came back, throaty and rueful. "You steer by luck, hani? You crazy mad, that course?"

"Do it all the time, *mahe.* Scare you?"

"Hani joke, a?"

"Got two kif docked down there. We go, they'll go. You got that patrol alerted?"

"Got," came that second voice.

"Ha," Pyanfar muttered. "You got your data; got all you want. Enough. We're getting out of here."

"A."

Assent. Pyanfar flung a glance toward Haral, across the separating console, and the contact went out. Chur flicked signals to the dock crew. "Got us prioritied out," Chur reported. "No problem." The lines were coming loose. Telltales began to flash, wanting ports sealed. Haral put the seals in function, straight down the sequence. Screens in front of number-one post livened, Geran routing through the station scan image. The airlock grapple clanged into unlock, and the last of the seal-ports was firm. "Moving out," Pyanfar warned over allship, and cleared *The Pride*'s own grapples, her grip on station independent of the station's grip on her: those boomed into the housing, and undocking jets eased them clear.

It was a smooth parting, an easy push clear and a nosing toward an untrafficked nadir as *g* started up, a whine of the rotational engines. Comp flashed them their lane, and scan showed *Mahijiru* and *Aja Jin* moving down below the station rim off portside. *The Pride* gathered momentum, a solid *g* and a half now, outbound.

"Kif are breaking free," Chur said, com monitor. "Station advises."

"No scan confirmation," Geran said.

Pyanfar was already reaching for the shielded weapons switch, uncapped it and flicked it on: a ripple of lights advised the gunports were clearing. "Stay on that," she told Haral without taking her eyes off her own business. "No comp synch, not with the *mahe* in the way. Can't be taking one of them by mistake."

"Hope they're as considerate," Haral muttered.

"Huh."

"Kif are moving out," Geran said. "Number-two screen."

"Where's our escort?" Pyanfar wondered glumly. "—Op deck, stay braced. Listen in and take your cues."

"Escort moving," Chur said. "They're on intercept; station's got them scan-blanked."

"Understood." She darted a look at station-sent scan, on which they themselves showed as an oversized wedge, massed blip of ships in synch. Geran sent another image. *G* continued, dragging at the gut, straining her arm back against the elbow brace. The kif were not gaining, were maintaining a sedate acceleration in their wake.

Goldtooth and this stranger Jik: escort. She did not, she admitted to herself, understand the *mahen* order of things, no more than outsiders understood the stsho. Trading with them was one thing. Figuring out the limits of a *mahe* like Stasteburana was another. Goldtooth and this *mahe* friend of his, this ship which had come kiting into system in the hour of Tahar's exit—merchanters, maybe; but what she saw of *Mahijiru* and *Aja Jin* on vid was ominously lean, ominously trim with their cargo holds stripped off; a lot of space given to the power assembly on those two, a profligate lot of jump capacity masked by those missing holds, odd-shaped cores swelling in such fashion that they would cut into any reasonable geometry of tanks which had been strapped on. Vanes with strange dark interstices, like folding joints, vanes larger than ships of their mass ought to carry. It was a curious thing, that ships never *saw* each other; that they nosed up to station and stayed invisible behind station walls; that they existed as blips and dots and figures in comp, moving too fast for vid to pick up. Only now that they were in synch, a package moving at the same velocity and in sight of each other—

"Runner ships," Pyanfar muttered to Haral. "Look at our escort, cousin."

"Got that," Haral said quietly. "Got that, Captain."

Something new among the mahendo'sat. Something which had to have been very quiet for a long time. Ships like the kif runners. Hunter ships. Her mustache-hairs drew taut as if her nose had scented something. Gods: *Mahijiru,* out prowling about Meetpoint, out on the fringes of stsho space—

Hunting rumors? A crew lounging on the dock, loud and visible with repair they could have done inside as well. Two sets of hunters on the docks besides the kif themselves, and they had come sniffing round each other, each so cleverly assaying the other, she and the *mahe*—

"That gold-toothed bastard knew something," Pyanfar said. "From the very start he knew. Knew this Akukkakk; knew those kif ships; knew what was stirring out here."

Haral shot her a disquieted look.

"Knnn," Geran said suddenly, and vid went off and another

image came in, sectorized on the mass of knnn ships, which were no longer stationary.

"Gods," Chur muttered, "here we go."

"Never mind the rotted knnn," Pyanfar said. "Watch the kif; op, take that sectorized image and keep us posted."

It vanished from her screen; Tirun acknowledged recept below. Behind them, on the image which turned up, the kif started now to move.

"Got us knnn," Goldtooth's voice cut in, transferred from Chur's board.

"Nuisance," Pyanfar said. "You know more than that, *mahe*? What more do you know? About how you were hunting trouble at Meetpoint?"

"Got no need hunt. *Hani* in port."

"Captain." Tirun's voice. "Decreased interval."

She was watching it. Flexed her claws carefully on the togglegrip. "Moving out," she told the *mahe*. "Going to boost up and test; clear my field, understand? No more time here."

"A."

She moved the control. *The Pride* kicked up to widen the interval between herself and the *mahe*. The number-one screen flicked from scan to a bracketed star; the images shifted one screen over and dumped the vid entirely. On scan the kif fell farther and farther behind, chancing nothing with the patrol.

And the knnn—the knnn streamed along in a manic flood, accelerating as they went, a few points off their course.

"Interval achieved," Haral said.

"Boosting up," Pyanfar warned the others. She hit the jump pulse, lightly, swallowed against the queasiness and saw the instruments sorting themselves out at the new velocity.

"Clear," Haral said. "All stable. Coming up on jump."

"Stand by the long one," Pyanfar advised the crew below. Cast a last and frantic look at scan, where *Mahijiru* and *Aja Jin* had fallen behind on estimated-position. No communication possible now; they were too much lag apart. It was the position she wanted, the *mahe* running at their tail; their nose they could take care of themselves. Best to flare through any ambush where they were going and not be the second or third ship in, as *Starchaser* had been at Kita, after the nest had been stirred and the kif wakened.

Luck, she wished the *mahe.* In spite of other things. In spite of deceits; in spite of *mahen* purposes which had nothing to do with hers. *Luck,* she thought, and: *conniving liar.*

The course was flashing on the screen, a jump first for Ajir System, and through it to Anuurn itself, the straightest course and the most vulnerable to ambush; but they were out of time for finesse.

"Ready," she warned the crew.

They reached their point. *Mahijiru* would be after them, gliding on their tail; and *Aja Jin,* that other of Goldtooth's ilk. . . .

. . . all the way.

A wail from com as they came up, a buoy, Ajir marker dopplered into nonsense. Mahendo'sat/hani cooperative, this station, full of traffic and hazards in the jump range for a lunatic chase to come streaking through, velocity unchecked: a second time to try the maneuver that had failed at Kita, had failed, with damage to the ship. Gods help any other incomer who chanced to be in the way.

ALERTALERTALERT, *The Pride* wailed, capsuled transmission: *mahe escort behind. Likely hostile action. Beware of kif insystem and out. Launch all system defense. Take precaution. Two ships following us are escort. Next is trouble. Casualties in previous attacks:* Handur's Voyager; Faha's Starchaser. *Kif attack on non-Compact unarmed ship, three alien casualties.* ALERTALERTALERT. . . .

Chaos would break loose at Ajir: kif at dock might take exception to it; Handur might be here to hear it, and Faha.

If the kif were not waiting here, in ambush already. . . .

The mass that was Ajir, a yellow sun, loomed ahead: Ajir, askew from most stars of the region, wearing its belt of worlds and debris rakishly aslant—hazard, Pyanfar's memory kept warning her, distant and fogged in the muddle of post-jump, of extreme velocities and instruments feeding them only the skim of reality, too fast, too fast. . . .

"Where *is* it?" she asked of Haral—for the gods' sakes, homestar . . . a blind newborn could sense it from Ajir, could feel it, head for it however shaken in jump: their bow was toward it.

"Locked on," Haral's slow voice purred through the madness, slow, when they were pushing *c* and the system was whipping past in unreality, moving while they drifted through movements: one dopplered star was clear for them, zeroed in the brackets, and all the rest had gone mad. . . .

Home.

Weeks, in the time/notime of jump. . . .

They were in. Hard to think, to begin the dump sequences. The ship would take over when manual intervention failed utterly; would dump velocity and glide them to an outsystem halt, still within return range. Easier to let it slide, let the system blur past, let the machinery take over—

No. They were on manual override from the last one. Machine-rules were already violated. Pyanfar lifted the arm, saw with her dazed vision Haral, who had begun the same desperate struggle, slow and sickly in the aftermath of their arrival. A warning light was blinking, not the same malfunction, but outside alert: com recept—beacon—

They dumped down and went totally blind for an instant. Anuurn beacon welcomed them out of it; their own alert was still going, crying havoc where they went. She got her hand up, signaled Chur with a blinker; after an interminable moment it went out.

Second dump. There was Tully's voice over the open com, and Hilfy's comforting him—Hilfy, who not so long ago had ridden sickly through the jumps, now steadied their passenger.

"Getting image," Geran said. "There are ships out here."

None in their way; Geran would not be so calm. They were zenith of everything and everyone.

"Getting course input," Haral said, and the screen shifted, lines blinking and calling for matchup, the lane assignment from the buoy.

Third dump. Pyanfar swallowed heavily and looked at scan again as it sorted itself out. "Image aft," Geran said: it went to number-two screen. *Mahijiru.* The wavefront was running up their backslides, where that ship and its partner were aimed if they delayed dump.

"Too close, *mahe*," Pyanfar muttered.

Final dump. They hit course, down the slot and true, on Kilan Station's guidance. "Transmit intent to dock at Gaohn," Pyanfar said. That was the innermost of the two stations of Ahr System, that about Anuurn itself. The signal went out; the acknowledgment flashed back from one of the robot buoys, automatic routing, approach as routine as any incoming merchanter.

"Dump behind us," Chur said. "Second arrival; both our friends are in."

"Transmit instructions to ignore routing and stay on our tail. Give them a signal."

"Station scan," Geran said, "is showing a lot of ships. A *lot* of ships."

Pyanfar looked. Six major planets about Arh: Gohin, Anuurn itself, Tyo, Tyar, Tyri and Anfas—with assorted moons, rings and planetoids. Anuurn alone was comfortably habitable; and Gaohn station circled it; and there was Kilan Station which supported the little colony on Tyo. There was always traffic. Hani were not the colonists that mahendo'sat and stsho and even knnn tended to be: but here, in home-system, there was always traffic, from little ships which plied the system to the greater ones which jumped in from other stars; there was the huge null-*g* shipyard of Harn Station, where all hani ships were born and where they came for refitting and repair.

But there were twice the usual number, easily twice, ships in offlanes positions, waiting; ships in clusters; ships by groups of four and five.

"I don't like that," Haral said.

"Not all ours," Pyanfar said. And after a moment: "He's *here*. Goldtooth said it; the kif at Kirdu said it. *Hinukku*'s come here. After revenge."

No one said anything. The minutes crept up on the chronometer. *The Pride* was sending her own signal, computer talking to computer. A telltale flashed and a signal came over com. "*Mahijiru*," Chur said. "*Aja Jin*. Both moving up on our track."

"Blink them a comeahead," Pyanfar said. "Tightbeam; nothing more."

"Permission to move about," Tirun sent from lowerdeck.

"Denied. Got a situation here. Stay put."

"Understood," Tirun answered.

Chur leaned down, opened the cabinet by her post and brought out a bottle, sucked a bit from it and passed it on; it went to Geran and to Haral; finally into Pyanfar's hand with an exact quarter visible through the opaque plastic. She sipped at it, her mouth like paper and tasting days stale; her hand left shed fur on the moist bottle when she dropped it into the wasteholder. The salt and the moisture helped, took some of the shakes from her limbs. There was still a misery in her back and in her joints, a tendency for her eyes to blur. Not easy on the body, double-skipping. Bodies were not designed for such abuses. She thought of docking, of having to walk about, to deal with possible trouble—

To get a shuttle and to get downworld with all else hovering about them. . . .

Something clenched about her gut, protesting. She looked at scan, their own, tightscan, number-four screen, where a friendly blip was moving up into intercept. Another blip showed on the edge of the screen.

"Got synch," Goldtooth's voice came through. "Jik come up otherside."

"Got too many ships," Pyanfar said, signaling Chur to put the transmission through. "Want you where you are, *mahe*."

A *mahen* chuckle. "A."

"Rot your hide."

She shut it down.

"Got station contact," Chur said. "They don't say anything out of the way; normal approach instructions."

"Three berths," Pyanfar said. "Together. Tell them to clear something if they don't have it. Talk them into it."

It was a long interval. They still had lagtime from station. "Stationmaster," Chur said finally, "intervened to grant it. We've got twenty through twenty-two."

"Comment?"

"Nothing," Chur reported.

Trouble. Pyanfar's ears flicked. If they could demand ships shunted about and get their request it was because they had a right to it; and if they had a right to it, then there *was* an emergency in progress. Homecoming kin had right-of-way . . . in situations of death, of challenge, of disasters.

"System's quiet," Chur reported. "I'm not getting idle chatter. They're not volunteering any information, Captain."

"Kif," Pyanfar said. "Outsiders present."

Tully said something from belowdecks. Went silent. Hilfy's voice followed, talking to him, low and urgent.

"Let's not have any panic down there," Pyanfar said. "Tully. Quiet. Take orders, hear?"

"Understand," Tully said.

The minutes crawled past. Jik's *Aja Jin* came into position, so that *The Pride* went flanked by the *mahe*. "Goldtooth," Pyanfar said. "You come onstation with me; want your friend stay out of dock and watch, a?"

"A," the answer came back, short and sweet; from Jik no word. He would do it, Pyanfar thought. Station was sending specific instructions: Haral was attending that, inputting it for comp. She hit the shunt which dumped the data onto Haral's screens, with a blinking warning that control of the ship came with it: Haral nodded, accepting it without missing a keystroke. Pyanfar loosed her restraints, swung her cushion about and assayed to get her feet under her.

"Get to the bridge," she told those below, leaning over com. "Aye," Tirun sent back. Pyanfar walked about a bit, unsteady on her feet, bent down enough to get some of the dried food out of storage by her own console. Chips and bottles of salts. She opened them, put them in reach of Haral and Geran and Chur, chewed on a bit of dried meat and washed it down with half a bottle of the liquid. Dehydrated. The jumps took *some* time off bodies. She walked about trying to get the needling pains out of her joints, heard the lift in function and then steps coming down the corridors.

"Captain."

Knnn-song wailed out of com.

"Gods and thunders!" Pyanfar spat. "Location on that."

"Ahead of us," Geran said. "One of those ships moving up on station."

Tirun and Hilfy and Tully had arrived, stood together in the archway which opened onto the bridge, silent in the grating sound which ran the scale.

Knnn never called at Anuurn. Never, till now.

"It overjumped us," Pyanfar said with—she reckoned—commendable calm. "If that's our knnn, it just overjumped us by at least an hour."

"Fast bastard," Tirun muttered.

"Mahijiru," Chur said, "asks if we notice."

"Cut that thing off," Pyanfar said. "Tell *Mahijiru* yes, we did notice." She pricked up her ears with an effort, flicking the rings into order on the left. "Hilfy. Tully's channel." Hilfy turned her pager onto broadcast. "Tully—we're home now. Anuurn. Got trouble here."

"Kif," Tully said. "I hear. Hani—make deal with them?"

"Papers," Pyanfar said sharply, and when Tully's hand went to his left pocket: "You keep those with you. You're registered; you've got a number in the Compact. No. No way the kif can take you by law. Going to have one lot of mad kif, maybe; maybe some mad hani. But they can't take you, except by force."

"Fight them."

"You take my orders. My crew, my orders."

"Pyanfar." Tully thrust out his hand to stop her from turning away. *"I don't go from you."*

Pyanfar flattened her ears, staring up into Tully's pale, distraught eyes. "I don't need someone making me conditions. You do what I tell you."

"Do. Yes. I go on this ship. With you. #### give ### hani I quick dead."

"We've got troubles enough, Outsider. Hani troubles as well as kif. Let be."

"With you. Long time voyage. With you."

"I'm not your kin, rot you. You come on my ship, you make me trouble—what in a *mahen* hell do I owe you?"

"Dead, outside. *Need* you."

"Huh." Male. The shout left a quiet after it. Alien male, but all the same she saw the line drawn, the edge past which there was no thinking . . . their patient, docile Outsider. She cuffed his arm, claws not quite pulled. "You listen, friend Tully; you *think,* rot your hide. We go off this ship, we, you, we come back, you come back with us. Hear?"

"Come with you?"

"I say it."

He flung his arms about her; sweaty, reeking as he was, as they both were, he hugged her with abandon. She freed one arm and the other and shoved him off in indignation, which in no way changed the look in his eyes.

"Do all you say," he said.

"By the gods you'll do it. You do something wrong and I'll notch your ears for you. You keep that brain of yours working or I'll rattle it like a gourd. Can you do that? Can you look at a kif and not go crazy?"

That took a moment's thought. He nodded then. "Get them other time," he said confidently, waved a hand toward the wide infinite. "We go find kif other time pull their heads off."

The mangled extravagance appealed to her; he did, with his

clear-eyed insanity. She cuffed him harder and got a moment's shock, not temper—like Khym, like her own easygoing Khym, where Kohan would have swung and cursed at the sting. She was reassured, that he was capable of restraint, that a cuff on the ears stood a chance of getting his attention; that blunt-fingered and slender as he was, a couple of them could hold him if they had to. "If we get out of this," she promised him, "we go skin some kif. Next trip out. I take you with me."

That was premature. They owned nothing to give away, least of all the disposition of the Outsider. Lose Chanur, she thought with a chill, and they could make no more promises at all; but confidence burned in Tully's eyes, a trust that he was theirs.

Gods. *Theirs.* Theirs for managing, for using, for finding the location of his distant people before the mahendo'sat or the kif could do so, and making a wedge for Chanur trade. But it was Hilfy's kind of a look he gave her. Worship . . . not quite. Absolute belief. She looked at Hilfy to be sure and found the same. Looked disquietedly at the others, at Haral and Geran and Chur and Tirun, who had their own rights on this ship which was theirs as well as hers, who had been here longer and knew better and had to know what the odds were. It was there too—quieter, but as crazily trusting. She talked about going kif-hunting and they gave her that kind of stare.

"Keep it sane in here," she said. "I'm going to clean up. Tully, for the gods' sake, *bathe.*"

She stalked out. *The Pride* streaked on toward station. She had no doubt that some of those ships out there were kif, and that there was at least the remote possibility that the kif might face about and start a run at them in some berserk notion of revenge.

If this Akukkakk saw no other possibility, he might. But his presence here, before her, indicated that he knew that she had to come here; and why; and that he had a chance of revenge far wider than one ship, a handful of deaths.

It was Chanur he was aiming at. His information was accurate enough to have brought him here. Somewhere, hani had talked; and he knew where to put the pressure on.

Faha, she thought unworthily, but the suspicion nagged at her. If not the Faha, others, who had talked too freely at some dock or—gods help them—Handur prisoners, taken alive at Meetpoint. She doubted the latter: the destruction had been thorough: and Goldtooth denied the chance of survivors. But someone, somewhere—had said enough in the wrong hearing. She put the thought away. It was too bitter.

She wore the red this time, red silk breeches and the best of her rings and the pendant pearl. Appearances. She combed and brushed until her mane and her beard gleamed red-gold highlights. She splashed on perfume, reckoned that some sweeter scent would hardly hurt Tully, and pocketed one of several vials in the drawer.

For Hilfy she pocketed something too. She went back to the bridge then, distracted herself with current reports on their approach—Hilfy was not there, nor were Tully or Geran or Chur, but Tirun had taken the number-three cushion next to Haral. "No trouble," Pyanfar observed.

"Routine so far," Haral said.

"I'll take it. Your turn." Pyanfar slid in at her place and Haral slid out of hers, weary and staggering in the use of cramped muscles.

"Getting some kif transmission," Tirun said after a moment. "Operational. They know we're here. Nothing more said."

"How many of them, do you reckon?"

"Station's given us an accurate count. Seven."

"Gods have mercy."

"Aye."

Pyanfar shook her head and called up the various images available to her screens. They were coming in under automatic at present, locked on station's guidance. Vid image filled one screen, Anuurn itself, blue and marbled with cloud. Beautiful. It was always beautiful on approach, never so spectacular as Urtur, but full of life. It conjured blue skies; and grassy plains and broad rivers and vast seas; it conjured colors, and scents, and textures, and a gut feeling which was different from all other worlds . . . for hani.

She watched at her leisure: with *The Pride* under automatic there was little else to do. A sweep of their second vid camera showed their *mahen* escorts riding slightly aft, two sleek killers, so precise in position they might have been one single ship.

"*Aja Jin* advises he'll drop back to guard as we go in," Tirun said.

"Understood."

"Still picking up signal from that knnn. Tried the translator on it. I get nothing but a docking matchup, aside from the singing."

"They docked?"

"Quarter hour ago. Gods know what station's going to do with them. No facilities except the emergency hookup. I don't get any outside transmission on that problem."

"Huh."

"Not a word from anyone else in system. Unnatural quiet."

"Kif docked?"

"All seven."

"Thank the gods for that. You sure?"

"Station's word on it."

Pyanfar laid her ears back, scowled. It was too cooperative all round, kif who put into station . . . something was crooked here. Badly out of trim. It was far too late to turn about. And there was Kohan and all of Chanur below, who had no such options to turn and run. Therefore *The Pride* did not.

"Station requests all weapons shielded."

Pyanfar considered a moment, reached to the board and complied. "Done," she said, wishing otherwise. Presumably *Mahijiru* did the same. *Aja Jin* had dropped behind them now, in a defensive position at their vulnerable tails.

"Got plan?" Goldtooth's voice reached her ears then, transferred from Tirun's board.

"Want you with me when we go out," she said. "You understand hani station rules. Know them all?"

"All," Goldtooth confirmed.

"See you on the dock."

Weapons, she meant to say: hani stations observed no weapons-rules. It was not a thing she wanted to discuss on com. She trusted that the *mahe* would turn up armed.

It was certain the kif would.

xi

Automation took them in to the last, trued to the cone. It was an easy dock. The grapples touched and locked on both sides. The instruction came up to access the line ports; *declined,* she sent back, refusing that mandated service. It was not likely, considering the circumstances, that station would quibble. No objection came back, only a pressure reading for the station itself and a recommendation to use the air shunt in the lock.

"They know it's trouble," Pyanfar muttered. "Tirun, someone's got to stay aboard. You're it, you and Geran. Sorry."

"Aye," Tirun muttered unhappily. No discussion. "Shall I page Geran and advise her?"

"Do that."

"Want both of you fit. If we can't get back, take command, your own discretion. Take the ship and get out of here, pick up crew at Kirdu—mahendo'sat or anything else; and make it count, hear me?"

Tirun's ears went down. "You're not planning on it."

"Gods no, I'm not planning on it. But if. *If,* old friend. If we lose—in any sense—neither hani nor kif sets hand to *The Pride.* That's firm."

"That's firm," Tirun said. "Tully—our problem or yours?"

"Mine," Pyanfar said. "He's walking evidence. And more problem than you need. You've got that tape; you've got an ally in the Kirdu stationmaster if it comes to that. I don't leave you any instructions. If something goes wrong, make up your own rules."

"Right," Tirun said.

The order split the sister-teams down the middle. If it came to that—Tirun and Geran would be a wounded half. But that was the way it went: she wanted Haral's size and strength with her, and Tirun was hardly fit for a fight. Chur was the smallest of the lot, but of the two remaining, the meanest temper. Pyanfar extended her hand in rising, pressed Tirun's shoulder. Practicalities. Tirun knew.

They gathered belowdecks, all of them, clean and combed, excepting Tirun, who had never gotten her turn at washing up. Tully wore a white stsho shirt belted hiplength about him, and a better pair of blue breeches—Haral's likely, who had been sharing clothes with him. Pyanfar looked the party over; and remembering the perfume in her pocket, took it out and tossed it at Tully. "All things help," she said. Tully unstopped it and sniffed, wrinkled his nose and looked doubtful, but when she mimed putting it on, he splashed some on his hand and wiped his beard and his throat. He coughed, and thrust the bottle into his own pocket.

"Another matter," Pyanfar said, and took a fine gold ring from the depth of her lefthand pocket, offered it to Hilfy and had the satisfaction of seeing the look in Hilfy's eyes. "I won't take you anywhere ringless. If we meet some kif, or even politer company —you'd better look like where you come from, hear, imp?"

"Thank you," Hilfy said, looked uncertain with it, and flustered; but Geran tugged her head over on the spot and bit a neat place for it, deftly thrust the earring through for her and fastened it. "Huh," Pyanfar said, there being her niece with her first gold shining in her ear and pride glowing in her eyes. "Come on. Let's find out what's waiting out there.—Tirun, Geran, you keep that lock sealed for everyone but us, no matter how bad it gets to sound, no matter what they offer you. Get on the com in op. Tell Goldtooth to get moving."

"Aye," Tirun said. Neither Tirun nor Geran was pleased with the onship assignment—Geran was trying to be cheerful, and not succeeding: "Take care," Geran said, patted Chur's shoulder. "Luck," Tirun said, last, and Pyanfar nodded to the others and walked with them down the corridor, leaving Tirun and Geran to get to business: she and Haral and Chur, and Hilfy; and Tully, who looked back, when none of the rest of them did, with a forlorn expression.

Pyanfar went first into the airlock, waited for Tully, hand on the hardness of the pistol she had in her pocket—as all of them had but Tully. He hurried in with them and Haral closed the inner hatch. One further insane moment Pyanfar debated with herself, then made up her mind and opened the locker by the outer hatch, took out the pistol they kept there and gave it to Tully. "Pocket," she said when he looked anxious surprise at her. "Pocket. Don't touch it. Don't think about it. If *I* fire, you can, hear? If you see me shoot, then you shoot. But I won't. It's civilized here. Hani don't take nonsense from the kif and kif know that. If the kif get nasty they find themselves more hani than they know how to run from. Promise you. You draw that at the wrong time and I'll skin you."

"Understand," Tully said fervently. He thrust the pistol into his pocket and put his hands demonstratively in his belt at his back. "I take orders. I don't make mistake."

"Huh." She touched the bar. The airlock's outer seal opened for them and her ears popped with the pressure change as the cold air of dockside sucked through the access tube. Sounds outside echoed, nothing out of the ordinary. Pyanfar led the way onto the rampway plates, around the curve and down toward the grayness of the dockside, with all its metal and machinery.

The translator was out of pickup range now: Tully became effectively deaf and mute. Pyanfar looked askance at him as they walked out the arch of the farside lock, onto the dockside itself. He was sticking close to Chur and Hilfy, or they to him, while Haral brought up the rear, tall and solid and looking like business with her scars and her be-ringed left ear. Haral had instinctively planted herself back there to guard the rear and quite possibly to head off Tully if he should lose his head. The latter was not likely, Pyanfar thought with some assurance. Old hunter that she was, she had some sense which way things would dart in a crisis, and she had Tully figured for the other direction. She directed her attention sharply ahead, where dockworkers had set up cord barriers—where a station official, Llun house or one of half a dozen other Protected families which kept the station, made her body the gateway, guard enough for a hani station, where civilized folk knew what they would touch off if they harried a warder representing her family and her family's post.

Llun, that guard, if the set of the ears was any true indication, a mature hani in the black breeches of officialdom immemorial. The Llun drew a paper from her belt as they approached her, and offered it, not without an ears-down look at Tully: but the Llun kept her dignity all the same. "*Ker* Chanur, you're requested for Gathering in the main meeting area. You're held responsible for all the others of your party; it's assumed the *mahen* ship is under your escort."

"Accepted," Pyanfar said, taking the paper. The Llun moved aside then to let them pass, impeccable in her neutrality. A little distance away, at the next berth, a similar barrier was set up about *Mahijiru*'s access. "Come," Pyanfar said to the others, and walked in that direction, took the chance to scan the official summons. "Charges filed," she said. "Compact violations and piracy."

"Rot them," Chur muttered.

"We're going to get that shelved," Pyanfar said, looked up again and let her jaw drop as Goldtooth led a good number of *mahe* down onto the dock, a Goldtooth resplendent in dark red collar and kilt, glittering with *mahen* decorations. "By the gods, look at him."

"Merchanter," Haral spat. "And I'm kif."

"Come on," Pyanfar said to her company. Goldtooth offered his papers to the hani on guard, but the guard waved him through unquestioned; the *mahe* and his crew walked out to join her in the walk toward the main dockside entry, a towering dark crowd of mahendo'sat. Sidearms, openly carried, businesslike heavy pistols strapped to the right leg. Decorations, worn by more than one of the group.

"Where we go?" Goldtooth asked.

"Gathering. *Ihi*. Place where we sort things out. Hani law here, *mahe*. Civilized."

"Got kif here," Goldtooth muttered. "Got Jik watch our tail."

They entered the corridor. It stretched ahead, polished, clean, uncommonly vacant. No young ones about, precious few of anyone except officials in uniform, a very few hani dressed like spacers, who watched in silence and stepped well aside.

"Too few," one of the *mahe* observed. Goldtooth made a low sound, uninformative.

"Too rotted few," Pyanfar said. She turned a necessary corner, saw the doors of the meeting hall ahead, double-guarded. She took no more thought of her companions then, of *mahe* or Outsider or kinswomen, flicked her ears to settle the rings in place and waved a grand gesture to the black-trousered hani who stood there.

"Chanur," one said. The doors whisked open, and a milling, noisy crowd of hani were gathered beyond—a crowd which retreated in growing quiet as they swept into the room. Pyanfar stopped in the midst, looked toward the Cardinal point of the room, at the station authorities who gathered there, at Llun and Khai and Nuurun, Sahan and Maura and Quna, evident by their position and by the posted Colors in front of which they stood.

And kif, to their right, a cluster of black robes. A pair of stsho. Pyanfar's nose wrinkled and her ears flattened, but she lifted them again as she faced the Llun, who stood centermost and prominent among the station families. She held up the paper and proffered it for a page who retrieved it and took it to the Llun senior.

"Chanur requests transport downworld," Pyanfar said quietly. "Our claim has precedence over any litigation."

The Llun senior—Kifas Llun herself, broad and solid and unmistakable in her gold and her dignity, unhurriedly took the paper, thrust it into her belt, and looked again at Pyanfar. "A complaint of piracy has been filed by Compact law; by treaty, this station has obligations which have precedence."

"The rights of a family when questioned bear on treaty law and define the *han*. Our place is in question."

The Llun hesitated, mouth taut. "Challenge hasn't yet been issued."

"Yet. But it will be now—won't it, *ker* Kifas? You know it; and I know it; and there are those here flatly counting on it. Point of equity, *ker* Kifas. Point of equity."

There was long silence. The Llun senior's ears lowered and lifted. Her nose wrinkled and smoothed again. "Point of equity," she declared. "The composition of the *han* is in fact in question. Family right takes precedence. The hearing is postponed until Chanur rights and Mahn have been settled."

"*No*," said a familiar, kifish voice. Among the tall, black-robed figures there was a stirring, and Pyanfar moved her hands to her hips and close to her pockets. More of the kif moved—to the outrage of the hall, the whole kifish contingent left the rim of the meeting hall and came out to the center of it. The stsho moved with them, gangling pale figures, sorrowfully gaunt, their pastel patterns asymmetric and erratic on their white skins, their persons in disarray and their heads drooping. And one kif stood taller than the rest, his stance that of authority among them. Pyanfar pursed her lips, eyes broad-focused on all the kif, well toward a dozen of them and, gods knew, armed beneath those robes.

"Akukkakk," she said.

"We protest this decision," the kif said to the Llun. Not whining, no: he drew himself up with borderline arrogance. "We have property in question. We've suffered damages. This Outsider and these *mahe* are in question. I claim this Outsider for kif jurisdiction; and I claim these *mahe* as well for crimes committed in our territories. They're from the ship *Mahijiru*, which is wanted for crimes contrary to the Compact."

"Tully," Pyanfar said. "Papers."

He moved up beside her and gave them to her, rigidly quiet. She offered the papers to the page, who took and read them.

"Tully. Listed by Kirdu Station authority as crew, *The Pride of Chanur*, with a *mahen* registration number."

"The connection is obvious," the kif said. "I charge this Outsider with attack on a kif ship in our territories; with murder of kif citizens; with numerous atrocities and crimes against the Compact and against kif law in our territories."

Pyanfar tilted her head back with a small, unfriendly smile. "Fabrications. Is the Llun going to tolerate this move?"

"In which acts," Akukkakk continued, "this Chanur ship and all its crew intervened at Meetpoint, with the provocation of a shooting incident on the docks, the killing of one of my crew; with the provocation of a hani attack in the vicinity of the station, in which we defended ourselves. In which attack this *mahe* intervened and took damage, a reckless act of piracy—"

"Lie," Goldtooth said. "Got here papers my government charge this kif."

"A wide-reaching conspiracy," Akukkakk said, "in which Chanur has involved itself. *Ambition,* wise hani. Don't you know the Chanur . . . for ambition? I am kif. *I* have heard . . . the Chanur have maintained a tight hold over the farther territories where your ships go, private for themselves and their partisans. Now they deal with the *mahe,* on their own; now they make separate treaties with Outsider forces, contrary to the Compact, for their own profit. Kif relations with the *mahe* are not friendly; we *know* this particular captain and his companion who hovers armed and waiting just off the station perimeter, threatening our ships and yours. This is your law? This is respect for the Compact?"

"Llun," said Pyanfar, "this kif is disregarding the station's decision. I don't need to specify the game he's engaging in. The law protects the *han* from such outside manipulations. These charges are a tactic, nothing more."

"No," said a voice from the gallery behind. A hani voice. A voice she had heard. Pyanfar turned, pricked up her ears as she saw a whole array of familiar faces on the other side of the hall. Dur Tahar and her crew; and the Faha beside her.

"This is not," the Llun said, "a hearing. The kif delegation has its right to lodge a protest; but the matter is deferred."

Dur Tahar walked forward, planted herself widelegged. "What I have to say has bearing on the protest. The kif's right that the Chanur's gone too far, right that the Chanur's made deals on her own. Ask about a translator tape the Chanur traded to mahendo'sat and denied to us. Ask about this Outsider the Chanur claims as crew. Ask about deals worked out in Kirdu offices which excluded other hani and created incidents from there to Meetpoint."

"By the gods, *ambition!*" Pyanfar yelled, and crooked an extended claw at the Tahar's person. *"Ambition's* a spacer captain who'd side with a hani-killing kif to serve her house's grab for power. Gods!" she shouted, looking about the room at strange faces, at unknowns, insystem crews and landless on Anuurn for the most part. "Is there anyone here from Aheruun? Anyone from that side of the world, someone here to speak for the Handur ship this kif killed at Meetpoint, while they were nose-to-dock and had no idea there was any trouble in the system? *Ambition*—is the Tahar, who left us at Kirdu crippled and alone and came running home to use the information to Tahar advantage, who sides with the kif, who hit three hani ships and a fourth ship from outside our space, a kif who's terrorized these wretched stsho into coming here with gods know what story, a kif who's created a crisis involving the whole structure of the Compact. By the gods, I know what blinds the Tahar to the facts—but you, *you,* Faha—great gods, they killed your kin, and you stand there taking the part of the *hakkikt* who had you boarded? What's happened to your nerve, Hilan Faha?"

Hilan opened her mouth to answer, stepping forward, ears back, eyes wild. The kif howled and clicked, drowning whatever she tried to say, and howled until Akukkakk himself lifted a bony gray arm and shouted, turning to the Llun. "Justice, hani, *justice.* This lying thief Chanur was involved from the beginning, private ally of the mahendo'sat, an agent of theirs from the beginning, involved with them in attacks, reckless attacks into our territory which we do not forget."

"This kif," Goldtooth roared, louder still, *"hakkikt.* Killer.

Thirty ships his. Make all kif together, this *hakkikt*. Make move new kind trouble in Compact, got no care Compact, spit at Compact." He strode forward, pulled a wallet from his belt and slammed it into the hands of the page. "Papers say from my government truth. Hani and *mahe* hunt this one, yes. Got kif run from *mahe*, move into territory this new Outsider, this Tully. Big territory. Big trouble. I make truth for the *han;* I make liar this Akukkakk *Hinukkui.* I witness at Meetpoint; this kif *lie.*"

"Danger our station," the stsho stammered, thrust forward by the kif. "We protest—we protest this incident; demand compensation—"

"Enough," the Llun said over all the uproar, and hani noise died quickly; kif commotion sank away likewise.

"Llun," Hilan Faha said in that new quiet.

"Enough," the Llun said, scowling. "The kif has his right to protest and to advance a claim. But since that claim exists, all sides have a right to be heard. There's a further statement entered in this cause."

She took a card from her belt, thrust it out for the harried page, who took it in haste and thrust it into the wall slot which controlled the hall viewing screen. It flared to life, rapid printout.

stsho	kif	knnn	(*)	hani	*mahe*	tc'a
station	ship	ship	ship	ship	ship	self
trade	kill	see	here	run	watch	know
fear	want	see	hani	escape	help	knnn
violation	violation	violation	violation	violation	violation	self
Compact	Compact	Compact	Compact	Compact	Compact	Compact
help	help	help	help	help	help	help

Tc'a communication, matrix communication of a multipartite brain, simultaneous thought-chains. Pyanfar studied it, took a deeper breath, and Goldtooth looked, and the kif, and all the hani.

"It's our shadow," Haral murmured. "It's the tc'a with that rotted knnn."

"It got itself an *interpreter,* by the gods," Pyanfar muttered, and a vast grin spread across her face. "Got itself that tc'a off Kirdu and it's talking to us, gods prosper it. . . . See that, kif?

Your neighbors don't like your company, and someone else saw what happened, someone you can't corrupt."

"We've got a major crisis thanks to you," Dur Tahar cried, thrusting herself between Pyanfar and the Llun. "Gods blast you, Chanur, that you can find anything encouraging in knowing the tc'a are involved in this mess. *Knnn* mobbed my ship outbound from Kirdu, knnn, like in the old days of dead crews and stripped freighters. Are you proud of that, that you've gotten *them* involved? I call for the detention of this Outsider pending judicial action; suspension of this *mahe*'s permit and papers; for the censure of the captain of *The Pride of Chanur* along with all her crew and the house that sponsors her meddling."

"But nothing for the kif?" Pyanfar returned. "Nothing for a kif adventurer who murdered hani and *mahe* and provokes a powerful Outsider species, with all *that* might mean? *Ambition,* Tahar. And greed. And cowardice. What have you got from the kif? A promise Tahar ships will be safe if this dies down? I turned down a kif bribe. What did you do when they made you the offer?"

It was a chance shot, a wild shot; and the Tahar's ears went back and her eyes went wide as if she had been hit hard and unexpectedly. Everyone saw it. There was a sudden hush in the room, the Tahar visibly at a loss, the kif drawing ever so slightly together, the stsho holding onto each other. It was bitter satisfaction, the sight of that retreat. "Bastard," Pyanfar said, with a sudden rush of sorrow for the Tahar, and for the Faha who stood there in that company, ears fallen. Akukkakk stood with his arms folded, kifish amusement drawing down the corners of his mouth and lengthening his gray, wrinkled face.

"He's laughing," Pyanfar said. "At hani weaknesses. At ambition that makes us forget we don't trade in all markets, in all commodities. And at his reckoning we'll trade again to get our ships moving again outside our own home system—because there are more kif out there than you see, and hani won't all fight. Hani never do. Hani never have. And I've been stalled long enough. I was promised transport downworld and I'm taking it. I'm going home and I'm coming back, master thief, master killer—and I'll see you in that full hearing."

Akukkakk no longer laughed. His arms were still folded. The kif were all very quiet. The whole room was. Pyanfar made a stiff bow to the Llun, turned and walked for the door, but Goldtooth and his crowd lingered, facing the kif. Tully slowed and looked back, and Pyanfar did, scowling.

"Goldtooth. You come. I'm responsible for you, hear? As the Tahar's made herself responsible for this kif onstation. Come on."

The Tahar said nothing to the gibe. That was the measure of their disarray.

"Got friend," Goldtooth said to Akukkakk. "This time, got friend, and not at dock. You docked good, kif, got you nose to station. Maybe you ask hani give you safe escort, a?"

Akukkakk scowled. "Perhaps. And perhaps Chanur will be so kind as to do that herself. When she comes back from Anuurn."

A chill wind went wandering across Pyanfar's back. She stared a moment at the kif, thinking over the odds. The Llun and the insystem merchanters were thinking likewise, surely, what they might logically *do* with seven kif ships and two *mahe* hunters.

"Give me," Akukkakk said, "the Outsider. Or the translation tape. It's not so much. I can get it from the *mahe,* sooner or later."

"Ha, like you get from hani?" Goldtooth muttered.

"What hani give," Pyanfar said darkly and with distaste, "is a matter for the *han.* Consensus. Maybe, *hakkikt.* Maybe we'll talk this thing out, with assurances on all sides. Before it damages the Compact more than it has already."

The quiet persisted, on all sides. The stsho stared back at her from haunted pale eyes, the kif from red-rimmed dark ones, hani from amber-ringed black. Kif faith. She turned her back, retreated as far as the door of the chamber, and this time Goldtooth and his crew were with her—and Tully, whose face was pale and beaded with sweat.

The door opened and sealed again at their backs. They passed Llun guards. The corridor stretched ahead, empty.

"Going to my ship," Goldtooth said. "Going to back off and keep watch these kif bastard."

"Going to the shuttle launch," Pyanfar said. "Got business won't wait. Got stupid son and trouble in Chanur holding. Life and death, *mahe.*"

"Kif find you go, make one shot you shuttle. Jik make you escort, a? Run close you side, make orbit, get you back safe."

She stared up at the *mahe's* very sober face, reached and clasped his dark-furred and muscular arm. "You want help after this, *mahe,* you got it. Number-one help. This kif lies. You know it."

"Know this," Goldtooth said. "Know this all time."

Their ways parted at the intersecting corridor. Pyanfar pointed the way back to the dock, a straight walk onward, and Goldtooth took it, his crew with him, a dark-furred, tall body moving off down the hall. Pyanfar motioned her own group the other way, which curved toward the shuttle launch.

Steps hurried after them, clawed hani feet in undignified haste. Pyanfar looked about as the rest of her party did, saw a young and black-trousered stationer come panting toward her. The youngster made a hasty bow, looked up again, ears down in diffidence. "Captain. Ana Khai. The station begs you come. All of you. Quickly and quietly."

"Station gave me leave for my own pressing business, young Khai. I'm due a shuttle downworld. I'm not stopping for conferences."

"I was only given that word," the Khai breathed, her eyes shifting nervously over them. "I have to bring you. The Llun is there. Quick. Please."

Pyanfar glared at the young woman, nodded curtly and motioned the others about to follow the messenger. "Quick about it," Pyanfar snapped, and the youngster hurried along at the limit of her strides, hardly keeping ahead of them.

It was, as the Khai had said, not far, one of the secondary meeting rooms at which door a whole host of stationers and no few insystem spacers hovered, a crowd which parted at their approach and swarmed in after them.

The Llun indeed. The old man of the station, sitting in a substantial cushioned chair and surrounded by mates/daughters/nieces and a few underage sons, without mentioning the client familiars, the black-trousered officials, the scattering of spacer captains. Kifas Llun was there, first wife, standing near him, and there were others of other houses. A Protected house: the Llun could not be challenged, holding too sensitive a post, like other holders of ports and waterways and things all hani used in common, and he had slid past his prime, but he was impressive when he got to his feet, and Pyanfar exchanged her scowl for a respectful nod to him and to Kifas.

"This trouble," he said, and his voice shook the air, a bass rumbling. "This Outsider. Let me see him."

Pyanfar turned and gathered Tully by the arm. There was a panicked expression in Tully's eyes, a reluctance to go closer to the Llun. "Friend," she said. "He."

Tully went, then, and Pyanfar kept her claws clenched into his arm to remind him of manners. Tully bowed. He had that much sense left. "Male, *na* Llun," Pyanfar said quietly, and the Llun nodded slowly, his heavy mane swinging as he did so and his mouth pursed with interest.

"Aggressive?" the Llun asked.

"Civilized," Pyanfar said. "But *mahe*-like. Armed, *na* Llun. The kif had him awhile. Killed his shipmates. He got away from them. That's where this started. We have a translator tape on him. We'll provide it with no quibbles. I want it on record he gave it freely, for his own reasons. In the Tahar matter—that's a *han* question. I didn't trust the Tahar as a courier. Gods witness—I'll be sorry to be right. And by your leave, *na* Llun, I'll be back to answer your questions. There's a matter of time involved. I was given leave to go."

"Challenge has been given," Kifas Llun said, and Pyanfar darted her a hard look. "Only now the word came up."

Pyanfar thrust Tully back to Hilfy's keeping and started away without a word.

"*Ker* Chanur," Kifas said, and she cast a burning look back. "A quicker way: listen to me."

"I'll want a com link," Pyanfar said. "Now."

"Listen, *ker* Chanur. Listen." Kifas crossed the room to her and took her arm to stop her. "Our neutrality—"

"Gods rot your neutrality. Keep the kif off my back. I've got business downworld."

"Got a ship," one of the insystem captains said unbidden, a hani of Haral's build. "She's old, *ker* Chanur, but she can set down direct on Chanur land, that no shuttle can do. Tyo freight lander: *Rau's Luck*. I'm willing to set her in the way of trouble if Chanur's minded."

Pyanfar drew in a breath and looked at the aging captain. Rau was no downworld house. Insystem hani, landless and unpropertied except for a ship or two, unless they were Tyo-based, colonials.

"Your word is worth something," Kifas said, "Pyanfar Chanur.

We're bound by the Compact. We can't do more than pin these kif at the station. You've got the *mahe* for help. You can do more than we can. Chanur has two more ships in that might be of use. Tahar—"

Kifas did not finish the statement; her ears flicked in discomfort.

"Yes," Pyanfar said. "*Tahar*. I'm not so sure I'd rely on their ships either at the moment."

"We can't muster a defense," Kifas said. "Your captains are downworld with most of the crews. So are others. We've got kif at dock for as long as we can keep them, but you said yourself—there may be others."

"You've got the insystem captains."

"Against jumpship velocity—"

Pyanfar looked about her, at the spacers present. "Go to the jumpships you can reach; you can fill out crews. Take orders. No matter what house. Get those ships able and ready. I'll get the Chanur captains back here; and any others I can find. In the meantime, keeping those ships ready to go will be the best action with the kif." She looked at Kifas Llun, grim sobriety. "Your neutrality is in rags. Give me one of your people. To bring witness down there to what's going on. I have to get moving. Now. *Mahijiru* and *Aja Jin* will keep the kif pinned and the way open.—If I don't move, *ker* Llun . . . the upheaval in the *han* is going to make differences, differences to more than Chanur. Tahar's down there, I don't doubt they are. Standing in line to get a share of the spoils. You're already in it. I'm not going to let Chanur go under."

"Rau," Kifas Llun said. "You're ready to go?"

"On the instant," the Rau captain said.

"Ginas," Kifas said, with a gestured signal to one of her people. "Go with the Chanur. Talk to them. Answer what you're asked. You're at her orders."

The one singled out bowed. Kifas offered the door, a sweep of her hand. "*I* Llun," Pyanfar murmured in a quick bow of courtesy toward Kifas and toward *na* Llun, who had seated himself again. Then she turned and swept her own company, the Llun messenger included, toward the door, following the Rau captain. "This way," the Rau said, indicating a turn which would take them toward the small-craft docks.

Kohan, Pyanfar persuaded herself, would not have taken challenge immediately as it was offered, not knowing that she had reached the system; and surely he knew by now: it was routine that a house was notified when a ship belonging to it made port. The timing of it argued that his enemies knew; and surely Kohan did. He was too wise to be catapulted into any such thing without some preliminaries. She relied on that, with all her hopes.

Two hours by plane from the shuttleport to the airport that served Chanur and Faha and the lesser holdings of the valley. With the Rau's proposal they saved that much time; and on that too she relied.

And on a pair of *mahe*.

And gods grant that Akukkakk saw some hope for himself. If one of those kif ships got a strike signal off, if the kif was bent on suicide—he might accomplish it, if there were more kif ships lying off out of scan range. Maybe five, six hours lag time for message and strike. With luck, the kif did not know that the hani ships gathered in system were on skeleton crew; with luck the kif would regard them as a threat . . . if no one had talked.

"That ship of yours," Pyanfar said to the Rau. "Armed?"

"Got a few rifles aboard," the Rau said.

xii

There was no access ramp for an insystem workhorse, only a dark tube into a chill and dimly lit interior directly off the dock. The Rau dived in first and shouted to her crew, a thundering and booming of feet on the uncushioned plates. The air was foul, stinging to the nose. Pyanfar came aboard seconds after the captain of the *Luck,* put a hand on the hatchway as she stooped to enter and drew the hand back damp with condensation—seals leaked somewhere in the recycling systems. Gods knew what the margin was on life-support. She worked her way past lockers to the control pit of the probe, trusting Haral and Chur to get everyone else aboard and settled.

"Name," she asked of the Rau captain, dropping down into the three-cushion pit, waist-high, and ducking under the overhead screens. "Nerafy," the captain said, nodded back toward her presumed co-pilot and navigator who were dropping into the pit on the other side. "Tamy, Kihany."

"Got us an escort," Pyanfar said. *"Mahe*'s going to see we get there and back; move it. No groundlings in this lot. Will you give me com?"

"We're going," Nerafy said, sinking into her cushion. The hatch boomed shut, deafening. "Kihany: it's Anuurn we're headed for. Get the captain that link."

Repulse cut in. Pyanfar hand-over-handed her way around the back of the cushions to the com/navigation board and braced herself with feet and a hand on the rim to lean over the board. "I want," she said, ignoring the contrary slams of *g* against which she shifted without thinking, "relay to *Aja Jin. Mahe.* Get that ship first."

It took a moment. A *mahe* voice came crackling through. They lost *g* as *Rau's Luck* executed a wallowing maneuver, acquired it again. "*Aja Jin.* Have you got us in watch? Track this signal."

"Got," the comforting answer returned. "Got. We watch."

"Out," Pyanfar said. She broke it off, not anxious to have long conversations with kif to pick them up. The mike in hand, she tapped the harried navigator on the shoulder. "Next call: satellite to ground station Enafy region, area 34, local number 2-576-98. Speak to anyone who answers."

The navigator threw her a desperate glance, shunted her functions to the co-pilot and started working, no questions, no objections: "What landing?" the co-pilot was asking.

"First we get there," Nerafy said. "Got ourselves a rescue run. Speed counts."

"Map Coordinates 54.32/23.12," Pyanfar said, listening to the one-sided com. They were in contact with Enafy. In a moment more the navigator held up a finger and she tucked the plug into her ear and applied herself to the mike. "Chanur," she said, shaking, but that was from the cold. "Is Chanur answering?"

"Here," said a voice from the world, distant and obscured by a bad pickup. "This is Chanur Holding."

"This is Pyanfar. We're on our way in. Who's speaking?"

There was a moment's silence in which she thought the contact was lost. "It's Aunt Pyanfar," that voice on the other end hissed within the mike's pickup. "For the gods' sake, tell Jofan and hurry!"

"Never mind Jofan, whelp! Get Kohan on and hurry up, you hear me?"

"Aunt Pyanfar, it's Nifas. I think *ker* Jofan's coming . . . The Tahar are here; the Mahn have challenged; Kara Mahn has; and Faha's gone neutral except Huran's still here; and Araun and Pyruun have called that they're coming. Everyone's gathered here. They knew—Aunt Jofan, it's—"

"Pyanfar." Another voice assumed the mike. "Thank the gods. Get here."

"Get Kohan on. Get him. I want to talk to him."

"He's—" Jofan's voice trailed off or static obscured it. "I'll try. Hold on."

"Holding." Pyanfar rested the back of the hand which held the mike against her mouth, shifted her body in pain: they were under acceleration now. The rim of the pit was cutting into her back. She achieved a little relief, found all her limbs shaking against the strain, the physical effort of the position she maintained. She watched the screens, seeing something else moving on scan. *Aja Jin,* she hoped. It had better be.

"Pyanfar." The deep voice, static-ridden, exploded in her ear. Kohan, beyond mistake. *"Pyanfar."*

"Kohan. I'm in transit. I'm coming. How much time, Kohan?"

A long silence.

"Kohan."

"I'll wait till you get here. I think I can stall it that long."

"I'm coming in on a direct landing. I want you to stay inside and hear nothing and see nothing. I have something with me. Something you'll find of interest."

"This Outsider."

"News has got there."

"Tahar—make charges against you."

"Already settled. Settled. You understand?"

There was another prolonged silence. "I have my wits about me. I knew you were on your way. Had to be here if this crowd showed up in such graceless haste."

She let go a long breath. "Good. Good for you. You keep at it."

"Where's Hilfy?"

"Fine. Fine and safe. I'm on my way. Now. No more talking. We've got business. Hear?"

A breath crackled through the static. "I'll work that Mahn whelp into a fit of his own." It began to sound like a reassuring chuckle. "I'll sit inside sipping gfi and enjoying the shade.—Move, Pyanfar. I want you here."

"Out," she said. She handed the mike back, a strain of her arm against acceleration, let the arm fall back and shivered as she realized how long that conversation had been, how clear it was who was speaking from this shell of a ship. They were on directional to the satellite: perhaps no one had picked it up.

"Got it set up," Nerafy said.

"I'm going back to my crew," Pyanfar said. She edged her way out of the pit, one foot against the bulkhead. "Safety line," the captain advised her; she saw it, and tucked down, gained the braking clip on the line and wrapped her hand into it. Launched herself down the long pit of the central corridor, past moisture-dewed metal and aged plastic lighting panels, her own weight and a half on her arm. She reached the barriered recess of cushions where the others had snugged in and Haral snagged her, hauled her with difficulty over the padded safety arm which closed off the compartment, and in several hands, one pair alien, she let herself collapse into the cushions with the rest of them. "Got contact with Kohan," she breathed, sorting her limbs out from among the rest of them. "He's going to stall."

Hilfy's face. She saw that tight-lipped relief and felt a little dismay for the girl who had come onto *The Pride* a voyage ago and the woman who stared back at her, self-controlled and reckoning the odds.

"Got contact with the *mahe* too," Pyanfar said. "They're with us." She cast a look past Chur and Haral to the Llun, Ginas, who nodded, a flat-eared and anxious stare in return. "You don't," Pyanfar said, "have to make the return trip. There's no reason for you to, *ker* Llun. We just get you down safe the one time, that's all."

"Appreciated," the Llun said tautly.

"Captain." Haral thrust a package of chips into her hands, and a bottle of drink. Pyanfar braced the bottle in her lap and hooked a claw into the package, hands trembling with the prolonged strain, used the claw to punch double holes on the plastic bottle-cap and spout. The food helped, however difficult to swallow in the acceleration stress. She offered some to the others.

"We've had ours," Chur said. Bodies squirmed down the line, everyone settling. Tully tried to talk, hand signs and mangled words, and Hilfy and Chur communicated with him as best they could, speaking slowly, something to do with the ship and atmosphere. He was cold; they held onto him and settled finally. Pyanfar rolled a strained glance at Haral and then closed her eyes, numbed by misery.

There was no more that she could do for either situation, the one on the ground or the one on station. Kohan's nerves would be on the ragged edge by now. This go-and-stop-again psyching for challenge would wear at him by the hour. Like nerving oneself for a jump and walking back from it. The second effort was a harder one. A from-the-heart effort. Gods knew how long the situation had been sawing at Kohan's nerves. Months. Since the night Hilfy left. Since before that—when he saw Khym Mahn likely to fall to challenge. There was a point past which he would heave up any

food he tried to eat, wake all night, wearing his strength down
with pacing, with the constant adrenalin high which would wear
him to skin and bone within days. Huran and some of the other
mates had stayed. There were his youngest couple of sons, who
had run for the borders if they had any sense, not to linger within
his reach. There were a score of daughters, who might muster
worth enough to see that he ate and slept as much as possible
approaching this time. Daughters, mates, and with the captains in,
several more half-sisters, who were most reliable of the lot. But
there were grown Chanur males who might come straying back
from exile to key up the situation further—returned from Hermitage, from wandering, from gods knew what occupations which
filled the lives of males in the sanctuaries. Always, at challenge,
there were those, hopeless, keyed up, and dangerous, hanging
about the fringes.

As for young Kara Mahn, he was probably good. He had taken
Khym, who had survived thus far more by wit than by strength.
Kara had promised both size and intelligence, the last time she
had seen him. Chanur blood, after all, Chanur temperament. She
cursed her own stupidity, in seeking after a mate like Khym, a
quiet and peaceful domicile, a mountain hideaway and Khym, a
resting place, a garden like a dream. Khym had listened to her sto-
ries, soothed her nerves, made her laugh with his wit; an ideal
mate, without threat to Chanur's interests. But gods, she had never
thought what she left behind in that place, her own Chanur-
blooded offspring, larger than Khym's daughters and sons of local
wives, larger, and stronger, and—if such things could be inherited—
quarrelsome and demanding.

Nothing like family loyalty. Her son yearned after his Chanur
heritage so much he wanted to take it for his own.

Betterment of the species, hani philosophers had called it.
Churrau hanim. The death of males was nothing, nothing but
change happening; the *han* adjusted, and the young got sired by
the survivors. One man was as good as another, and served his
purpose well enough.

But by the gods it was not true, there were the young and the
reckless who might, on a better opponent's off day, win; there
were challenges like the one shaping up against Chanur, which involved more than one against one.

And sometimes—gods—one loved them.

She slept somewhat, in the steady acceleration, in sensations so uncomfortable numbness was the best refuge; and in the confusion of jump and time, her body was persuaded it was offshift or perhaps the shift past that.

A new sensation brought her out of it, weightlessness and someone hauling her out of a drift as a light flashed. "About to make descent," Haral said, and Pyanfar reached for a secure hold in preparation.

It was a rough descent: she expected nothing else. She had no idea of the shape of the lander, but it was not one of the winged, gliding shuttles. The lander hammered its way down after the manner of its kind, vibrating stress into the marrow of living bones and vibrating skin and tissues and eyes in their sockets, so that there was nothing to do but ride it down and wish desperately that there was a sight of something, something to do with the hands, some sequence which wanted thinking about and managing.

There was a time she simply shut her eyes and tried to calculate their probable position; she had, she decided, no love of riding as a passenger. Then the sound increased and the stresses changed—gods, the noise. She heard what she fervently hoped was the landing pods extending.

They were in straight descent now, a vibration of a rhythmic sort.

Touch, one pod and then the others, a jolt and a series of smaller jolts, and silence.

Pyanfar flicked her ears with the sudden feeling that she was deaf, looked about her at her shaken comrades. Down was different than before: the gimbaled passenger section had reoriented itself and the central corridor was flat and walkable. "Out," Pyanfar said. "Let's see where they set us down."

Hilfy unlocked the padded safety barrier, and they went. Hydraulics operated noisily and when they had come as far as the control pit, daylight was flooding in onto the metal decking from the open lock.

The others descended. Pyanfar delayed for an instant's courtesy, a thanks for the Rau crew who were climbing out of their pit, their ship secured. "If you come," Pyanfar said, "well, you're welcome in Chanur land. Or if you stay here—we'll be bringing more passengers as quickly as we can."

"We'll wait," Nerafy Rau said. "We put you close, Chanur. We'll have the ship ready for lift. We'll be waiting."

"Good," she said. That was her preference. She ducked under the conduits and swung down onto the extended ladder, scrambled down to the rocky flat where they had landed, in the generally wedge-shaped shadow of the lander. The air smelled of scorch and hot metal; the ship pinged and snapped and smoke curled up from the brush nearby.

Midday, groundtime. The shadows showed it. Pyanfar joined the others and looked where Chur pointed, to the buildings which showed on a grassy horizon: Chanur Holding; and Faha was farther still. And the mountains which hove up blue distances on their right—there lay Mahn Holding. Close indeed.

"Come on," Pyanfar said. She had made herself dizzy with that outward gaze, and shortened her focus to the rocky stretch before her. Horizons went the wrong way; and the colors, gods, the *colors*. . . . The world had a garish brightness, a plenitude of textures, and the scents of grass and dust, and the feel of the warm wind. One could get drunk on it; one had enough of it in a hurry, and the sight filled her with a moment's irrational panic, a slipping from one reality to the other.

"Not so far," Hilfy panted, latest from the world. "They'll have heard that landing. He'll know."

"He's got to," Haral agreed.

So will others, Pyanfar thought, deliberately slowing her pace. Rushing up exhausted—no, that was not the wise thing to do. Tully checked his long strides as they did; the Llun who had trailed behind them caught up. Manes were windblown, Tully's most of all. The sun beat down with a gentle heat: autumn, Pyanfar realized, looking about her at the heavy-headed grasses, the colors of the land. Insects started up in panic, settled again.

"They'll surely send a car," Chur said. "If they've spotted us."

"Huh," Pyanfar said; it was her own hope. But none had showed thus far, no plume of dust, nothing of the sort. "They may," she said, "have their hands full. No good any of them leaving, not if things are heating up."

No one answered that. It required no response.

She kept walking, out to the fore of the others. Familiar ground, this. She had known it as a child. They reached a brook and waded it ankle-deep, came up the other side, and by now Tully was limping—"He's cut his foot," Chur said, supporting him while he lifted it to examine it. "You come," Pyanfar said unforgivingly, and he nodded, caught his breath and kept going.

Not so far now. They joined the road that led to the gates, easier going for Tully, for all of them. Pyanfar wiped her mane from her eyes and surveyed the way ahead, where the gold stone outer walls of Chanur Holding stretched across the horizon, no defense, but a barrier to garden pests and the like—the open plains lapped up against it in grassy waves. Beyond it—more buildings of the same gold stone. There would be cars . . . the airport was behind them, down the road; they would have come in from there, all the interested parties and the hangers-on, save only the adventurers from the hills, from Hermitage and sanctuaries, who would come overland and skulk about the fringes; vehicles would have driven in along this road, gone through the gates, parked on the field behind the house . . . that was where they always put visitors.

When their uncle had fallen to Kohan—

The years rolled back and forward again, a pulselike jump, leaving her as unsettled. Homeworld . . . with all the mindset which took things so easily, so gods-rotted eagerly.

Nature. Nature that made males useless, too high-strung to go offworld, to hold any position of responsibility beyond the estates. Nature that robbed them of sense and stability.

Or an upbringing that did.

The grillwork gates were posted wide, flung open on a hedge of russet-leaved ernafya, musky-fragrant even in autumn, that stretched toward the inner gates and the house, an unbroken and head-high corridor. She passed the gate, looked back as the others overtook her, and in turning—

"Pyanfar." Someone came from among the hedge, a rustling of the leaves; a male voice, deep, and she spun about, hand to her pocket, thinking of someone out of sanctuary. She stopped in mid-reach, frozen by recognition a heartbeat late—a voice she knew, a bent figure which had risen, bedraggled and disfigured.

"Khym," she murmured. The others had stopped, a haze beyond her focus. The sight hurt: impeccable and gracious, that had been Khym; but his right ear was ripped to ribbons and his mane and beard were matted with a wound which ran from his brow to chin; his arms were laced with older wounds, his whole body a map of injuries and hurts, old and new. He sank down, squatting on the dust half within the hedge, his knees thrusting out through the rags of his breeches. He bowed his filthy head and looked up again, squinting with the swelling of his right eye.

"Tahy," he said faintly. "She's inside. They've burnt the doors down . . . I waited—waited for you."

She stared down at him, dismayed, her ears hot with the witness of her crew and of the Llun—on this wreckage which had been her mate. Who had lost that name too, when he lost Mahn to their son.

"They've set fires in the hall," Khym stammered, even his voice a shadow of itself. "Chanur's backed inside. They're calling on *na* Kohan—but he won't come out. Faha's left him, all but—all but *ker* Huran; Araun's there, still. They've used *guns,* Pyanfar, to burn the door."

"Kohan will come," Pyanfar said, "now. And I'll settle Tahy." She shifted her weight to move, hesitated. "How did you get to Chanur? Kohan knows?"

The whole eye looked up at her; the other ran water, squinted almost shut. "Walked. Long time ago. Forget how long. *Na* Kohan let me . . . stay. Knew I was here, but let me stay. Go on, Pyanfar. Go *on*. There's no time."

She started away, down that road which led to the house, not without looking back; and Hilfy walked beside her, and Chur and the Llun, but Tully—Tully had lingered, stared down at Khym, and Khym reached out a hand to stay him, only looking. . . .

Khym, who had delighted in the tales she brought him, of strange ports and Outsiders, and he had never seen a ship, never seen an Outsider, until now—

"*Tully!*" she called, and Haral caught him by the arm and brought him quickly. And then: "Khym—" she called. For no reason. For shame. Kohan had been as soft . . . when Khym had strayed here in his exile, hunting some better death than strangers.

He looked up at her, a slow gathering of hope. She nodded toward the house, and he picked himself up and came after them: that much she waited to know. She turned on the instant and set a good pace down the dusty road, eyeing the hedges which followed its bending. Ambush, she thought; but that was an Outsider way, something for kif and *mahe,* not hani on Gathering.

Still. . . .

"Scatter," she said, with a wave of her arm to her crew. "The garden wall: get there and we'll settle this daughter of mine. Hilfy: with Haral, Tully—Chur, you take him. *Ker* Llun, you and I are going through the gate."

Ginas Llun nodded, her ears flat with distress, and while the others scattered in opposite directions through the hedge, Pyanfar thrust her hands into her belt and strode along at a good pace around the bending of the road and toward the inner gates. A step scuffed behind her, and that was Khym: she turned to look, to encourage him with a nod of her head, herself in gaudy red silk; her companion in official black; and Khym—grimy rags that might once have been blue. He came near her, beside her, limping somewhat; and gods, the waft of infection in his wounds—but he kept their pace.

They could hear it now, the murmur of voices, the occasional shout of a voice louder than the others. Pyanfar's ears flattened and pricked up again; a surge of adrenalin hit fatigued muscles and threatened them with shivers. "It's not challenge," she muttered, "it's riot."

"Tahar's here," Khym said between breaths. "*Na* Kahi and his sisters. That's second trouble. It's set up, Pyanfar."

"I can bet it is. Where's our son's brains?"

"Below his belt," Khym said. And a few steps later, with the sounds of disorder clearer in the air: "Pyanfar. Get me past Tahy and her crowd and I can make a difference in this . . . take the edge off him. That much, maybe."

She wrinkled her nose, gave him a sidelong glance. It was not strict honor, what he proposed. Neither was what Tahar intended. Their son—to end him by such a maneuver—

"If I can't stop it," she said, "—take him."

Khym chuckled, a throaty rattle. "You always were an optimist."

They rounded the last curve, the gate ahead, wide open toward the gardens, the aged trees, the vine-covered goldstone of the Holding itself. A crowd surged about the front of the house, trampling the plantings and the vines. They shouted, taunts and derision toward Chanur; they rattled the bars of the windows.

"Rot them," Pyanfar breathed, and headed for the gate. A handful of Mahn spotted her and set up an outcry, and that was all she wanted. She yelled and bowled into them with Khym at her side, and the Mahn retreated for reinforcements in the garden. "*Hai!*" she yelled, and suddenly there were Hilfy and Haral atop the wall, and a peppering of shots into the dirt in front of the Mahn, who scrambled for cover.

"Get the door," Pyanfar yelled, waving at them, and they jumped and started running. More of the Mahn and some of their

hangers-on were on the colonnaded porch, and suddenly Chur and
Tully were on the low garden wall which flanked that, Chur yell-
ing as if encouraging a whole band of supporters. The Mahn
darted this way and that, herdwise, and scattered from the door in
the face of the three-way charge. Pyanfar raced up the steps and
converged with Haral and Chur, gun in hand, burst through the
doorway half a step ahead of them, into dimmer light and a chaos
of bodies and the reek of smoke. It was a huge room, lit from
barred windows, the wreckage of double doors at the end. Hani
there turned and faced their rush in a sudden paralysis, a hundred
intruders who stared at levelled Chanur guns.

Some moved; young women put themselves into the fore of
things. Others shifted about the fringes, carefully. Voices echoed
deep within the halls. Pyanfar kept the pistol braced in her two
hands, her eyes wide-focused, taking in all the movements.

That young woman—her own image, red-gold mane and stature
more than her Mahn sisters: Tahy. Her focus narrowed. The
young man—gods, tall and straight and broad-shouldered . . .
years since she had seen them. Longer years for her planetbound
daughter and son, growing-up years; and they had allies . . . a
score of Mahn youths, male and female; and about the walls of
the room—Kahi Tahar, *na* Kahi, the old man, Chanur's southern
rival; and others—senior women of holds she suspected as Enaury
and others of Tahar's hangers-on, here for the scavenging.

"Out of here," Pyanfar said. "Out of here, all of you."

"Guns," Tahy spat. "Is that the way of it? We have our own. Is
that what you choose, while *na* Kohan hides from us?"

"Put them away," Pyanfar said. She pushed the safety back on,
pocketed hers. In the tail of her eye Haral did the same, and the
others followed suit. "Now," Pyanfar said. "You're somewhat
strayed from the field, son of mine. Let's walk this back out where
it belongs."

"Here," Kara said.

A movement in the corridor behind the Mahn: Pyanfar noted it
and drew in her breath. Chanur. A good score of the house. And
Kohan, a head taller than the others.

"*Hold it,*" Pyanfar shouted, moved suddenly to the side, distraction. The invaders shifted in confusion and hands reached for
weapons, a moment's frozen confusion and suddenly Chanur at
the Mahn's backs. The Mahn retreated in haste, backing toward
the wall that had been at their left, but Tahy and her companions

who thrust themselves between Kara and Kohan quick as instinct; Pyanfar dived for the other side, Haral and Chur and Hilfy moving on the same impulse, interposed themselves. She touched Kohan's overheated arm. He was trembling. "Back," she said. "Back off, Kohan." And to Tahy: "Out. No one wins here. If Kohan delayed—it was my doing; and I'm here. With Ginas Llun, who'll back up what I say. With an Outsider, who's proof enough we've got trouble. We've got kif at the station: they've called the captains in . . . to defend Gaohn. It's like that up there. We can't afford a split in the *han*."

Tahy gave a negative toss of her head. "We hear a different story—all the way. No. You want to settle something on our own— we'll oblige you. Kohan need help, that you had to drag *him* up out of the brush? We'll settle that."

"Station's *fallen*," a voice said out of Chanur ranks, and one of the captains thrust herself forward, Rhean, with crew in her wake. "Word's on the com: they've called for help—it's no lie, *ker* Mahn."

Noise broke out in the room, a ripple of dismay through all those present. The Llun strode into it, neutrality abandoned. "How long ago? Chanur . . . how long?"

"Message is still going," Kohan answered, self-controlled, though his breath was coming hard. "Kara Mahn. I forget all this. It's over. Leave now. We'll not talk about it."

Kara said nothing. There was a glassy look in his eyes. His ears were back. But Tahy looked less sure of herself, motioned the others back.

"You've got your chance," Pyanfar said quietly, evenly. "Listen to me: you've got Mahn. Tahar's not your ally. You go on with this challenge, and Tahar's here to take on the winner; worn down, you understand me. To take two holdings. Their ambition's more than yours. The Llun can tell you that—a Tahar captain, dealing with the kif—"

"Rot your impertinence," Kahi Tahar shouted, and one of his sisters interposed an arm. "A lie," that one said.

"Perhaps," Pyanfar said levelly, "a misunderstanding. An . . . excess of zeal, a careless tongue. Back out of here. We may not pursue it.—Tahy . . . out of here. The Compact's close to fracturing. It's not the moment. Get out of here."

"*Na* Mahn," Kohan said. "It's not to your advantage."

"You'll lose Mahn," Khym said suddenly, thrusting past Hilfy.

"Hear me, whelp—you'll lose it . . . to Kohan or to Kahi. Use your sense."

Kara was past it. The eyes were wide and dark, the ears flat, nostrils wide. Suddenly he screamed and launched himself.

And Khym did. Pyanfar flung herself about, bodily hurled herself at Kohan as her crew did, as Hilfy and Huran Faha and Rhean and her crew. He backed up, shook himself, in possession of his faculties: Pyanfar saw his eyes which were fixed on the screaming tangle behind her—herself spun about, saw Khym losing the grip that would keep Kara's claws from his throat.

"Stop it," she yelled at Tahy, and herself waded into it, trying to get a purchase on either struggling body, to push them apart. An elbow slammed into her head and she stumbled, hurled herself back into it, and now others were trying to part the two. "*Tully!*" Hilfy shouted; and suddenly a fluid spattered them, straight into Kara's face, and over her, stinging the eyes and choking with its fumes. Kara fell back with a roar of outrage; and she did, wiping her eyes, coughing and supported by friendly hands. Chanur had hold of Tully, she saw that through streaming eyes, his arms pinned behind him, and Khym was down, and Kara was rubbing his eyes and struggling to breathe. She caught her breath, still coughing, shook off the hands which helped her. She knew the aroma, saw the small vial lying empty on the floor—the smell of flowers got past her stinging nasal membranes. "Tully," she said, still choking, reached out a hand and pulled him to her by the back of the neck, shook him free of the Chanur who had seized him—patted his shoulder roughly and looked across at her son, whose eyes were still running water. "Break it off, *na* Kara. You have Mahn. Call it *enough*."

"Off my land," Kohan said. "Tahar. Be glad *I* don't challenge. Get clear of Chanur Holding. *Na* Kara: a politer leave. Please. Priorities. I'll not come at you now. I could. Think of that."

Kara spat, turned, stalked out, wiping his eyes and flinging off offered help, divested of his impetus, his dignity, and his advantage. Tahy remained, looked down at Khym, who had levered himself up on his elbows, head hanging. She might have flung some final insult. She bowed instead, to Pyanfar, to Kohan, last of all to Khym, who never saw it. Then she walked out, the other Mahn before her.

Tahar lingered last, *na* Kahi and his sisters.

"*Out,*" Kohan said, and the Tahar's ears flattened. But he

turned and walked out of the hall, out the door, and took his sisters and his partisans with him.

Kohan's breath sighed out, a gusty rumble. He reached for Hilfy, laid his arm about her shoulders and ruffled her mane, touched the ring which hung on her left ear—looked at Pyanfar, and at Khym, who had struggled to his knees. Khym flinched from his stare and gathered himself up, retreated head down and slouching, without looking at him.

"Got no time," Pyanfar said. "Well done. It was well done."

Kohan blew a sigh, nodded, made a gesture with his free hand toward the rest. Nodded toward the door. "*Ker* Llun."

"*Na* Chanur," the Llun murmured. "Please. The station—"

"Going to be fighting up there?"

"No small bit," Pyanfar said.

"You handle it?"

"Might use some of the house."

"I'll go," Kohan said. "*I'll* go up there."

"And leave Tahar to move in on the boys? You can't. Give me Rhean and Anfy and their crews; whoever else can shoot. We've got to move."

Kohan made a sound deep in his throat, nodded. "Rhean, Anfy, Jofan—choose from the house and hurry it." He patted Hilfy on the shoulder, went and touched Haral and Chur in the same way—lingered staring at Tully, reached and almost touched . . . but not quite. He turned then and walked back. "Hilfy," he said.

"My ship," Hilfy said. "My ship, father."

It cost him, as much as the other yielding. He nodded. Hilfy took his massive hand, turned and took the hands of Huran Faha, who nodded likewise.

"Come on," Pyanfar said. "Come on, all of you. *Move*. I'll get her back, Kohan."

"All of you," he said. The others gathered themselves and headed for the door in haste, some delaying to go back after weapons. Pyanfar stayed an instant, looked at Kohan, his eyes, his golden, shadowed eyes; his ears were pricked up, he managed that. "That matter," she said, "this Outsider of mine—I'll be back down to explain it. Don't worry. Get Chanur back in order. We've got an edge we haven't had before, hear me?"

"Go," he said softly. "I'll get it settled here. Get to it, Pyanfar."

She came back and touched his hand, turned for the door,

crossing the room in a dozen wide strides and headed off the porch, where no sign remained of the attack but the trampled garden and a passing of vehicles headed down the road beyond the wall, clearing out in haste.

And Khym. Khym was there, by the gate, crouched there with his head on his folded arms. Fresh wounds glistened on his red-brown shoulders. He survived. He went on surviving, out of his time and his reason for living.

"Khym," she said. He looked up. She motioned toward the side of the house, that pathway which the others had taken to the back, where they could find transport. He stood up and came, limping in the first steps and then not limping at all. "I'm filthy," he said. "No polite company.".

She wiped her beard and smelled her hand, sneezed. "Gods, I reek for both of us."

"What is he?"

"Our Outsider? Human. Something like."

"Huh," Khym said. He was panting, out of breath, and the limp was back. They came along the side of the house, down the path by the trees at the back, and latecomers from the house reached them and fell in at their pace, carrying rifles. Khym looked back nervously. "It's all right," Pyanfar said. "You want to go, Khym? Want to have a look at station?"

"Yes," he said.

They reached the bottom of the hill, where Haral and Chur had started up two of the trucks, where a great number from Chanur were boarding, a good thirty, forty of them, besides those ten or so behind. Tully was by the side of one, with Hilfy. Pyanfar reached and cuffed Tully's arm. "Good," she said. "Up, Tully."

He scrambled up into the bed, surprisingly agile for clawless fingers. Hilfy came up after him, and Khym vaulted up with a weight that made the truck rock. Others followed.

Pyanfar went around to the cab, climbed in. "Go," she said to Haral, and the truck lurched into motion, around the curve and onto the road, toward the outer gates, flinging up a cloud of dust as they careened between the hedges, jolting into near-collision with the far post of the outer gate before they headed off across the field on the direct course toward the waiting ship.

Gods help us, Pyanfar thought, looking back at the assortment which filled the bed of the truck, young and old Chanur, armed with rifles; and a one-time lord, and Tully, and the Llun, who had decided to come back with them after all.

The ships had gotten off station to keep the kif there, and the kif were still there, indeed they were; were running the halls of station —kif loose with revenge in mind, a *hakkikt* who might see his own survival doubtful and revenge very much worth having.

She faced about again, feet braced against the jolts as the truck lurched over uneven ground. Haral fought the wheel with desperate turns and reverses, following the track they had walked now, the beaten line of their own prints in the tall grass, where there would be fewer hidden pits and hummocks.

"Hope *Aja Jin*'s still in place," Haral muttered.

"Hope *Hinukku* and the rest are," Pyanfar said, bracing her hand against the dash. "If we've got more kif than we had—if they've gotten a call out for reinforcements. . . ."

"Lagtime's on our side."

"Something had better be," Pyanfar said. "Gods, for a com."

Haral shook her head and gave all her strength to the wheel, slowed as they jolted toward the slope of the stream. The truck lumbered its way over the grassy bank, clawed its way over muddy bottom and rocks, slewed about and found purchase on the other bank, headed up again, with the ungainly wedge that was *Rau's Luck* growing closer and closer.

A light was flashing, sun-bright against the ship. Pyanfar pointed to it, and Haral nodded. The Rau saw them coming. Running lights began to flash, red and white, blink code.

It was the message they already had. Haral flashed the headlights, a desperate snatch back at the wheel.

Planetary speeds. In the time it had taken them to get this far from the house, a jumpship could cross an interworld distance. And perhaps some were doing that. The *han* was intact, the structure of Holdings which could decide policies; but the loss of Gaohn Station—

She cursed herself, to have assumed any revenge would be too great for Akukkakk's pride, to strike at stations—he had done that —no one struck at worlds, not in the whole history of the civilized powers.

Except the kif . . . it was rumored that they had done so, in their own rise off their native world, in the contests for power. They had once struck at their own.

xiii

The engines put on thrust, a hollow roar of the down-world jets, and the *Luck* lifted. Pyanfar dropped into the rear of the dark control pit as the deck came up, hit heavily and crouching and tucked down, straightening the blanket and pillow she had gotten to pad her back in that nook, on the pit floor behind the Rau's three cushions. The captain lifted her hand, signal that her presence was noted, and reached at once back to the board in front of her. The *Luck* went on rising; the gear thumped up into the housings and the pressure mounted. Pyanfar discovered a pain in her shoulder and struggled a little against the blanket to relieve it.

Not so steep a lift compared to the angle at which they had landed: the lander *flew,* of sorts, vertical lift at first, and then an angled flight which still had aft for downside, *g*-wise. The primaries cut in with a thrust which settled all her gut differentially toward her spine.

Some of their company were well off, aft, in the padded passenger shell. Tully and Khym and Ginas Llun were settled there, in thick cushions, and Haral, to keep them company and settle problems. The unlucky rest rode the boards, tilting cushioned partitions expanded from the next bulkhead—blind, dark misery, packed in like fish, four across, the back of the next cushion tilting back and forth almost in one's face . . . gods, gods, to ride like that with the ship going into trouble aloft—she felt guilt for being where she was, in what relative comfort she had.

The co-pilot let an object fall to her. She reached with difficulty and gathered the plastic-wrapped article from the angle of the pit where it stayed fast, unwrapped the earplug and thrust it in. No information was coming in during their ascent, only static, but having the contact helped.

Station had gotten that one message off, had still been sending it out when ascent began, which meant that the station central command had been in hani control and that stationers had their hands full, sparing no one to answer questions. It kept going, meaning that the kif had not gotten to it to silence it—or that they had had no critical interest in doing so.

But the docks. . . . She pictured the workers fled in panic, disorganized, having no preparation against such an action as the kif had taken. Attacking stations was not a thing hani would do; therefore it was not reasonable, therefore there was no contingency.

Gods blast such thinking, and the complacency which fed it. Gods blast her own; and hani nature, that they ran each for their own fragmented concerns, because all the world was set up that way. She had had no choice in going home to Chanur, because a hani would go on with challenge while the house caught fire, until the fire singed his own hide. Hani always went their own way, disdaining outside concerns, pricklish about admitting they would not be in space at all but for the mahendo'sat explorers who had found them—but that was so. And hani went on doing things the old way, the way that had worked when there were no colonies and no outside trade; when hani were the unchallenged owners of the world and hani instincts were suited to the world they owned.

But, gods, there were other ecosystems. They had another one going, in the Compact itself; and they dealt with distances wider than the grassy expanses of Anuurn's plains; and with creatures of instincts which had proven equally capable of being right in other ways.

In one unimagined hell, the kif way had worked best; and gods, even the chi way had worked somewhere, lunatic as they seemed, incomprehensible to outsiders. And Tully—who sometimes made half sense, and at other times made none at all.

Had Goldtooth despised her for her desertion, because being hani she had had no choice but to go, in the face of every reason to the contrary? Shame pricked at her, the suspicion that all hanikind had failed a *mahen* hope, that hope which had lent those two ships; and that somewhere up above might be the wreckage of her *mahen* allies and *The Pride* itself, with a kif waiting to blow this shell of a lander to vapor and junk, along with the hani brain who had just figured out something critical to the species, far too late.

Madness. The angle had her brain short of oxygen. There was a grayness about her vision. She felt nothing any longer in her backside and her arms and her legs, and the pressure kept on building.

Engine sound changed. They were leaving the envelope of air, still accelerating. She blinked and struggled to move her neck, saw through a blur telltales winking in the darkness, saw a flare of light as the scan screen cleared. She blinked again, trying to see past the silhouetted arm of the co-pilot, making out something large and close to their position.

". . . *Luck*," a voice snapped through the plug into her ear, "this is *The Pride of Chanur*. We'll match with you and lock on." *Tirun*.

If she could have leaped up and shouted for joy she would have done so. Pinned by the *g* force, it was all she could do to smile, a strained and difficult smile, with her heart hammering against her ribs and the blood bringing pain to her extremities.

Then the *Luck*'s engines stopped, and she gasped a reflexive breath in the sudden relief. The invisible hand which had pressed her to the deck was gone, and she reached in a practiced hand-over-hand to the com board, drifting feet toward the overhead and tucking down again to reach the mike. "Hurry it, Tirun, for the gods' sake." And to the Rau: "Where are the kif? Can you pick them up?"

"Station's scan's off," the Rau navigator said. "Not just Gaohn's: Harn and Tyo too, completely down. We've got our own, that's all."

"Put on the rescue beeper," Pyanfar said, thrusting that dire news to a far recess of her mind. "*The Pride* can home on it. Let her automatics take you."

"Advice," the captain said. "Your job now, *ker* Chanur. Gods help us, we're stone blind to any jumpships moving out there."

"Keep her trimmed and constant and watch out for the shock." Pyanfar aimed herself back to the shelter of her padded nest in haste. "Those grapples will do the fine matching. Don't try the jets. She's moving under comp."

"Gods, it's on us," the co-pilot said.

"Closing," Geran's voice sounded through the com plug. "Stand by, *Luck*."

A proximity alarm started, quickly silenced from the board. Scan broke up.

"O *gods,*" said the navigator.

Pyanfar tucked, clenching the cushion support with all her strength.

Impact. The *Luck* rang and leapt and her body left the deck, grip scarcely holding; hit it again, shoved back as the grapples grated, shifted.

Held. There was a comforting silence. Weightlessness.

"Got trouble," Tirun's voice said. "Blow that lock out; we've got a tube the other side. For the gods' sake board, abandon ship. We can't defend you."

"*Haral!*" Pyanfar yelled down the core corridor. "*Everyone!* get forward!"

"Captain," Nerafy Rau said.

"Come on," Pyanfar said, hauled herself to the captain's cushion and hung there one-handed, staring down at her. "All of you . . . gods, come with us. We'll get you back to your ship if there's a chance of it. If not that, there's kif to settle with, and those people on the stations—will you die here with no shot fired?"

"No," the Rau captain said, and started unbuckling. The others did. Pyanfar completed the summersault and looked aft down the corridor, at a white-shirted human sailing up it narrowly in advance of a flood of armed hani. The Rau captain handed her way up from the pit and headed for the nearby lock and Pyanfar grabbed for the board and the mike as the crew left it. "Tirun! Where are the kif?"

"Gods know. *Mahijiru*'s running far-guard; tell you the rest when you get here."

The bodies of her companions tumbled about her. The lock powered inward and airshock rammed through in a cold gust. "Coming," Pyanfar said, and let the mike go, kicked at the nearest conduit and flung herself into the stream of bodies, into the dark and numbing cold of *The Pride*'s ship-to-ship grapple-tube. Extremities went numb. Breath stung in the lungs and moisture threatened to freeze her eyeballs. It *hurt,* gods, it hurt. A light glowed green as she arrived in *The Pride*'s null-*g* outer frame, a safety beacon, a guidance star far across the dark, marking the location of the personnel lift. A blue chain of glowlights dotted across the blackness toward it, the safety line. "Khym!" Pyanfar

shouted, thinking of his inexperience, "blue's the guideline, Khym
. . . Tully! go to the blue lights!"

"Got him," Hilfy's young voice shouted up ahead. "Got them
both."

A door opened onto the lift. Someone had gotten to it. A distant rectangle opened, blinding white, with a score of dark bodies
hurtling and struggling along the blue dotted course toward it,
large and small with distance, some like swimmers in the air, some
using the rope and propelling the swimmers along. Bodies collided
and caught each other and kept going, one after the other, into
that lift chamber, where they took on color and identity. Pyanfar
found herself slung along the final distance, hauled into the lift;
and among the last came the Rau, into that blinding glare.

"We're in," Chur was shouting into com. Haral shouted a warning and closed the lift door, and suddenly all the floating bodies
tended floorward as the car moved. "Brace!" Pyanfar snapped at
the novices, but experienced spacers grabbed them, and suddenly
the car thundered and slammed into synch with the rotating inner
cylinder. There was full *g,* and the lift slammed upward again,
with a queasy rear-of-the-car acceleration stress as *The Pride* put
on a gingerly movement. Something banged in the distance.—
"Grapple's clear," Haral said. The lift went on rising, past lowerdeck, to main. Feet found the floor; bedraggled groundlings
hugged those who had a hold on them, ears flat and eyes wild.

The car stopped and opened on main. Pyanfar thrust herself
through and out, raced down the main corridor for the archway of
the bridge, claws scrabbling on the decking against the gentle
thrust. Haral was hard on her heels. "Lowerdeck," Chur shouted
behind them. "Ride it back down where there's secure space." The
door closed; the lift hummed into function again. Pyanfar did not
look back. She hurled herself the last difficult distance, past Geran
and Tirun at the number three and two posts as Haral found her
place and slid into it. Pyanfar reached her own vacant cushion and
flung herself into it without a word. Scan images were coming up
on her screens, their position relative to the world and the station
—a dot that was knnn-symboled, hovering off apart from the chaos
of other dots, two marked *mahe,* and the horrid hazard near the
station, a horde of unidentifieds, debris sweeps that marked the
death of ships and the course of their remains.

"*Aja Jin* took damage," Tirun said steadily. "Kif invaded traffic
control on the station and knocked the scan out. Llun had their

hands full; everyone was boarding any ship at all. We broke out of dock and ran with the rest . . . figured they were screening incoming ships. Strike came in three quarters of an hour ago. Outbound now. We're headed back in to station, present course: *Fortune* got a landing party in. Several others got in after them. Proceed?"

"Keep talking. Go as we bear." She reached and hit the motion warning. "We're moving," she said over allship. "Brace; I'm going to keep the com open from our end. We've got troubles and I don't want any stirring about down there.—Tirun, what's the comp on that kif movement? Got a course plotting?"

The data flashed to the screen. "All stations have killed scan output. Some of the kif are out of dock but we don't know which. Only good thing in it, with station's scan stopped a good bit before the strike, they had only our last-known position to go on and the attack missed most of us. *Aja Jin* got it, being posted stationary; at least one freighter was hit and we think some of the kif, but we don't know who got hit, because no one's outputting much chatter and a lot of the freighters are scan-blanked and hiding. I figure they'll go for the fixed targets on the next pass—the station, *Aja Jin's* last position . . ."

"Anuurn, maybe."

Tirun threw her an ears-flat look.

"You've got it going," Pyanfar said. "I'll go with it. Give me the rest of your reckoning. Where do you reckon Akukkakk is?"

"I think he was one that got off station; and he can't have boosted fast enough to have run with the strikers. I figure he's one of those ships out there, quiet like all the rest of them. And we find out just which one he is when that strike force comes sweeping back in."

Pyanfar nodded. To take the maneuver they had handed him—the undocking of the freighters—and to turn it to his own advantage . . . that was very probable. That was Akukkakk's style, for which she had begun to acquire a sense: a pattern of movements, a tendency to up the stakes when challenged.

"He's going to go on sending them in against the station," she judged, "hammer it into junk. *That,* for a lesson for us. But he knows rotted well which one we are, cousins. We're all too conspicuous, and I've a notion which way he'll go when he can—even odds between us and *Mahijiru.* And since *Mahijiru's* got Jik by him . . ." She cast a glance at scan, where the *mahe* rode as a double blip hard by the kif position at station. "They'll be overriding their own scan, that strike force, but Akukkakk's going to have a good identified image for them. Gods rot him."

"We drop our people at station," Haral said from the fourth cushion, "and pull a tight turn, maybe; go sort that crowd out."

"Got to do something, that's sure.—Tirun: to you." She shunted back what activity her board had received. "Take us in. I'm going to talk to the others.—Going to need all the rest of you up here. Stay put, Haral."

"Right," Haral muttered.

Pyanfar turned the cushion, slid out of it, headed out of the bridge at a dead run into the direction of thrust, digging in for traction. She skidded to a collision with the wall at the lift, hit the call button and caught her breath while it came.

It arrived; she stepped in and waited while it sped her to the lowerdeck, tremors in her muscles, a tendency to shiver in what ought not to be a chill.

Lowerdeck main corridor. She found the Chanur gathered there, braced sitting in the passage, rifles in laps, the best security they could find near their exit. They scrambled up as she came . . . and there was Chur among them, and Khym; and Tully, with Hilfy; and the Llun and the Chanur captains and their crews. She went among them, caught Chur's arm and looked at the others. "You've understood?"

"Understood," Rhean Chanur said. "We try to get the stationers rounded up and if we have to ride through another strike— we get to core and try to wait your pickup after it's past. Gods help us."

"*The Pride* will be back, Rhean; that's your ship that forced the breach; your crew, gods look on them. I don't know what damage she may have taken. You'd better plan for any pickup that comes for you.—Anfy, same goes—any ship. Got insystemers filling jumpship posts, anything we can get. Gods know who's where.—The rest of you: if you use those guns, you pair up with the crews and give backup fire. Hit the wrong target and you'll kill your own allies, hear? Or blow a seal; keep your wits straight and know what's behind what you're shooting at. You go shooting on a station, hear me, you put your shots on the decking and work up their legs."

Young ears lowered in distress; eyes stared, black-centered. Hilfy's look was something else again, ears pricked, sober. Pyanfar stared at her, at once pleased and heartsick. No way to pull her out of it. No need. Those who went onto station and those who stayed with *The Pride* were in equal danger. Maybe more, for them on the ship. Akukkakk would see to it, given the chance.

"Approaching dock," Com said. "Stand by for braking."

"We'll not waste time," Pyanfar said quietly, to those about her. "Chur, Hilfy, you're all *The Pride* can send: do it right and get back. All of you—Khym . . . go with my crew, hear?"

He nodded. There was a pricklishness in the air. No one else would have been glad to take him. In Chur's and Hilfy's eyes there was no flinching. He glanced toward them and the remnant of his ears lifted in the look they gave him.

For her sake, she thought. Gods help them—if he got one of them killed, rushing into something blind-crazy.

Braking started. They braced against the corridor wall—hard thrust, and miserable for the approach. Pyanfar shut her eyes a moment, slid down to a crouch with the rest of them, content for the moment to be where she was and wishing to all the gods she could go with them.

Tully squatted down close to Hilfy. Pyanfar turned her head, tightened her mouth in consideration. That was the one who might bolt. That was the one, deaf to instructions, crazy with anger. Khym crouched further down, shamed, she knew, by his condition; by the distrust about him, the expectation that he would be more danger than help to his own side, prone to take his own way, prone to male temper and instability—Khym, who had saved all their necks and given them the chance to get aloft in time. Like Kohan, fretting in agony downworld, because he was trapped in Chanur Holding; and gods, he had won.

They lost *g,* made the shifts, such that bodies leaned against one another in the nudgings of the docking jets, and those who had a hold braced those who did not.

Contact. The last direction of *g* confirmed itself and the grapples clanged home, the access thumped into position. "Got contact with a hani force out there," Geran said. "You've got a clear exit. —Luck to you."

"Have some yourself," Chur called up at the com. "Hai, up there," Hilfy shouted, and the lot of them scrambled up in readiness to rush to the lock.

Pyanfar rose with the rest of them. "Tully," she said, and beckoned him. His face which had been eager took on an apprehension

of what she wanted. She beckoned a second time, with the Chanur
forces beginning to head down the corridor toward the lock, and
when he did not come she went after him and took him by the
arm, while Chur and Hilfy delayed.

"Go," Pyanfar said to the two. "Take care."

They went, in orderly haste, with the others, down the corridor
toward the lock. Pyanfar laid her ears back, felt Tully pull at her
hand.

"Ask," he said. "Fight them, Pyanfar."

"No," she said. "You can't hear orders out there, understand?
Come with me. Come up to the bridge."

If his pathetic small ears could have moved they would have
lain down, she thought; it was that kind of look. "Yes," he said in
a small voice. "Understand."

The lock opened and shut again shortly after. "Coming up,"
she called to the open com. "Easy on the undocking."

Tully came with her, running beside her. She got him into the
lift and he leaned against the wall with his eyes on hers, with pain
in those eyes, like Kohan's pain—shadowed eyes, his bright mane
tangled, his whole body shrunken with exhaustion and unhap-
piness.

"We go," she said as the lift opened onto the bridgeward corridor. "*We* get the kif, friend, find Akukkakk and settle a score,
ship and ship."

"There?" He made a wide gesture, infinity.

"This system. All too close." She strode through the archway
onto the bridge, grabbed Tully's arm and thrust him for the auxiliary seat next Haral's post, none so safe there, but nothing was.
She slid into her own well-worn cushion and fastened the restraints while Tirun ungrappled; took the controls as *The Pride*
acquired her own *g,* sent them out narrower than she would have
cut it with station authorities in a position to protest.

"Situation as-was?" she asked Tirun.

"Figure we've got a little under a half hour on that strike,"
Tirun said.

"Haral: to all ships. Got kif among us. Broadcast ID's, now—
house and origin—and get our own signal going."

"Right."

She put them over station. Vid showed the two *mahe* ships
clear enough, a scattering of ships which had never made it away

from dock, some wrecked, some trailing debris that streamed in the station's rotation.

Kif ships, three of them, still at dock, with their tails singed: *Mahijiru* had done that much.

From the *mahe* . . . nothing, neither signal nor output. But they started to move, one after the other.

"We've stirred something," she said. "Our friends have some notion they're not talking about."

"Getting ID input," Geran said.

Scan started acquiring data, positive ID's on hani ships. The knnn zigged and darted at some velocity, throwing off small ghosts that indicated boosts. Pyanfar ran her tongue over her teeth, refusing that distraction, watching the pattern of those ships as yet unidentified, as more and more identifications came in and *The Pride* increased her own speed. Another ship was moving in on dock, and another one behind, insystem haulers, at a standstill compared to their own building velocity. Ships were moving in random directions, not to be caught when the strike came in—at least that was their hope.

"Rot them!" Haral exclaimed. "Crippled even—look at that speed."

Jik, Haral meant. *Aja Jin* trailed debris, but the two *mahe* kept accelerating with no apparent impairment . . . straight into the thickest concentration of ships.

She eased up, shut down altogether. The *mahe* had given up flexibility, launched themselves into the heart of things, deliberate and less and less able to veer off and handle a turn. "Maintain our options," she said quietly.

Suddenly a freighter designated hani blossomed into chaff.

"Captain," Tirun said. Three unidentifieds in the vicinity acquired the enemy designation. *Mahijiru* and *Aja Jin* swept toward the group.

"Keep out of our way, rot you," Pyanfar muttered. Haral was on com, advising all ships in the area to head off the kif movement.

"Going to have the *mahe* in line of fire if they do a straight turnover," Geran said. "Fire headon—"

"Going to let the kif pass our zenith," Pyanfar said grimly. "That's our best side anyway."

"I've got it," Tirun advised her, throwing the safety off the armaments of the upper frame.

"Knnn's coming up," Geran said sharply, and the proximity alarm beeped as the high-velocity ship ripped from tail to bow, nadir, gone into the developing *mahe*/kif confrontation so fast scan developed them a line of likely course.

"*Mahijiru*'s compliments," Haral relayed.

Scan showed debris, hani, *mahe,* or kif was uncertain: positions were too close. Dots coincided and split as the kif moved toward them. Someone was hit, and suddenly the fight was headed *The Pride*'s way.

"Akukkakk's *there,*" Pyanfar said, beyond doubt what kif would rate *The Pride* his prime target, disregarding the *mahe* who had just attacked.

"Two ship now," Tully exclaimed. Scan showed the *mahe* still paired, no longer accelerating and probably braking for their return; showed hani moving on the kif from points of the sphere, and two active kif ships. The third was involved with a debris-track, near the knnn's erratic blip. "That kif they get."

"This pair we got," Tirun muttered. The double image was closing with them, less and less interval, with their own impetus added to the kif's oncoming velocity. The knnn was on the return now, streaking out of the vicinity of the debris-track. *Mahijiru* and *Aja Jin* were farther and farther away, obliged to lose velocity before they could make way on the kif's heading, too close to traffic for jump pulses to assist.

"Which one?" Tirun asked.

"Take the best target," Pyanfar said. "I can't tell." Hani jump-ships were on the near-scan now, several of them, hammering toward intercept with the kif, but not in time for *The Pride*. No place for a freighter, a race with the swift hunter-ships, even cargo-dumped. No way to win.

"*Now!*"

The kif ripped past them, zenith, and they fired. Screens broke up. Explosion slammed *The Pride* askew and red-lighted the boards. Pyanfar reached in an adrenalin time-stretch, fought the pitch and wobble. In the screen's clearing a new rapid image bore down on them, a high knnn wail in com.

It went past them, zenith. Pyanfar spun *The Pride* one hundred eighty degrees in a tail roll, anticipating a kif turnover and return pass, hoping to get a shot off. *Mahijiru* and *Aja Jin* would come, were coming, might get back in time. *The Pride* fired back as the guns came in line. The kif had proceeded into turnover as their respective momentum separated them, and fire came back, broke up screens, red-lighted remaining clear boards.

"*Got* one," Geran yelled. "Look at that bastard wobble. By the gods we got him!"

Fire from the other kept up. The interval was still increasing between them, but at a slower rate. It would be coming back . . . soon.

"Goldtooth," Pyanfar said, punching in the com, "rot you, hurry it a bit, someone out there hurry it."

The knnn was pulling about in a tight turn, one of those maneuvers a knnn could survive and hani could not. It zigged into the interval, into the line of fire.

"Good job," Goldtooth's voice reached *The Pride*. "Got—"

Com broke up. Scan suddenly went berserk, all the sensors blind . . .

. . . jump field. Gods, a jump field—in crowded space.

"Captain!" Tirun yelled, far away and suddenly close as the field let them go. Tully cried out, a miserable wail.

Something was *there*—where nothing had been, a massive presence, a vast blip on scan as it cleared, a monster located to starboard zenith. They were off their heading, displaced. Everyone was. Comp was flickering wildly trying to compensate. Pyanfar keyed into the system, trying to get sense out of it. Gods, the newcomer was *huge*. Scan had the other blips, that were the kif and the *mahe* and the hani and the solitary knnn—

"Captain." Haral's voice. Com went on broadcast again, a wailing chorus which overburdened the audio, noise vibrating above and below hearing, wounding the ears.

The huge blip broke apart, fragmented, not debris, but discrete parts of which one stayed central and the rest sped outward.

"*Knnn*," Pyanfar breathed. "Traveling in synch. Gods help us all."

"*Hani—*" Com crackled through the static, a familiar, kifish voice. "*Pyanfar Chanur—*"

The knnn ships moved together, a cloud of them, headed for the kif; and all at once the kif's outgoing velocity began to show increase—Akukkakk had way and he was throwing everything he had into it. Retreating. Unable to boost up; the knnn were too close, and closer yet.

The solitary knnn ship zigged and darted and joined the chase.

"*Chanur!*" Goldtooth said.

Pyanfar watched the screens, frozen in place. Hani voices came over com, panicked, questioning. The chase on scan gathered more and more velocity.

Suddenly came another output, a signal which made no sense to comp: scan started blinking on the ship-sized object the knnn had left behind, asking operator intervention.

An alien voice came over com, Tully-like and frightened.

Pyanfar cast a glance at Tully, who clung sweating and jump-shocked to the edge of the com counter, whose eyes stared wildly as the voice kept going.

"## ship," translator rendered the transmission from the new-comer. "## ship ## you."

"Com!" Pyanfar yelled at Haral and got it. Her heart pounded against her ribs. "This is the hani ship *The Pride of Chanur*. You're in hani space. *Friend,* hear?"

"Captain," Tirun cried, "Captain, the knnn—"

The translator response droned in her ears. Pyanfar stared at the screen, at a narrower and narrower gap between the knnn and the fleeing kif. "Tully," she said without looking around. "Haral—give him com. Give it to him."

The translator voice went out, cut. She flung an instant's look back, at Tully, who had gotten himself together, who had the mike in hand and talked a wild-eyed rapid patter at these creatures who had arrived in knnn synch, in a ship which had come in hauled like so much freight, unable to communicate with the knnn—

"Captain—"

She looked about again. Knnn closed with *Hinukku*, sur-rounded the kif, became one mass about it, as they had been massed about the Outsider ship at its arrival.

"Gods," Tirun muttered.

"They're *trading,*" Pyanfar said incredulously. "Like at Kirdu—gods, they're making a trade. An Outsider ship—for *Hinukku*. For Akukkakk."

"*Pyanfar!*" Goldtooth's voice came over com. "*You got sense these bastard?*"

"Human ship," Pyanfar said, punching in her still-active link. "The knnn just dropped a live cargo on us. Tully's kind.—They're still going, by the gods, the knnn are still going, outbound."

"*Kif ship leave station,*" Jik cut in. "*He go.*"

A solitary kif, of the crippled three at station . . . it was so: a lame kif without a tail, headed out on the course of the other lame kif, inching his way into retreat. "Right down the incoming strike track, that's their course," Pyanfar said, fairly shaking with excitement. "By the great and lesser gods, they're pulling out, they're going to run."

There was a sudden and major vacancy on scan, the characteristic scatter-ghost of a ship departed into jump—where the mass of knnn had been, enveloping *Hinukku*. A vast ghost, a ripple in space-time; and hard after it—a smaller ghost, their own knnn. Vanished.

The two remaining kif kept going, realspace and realtime, headed for the far dark and sending out a steady signal, telling of disaster.

Running for their lives.

"We got," Goldtooth said. "Got, *Pyanfar*."

"Got.—Gods know what we've got." She heard Tully still chattering back and forth with the newcomer, heard lilts and tones in his speech she had never heard. She looked back at him, who had all but usurped Haral's com board. He saw her. His face was wet. "Friend," he said to her in her own language. "All friend."

Gods knew what there was to say to the newcomers that the translator could convey without foulup. Gods knew how to cope with a dozen other Tullys equally confused and upset as he had been on his arrival.

"They come," she said slowly, distinctly. "Tell them they come to station."

"Come, yes."

She spun about again, toward the screens, started putting on thrust for a stationward course. Other ships were proceeding on that heading, the hani jumpships who had never slackened speed; hani who had kin on station; hani who had crew from station or who had dropped landing parties on the docks to try to assist the Llun.

Anything might be happening there, even now, with kif elsewhere in rout.

A hundred Outsiders plated in gold could not have interested her at the moment.

"Captain—" Geran said, and suddenly new data came up on the screens, and a familiar steady signal came over audio. "Station's broadcasting again, Captain."

She heard the *mahe* advise them of the obvious, heard the alien chatter from the Outsider, who must have picked it up, and the voices of hani sending anxious queries to station.

"Station is entirely secure," the answer came back. "This is Kifas Llun speaking. Resistance has ended and the station is entirely secure."

Pyanfar kept up the thrust, heedless of the lights which advised of damage. That rotted number-one vane was hit again; gods knew what else was gone, but the fine control was still there, and likewise their ability to brake. No limping in; no lanes established yet: they were all see-and-avoid.

Other signals came in. Harn Station was back on output; and then Tyo, reporting minor damage, minor casualties.

Hilfy, Pyanfar kept thinking, and Chur.

And Khym, at the bottom of her thoughts, Khym, for whom she had no hope.

But that was what he had come looking for, after all.

A sweat prickled on her nose. Breath came hard under the acceleration. The *mahe* traveled with them, and for its own reasons and in its own purpose, the Outsider ship came, outstripping slower insystem haulers for whom that voyage was the work of hours.

By the time they could get there, Gaohn Station might have some reckoning of the casualties.

xiv

The Pride opened accesses while *Mahijiru* eased into dock beside her, and Jik's *Aja Jin* stood watch toward that quarter of the system out of which some stray kif might still come . . . not expected, but they took precautions.

The Outsider ship came in more slowly still, permitted docking, but having to accomplish it without understanding the language, the procedures, and without compatible equipment. "Beside us," Pyanfar had told them simply. "You got vid? You see four grapples: airlock placed in center, understand? You go slow, very careful. You have trouble, you stop, wait, back off: small ship can come from station, help you dock. All understood?"

"Understand," the answer had come back through the translator. And the Outsider arrived, cautiously . . . wondering, doubtless, at the holed carcasses of kif ships nearby, at the signs of fire which pitted the adjacent section of the station torus.

Someone on the dock got a direct line hooked up. "Captain," Geran cried, her eyes shining amber. "Captain, it's Chur and Hilfy. They're *there,* both of them!"

"Huh," Pyanfar said judiciously, because there was a docking Outsider chattering in her other ear at the moment; but relief jellied her gut, so that she heard very little of the Outsider's babble at all. She looked at her crew, and at Tully, whose eyes had lighted at the news.

"They're safe," he asked, "Chur and Hilfy?"

"We're going out there," Pyanfar said, thrusting back from the controls. "All of us, by the gods." She stood up, remembered the tape they had duped on the way in and pocketed it. "Come on."

They came, off the bridge and long-striding down the corridor,

Tully too, rode down the lift and marched out the lock. If there was ever a time for running for joy, it was that last walk down the rampway; but Pyanfar held herself to a sedate walk, down the ramp, into the wide, fire-scarred dock where hani stood with weapons.

Chur and Hilfy and some of the other Chanur—o gods, Hilfy, with a bloodstained bandage round her side and leaning on Chur who had one arm in a sling. They smiled, in shape to do that, at least. Chur hugged Geran one-armed, and Pyanfar took Hilfy by both shoulders to look at her. Hilfy was white about the nose, with pain in the set of her mouth, but her ears were up and her eyes were bright.

"We got them," Hilfy said hoarsely. "Got behind them at the dockside while others came through the core and pushed them out to us. And then I think they got some kind of order, because they went frantic to get to their ships. That was the big trouble. One got away. The rest—we got."

"Khym."

Hilfy turned with some evident stiffness, indicated a figure crouched against the far side of the dock, small with distance. "*Na* Khym got the one that got me, aunt, thank the gods."

"Hit them hand to hand, he did," Chur said. "Said he never could shoot worth anything. He came across that dock and hit that kif, and gods, five of them never more than singed his fur. I don't think they ever saw a hani of his size—gods, it was something. They bailed out of cover and we got the leftovers."

Pyanfar looked, at once proud and sad, at that quiet, withdrawn figure. Proud of what he had done—Khym, who had never been much for fighting—and sad at his state and his future.

Gods, if they could only have killed him—given him what her son had not had the grace to give. . . .

Or perhaps Kara had sensed he could not kill him, that Khym Mahn backed to the wall was a different Khym indeed.

"I'll see him," she said. "We're going to get you two to station hospital."

"Begging pardon," Hilfy said, "station hospital's got its hands full. Rhean's got someone hit bad, and Ginas Llun—she's none too good either—and a lot of others."

"Hilan Faha," Chur said, "and her crew—they're dead, Captain. All of them. They led the way in for the core breakthrough. They insisted on it. I think it was shame—for the company they'd kept."

"Gods look on them, then," Pyanfar said after a moment.

"The Tahar—" Hilfy said bitterly, "got *Moon Rising* out and ran for jump. *Ran* for it. That's what they're saying on station. But the Faha wouldn't go with them."

"That'll be the end," Pyanfar said. "When that tale gets back to Enafy province, Kahi Tahar and his lot won't show their faces in Chanur land or elsewhere."

"*Hani,*" a *mahen* voice bellowed, and here came Goldtooth and crew, a dozen dark-furred, rifle-carrying mahendo'sat flooding toward them, towering over them. Goldtooth grabbed Pyanfar's hand and crushed it till claws reminded him to caution. He grinned and slapped her on the shoulder. "Got number-one help, what I tell you?"

Hani were staring at this *mahe*-hani familiarity. Her crew was. Pyanfar laid her ears back in embarrassment, recalled then what they owed Goldtooth and his unruly lot and pricked the ears up at once. More, she linked arms with the tall *mahe,* and gave the gawkers on dockside something proper to stare at. "Number-one help," she said.

"Got deal," said Goldtooth. "Got friend Jik repair, same you get at Kirdu. Chanur fix, a?"

"Rot you—"

"Got deal?"

"Got," she admitted, and suffered another slap on the shoulder. She looked at Tully, thinking of Chanur balance sheets, debits and credits. Looked at him looking at her with those odd pale eyes full of worship. Behind him an accessway had opened. His own kind had come, gods, a bewildering assortment, pale ones and dark ones and some shades in between.

"Tully," she said, signed with her eyes that he should look, and he did.

He froze for the instant, then ran for them, hani-dressed and hani-looking, ran to his assorted comrades, who were clipped and shaved and clothed top and bottom in skintight garments, shod besides. Hands reached out to him; arms opened. He embraced them all and sundry and there was a babble of alien language which echoed off the overhead.

So he goes, Pyanfar thought with a strange sadness—and with a certain anxiety about losing a valuable contact to others—to Llun, by the gods, who would be eager to get their own claws in; and

Kananm and Sanuum and some of the other competitors in port. Pyanfar shed Goldtooth's arm and crossed the dock toward the knot of humans, her own companions following her. Tully brought his people at least halfway when he saw her, came rushing up and grabbed her hand with fevered joy.

"Friend," he said, his best word, and dragged her reluctant hand toward that of a white-maned human, whose naked face was wrinkled as a kif's and tawny-colored like a hani's.

The captain, she thought; an old one. She suffered the handclasp with claws retracted, bowed and got a courteous bow in return. Tully spoke in his own language, rapidly, carrying some point—indicated one after another of them and said their names his way—Haral and Tirun, Geran and Chur and Hilfy, and the mahendo'sat at least by species.

"Want talk," Tully managed then. "Want understand you."

Pyanfar's ears flicked and lifted, the chance of profit within her reach after all. She puckered her mouth into its most pleasant expression. Gods, some of them were odd. They ranged enormously in size and weight and there were two radically different shapes. Females, she realized curiously; if Tully was male, then these odd types were the women.

"*We* talk," Goldtooth interposed. "*Mahe* make deal too."

"Friend," Pyanfar told the humans in her best attempt at human language. Tully still had to translate it, but it had its effect. "I come to your ship," she said, choosing Tully's small hani vocabulary. "Your ship. Talk."

"I come too," Goldtooth said doggedly, not to be shaken. Tully translated.

"Yes," Tully rendered the answer, grinning. "Friend. *All* friend."

"Deals like a *mahe*," Pyanfar muttered. But that arrangement was good enough for her. She suddenly conceived plans—for the further loan of two *mahe* hunter ships on a profitable voyage.

"Captain," Haral said, touching her arm and calling her attention to a cluster of figures coming out of the dockside corridor.

Llun were on their way—Kifas Llun herself in the lead of that group, come to answer this uncommon call at Gaohn Station, a score of black-trousered officialdom trailing after her.

They would demand the translator tape, that was sure. Pyanfar thrust her hands into her waistband. "Friends," she assured Tully, who gave the approaching group anxious looks, and he in turn re-assured his comrades.

"Hilfy," Pyanfar said, "Chur, no need for you to stand through this. Go to the ship. Geran, you go and take care of them, will you?"

"Right," Geran agreed. "Come on, you two."

No protests from them. Chur and Hilfy started away in Geran's keeping and Tully delayed them to take their hands one by one as if he expected something might keep him from further good-byes.

Gods, she had no desire to deal with the Llun or anyone at the moment. Her knees ached, her whole body ached, from want of sleep and from strain. She felt a span shorter than she had come across that blink from Kirdu. They all must. Tully too. She wanted—

She wanted to have time . . . to talk to her own, to find out who else of Chanur was hurt, to call Kohan. . . .

And somehow—to talk to Khym. To do something, anything for his misery, in spite of what others thought and said.

"Geran," she called out at the retreating group. "Khym too. Get him aboard and tend to him. Tell him I said so."

A small flick of the ears. "Aye," Geran said, and went off in Khym's direction while Chur and Hilfy made their own way back. Pyanfar turned to the arriving Llun with a dazzlingly cheerful smile, fished the tape from her pocket and turned it over to Kifas at once with never a fade of good humor.

"We register these good Outsiders, our guests, at Gaohn Station," Pyanfar said, "under Chanur sponsorship."

"Allies, *ker* Chanur?" There was a frown of suspicion on Kifas Llun's face. "Nothing the Tahar said weighs here now with us . . . but did you send for them?"

"Gods no. The knnn did that. Knnn who got a bellyful of kif intervention in their space, I'd guess; who found these Outsiders near their space and decided in their own curious fashion to see to it that they met reputable Compact citizens of a similar biology—snatched them up in synch, they did, and they took the *hakkikt* out the same way, may they have joy of him. They're traders, you know, *ker* Llun, after their own lights. I'll wager our human friends here don't know yet what's happened to them or how far they are from home or how they got here. They'll have drugged down and ridden out the jumps it took to get them here, and gods know how many that was or from where."

"Introduce us," the Llun said.

"I'll remind you," Pyanfar said, "that we and they have gone through too many time changes. We're not up to prolonged formalities. They're Chanur guests; I'm sponsoring them, and I feel it incumbent on myself to see that they get their rest . . . but of course they'll sign the appropriate papers and register."

"Introductions," the Llun said dryly, too old and too wise to be put off by that.

"Tully," Pyanfar said, "you got too rotted *many* friends."

It was what she expected, grueling, a strain on everyone's good humor, and entirely over-long, that visit to station offices. There was some restraint exercised, in respect to family losses, in respect to frayed and lately high tempers; in respect to the fact that for one time out of a hundred, hani had worked together without regard to house and province, and the cooperative spirit had not entirely faded.

There was gratitude to Goldtooth and the *mahe* ships, who got station privileges and repair. Gaohn Station was all too anxious to share the bill with Chanur, aching to get *Aja Jin* into the hands of Harn Shipyards, to be studied and analyzed during the course of the work. The mahendo'sat were evidently satisfied with the situation—smug bastards, Pyanfar thought, bristling somewhat as all hani did, at the unhappy truth that the mahendo'sat were always ahead of hani, that mahendo'sat technology which had gotten them into space in the first place was responsible for keeping them there. The mahendo'sat were apparently ready for their allies to see the hunter ships, at least. Rot the Personage and his small fluff with him.

Station was eager too for a look at the human ship; and doubtless the humans entertained some suspicions about that and everything else, but it was a fair question what they had in their power to do about it.

They were, at least for the moment, effectively lost.

"We find home," Tully said, "not far from Meetpoint. Know this. Your record, your ship instruments—help us."

"Not difficult at all," Pyanfar said. "All we have to do is send your records through the translator and get our charts together, right? We come up with the answer in no time."

"Mahendo'sat," Goldtooth said, "got number-one good reckoning location human space. Number-one good charts."

All too many friends indeed, Pyanfar reflected.

Tully went to his own, not without hugging her and Haral and Tirun, and shaking hands energetically with Goldtooth and with Kifas Llun and others—an important fellow among his people now, this Tully, surely; a person who knew things; a person with valuable and powerful friends. Good for him, she thought, recalling the wretched, naked creature under the pile of blankets in the washroom.

She made the call to Kohan, a quick call—her voice was getting hoarse and her knees were shaking—but it was good to hear that things on the world had settled down, that Kohan had gotten himself a good meal and that the house was back in some order.

While the world had been under kif guns, they had tidied up the house, cooked dinner, and started replanting the garden. Pyanfar lowered her ears at the thought, how little real the larger universe was to downworld hani, who had never thoroughly imagined what had almost happened to them; who heard about the terrible damage to the station as they might hear about some earthquake in a remote area of the globe, shaking their heads in sympathy and regretting it, but not personally touched—worried for their own kin, of course worried—and there would be hugging and sympathy at homecoming. But they set the world in order by replanting the garden and seeing Kohan fed.

Gods look on them all.

She went on the last of her strength to the hospital, to visit the Chanur wounded, because she was first in Chanur and it meant something to them; because she owed courtesy to Rhean, who sat with her mending crewwoman; because the news from home would do them good, these downworld Chanur not of the ship crews, who understood the necessity of planting gardens.

She checked with station command, that the Rau had found a way back to their ship, which another small freighter had managed to secure for them.

And then she and Haral and Tirun walked the long way back to *The Pride,* all of them hoarse and exhausted and finding the limit of their energy simply in putting one foot in front of the other. She limped, realized she had somehow broken a claw; thought with longing of a bath, and bed, and breakfast when she should wake.

But on *The Pride,* one thing more she did: she stopped by sick bay and looked in on Geran's charges, found Hilfy and Chur comfortably asleep on cots jammed side by side into the small compartment, and Geran drowsing in the chair by the door.

Geran woke as her shadow crossed her face, murmured bleary-eyed apology. Pyanfar shrugged. Tirun and Haral looked in at the door, leaned there in the frame, two worn ghosts.

"Khym," Pyanfar said, missing him.

"Cot in the washroom," Geran said. "By your leave, Captain. He wouldn't accept Hilfy's quarters, but she tried to insist."

"Huh." She edged through to see to Chur and Hilfy, saw their faces relaxed and their sleep easy, walked out. "Orders?" Haral asked in apparent dread. "Sleep," she said, and the sisters went their way gladly enough.

For herself, she walked on down the corridor to the washroom and opened the door.

Khym was safely tucked in bed, nested in blankets on a comfortable cot. One eye was bandaged. The other opened and looked at her, and he moved to sit up—clean, his poor ears plasmed together such as they could be, the terrible scratches on his arms and shoulders treated. Patches of his coat were gone where the scabs had been; his beard and mane were haggled up, doubtless where snarls had had to be snipped out.

"Better?" she asked.

"*Ker* Geran shot enough antibiotics into me, I should live forever."

Rueful humor. She sank down on the end of the cot, refusing, as Khym refused, to abandon a cheerful face on things. She patted his knee. "I hear you put a wind up the kif's backs."

He shrugged, flicked his ears in deprecation.

"You got your look at station," she said. "What do you think of it?"

Ears pricked up. "Worth the seeing."

"Show you the ship when you and I get some sleep."

"I can't stay up here, you know. You're going to have to find me a shuttle down tomorrow."

"Why can't you stay up here?"

He gave a surprised chuckle. "The Llun and others will say, that's who. Not many lords as tolerant as *na* Kohan."

"So station's their territory. So, well. I thought you might consider taking a turn in mine. On *The Pride*."

"Gods, they'd—"

"—do what? Talk? Gods, Khym, if I can carry an Outsider male from one end of the Compact to the other and come out ahead of it, I can rotted well survive the gossip. Chanur can do anything it pleases right now. Got ourselves a prize in this Outsider; got ourselves a contact that's going to take years to explore. I can deal with Tully; and with the mahendo'sat—a whole new kind of deal, Khym. Who's to know—if you stay on the ship—who's to question —when we're not in home territory? What do you think the mahendo'sat care for hani customs? Not a thing."

"*Na* Kohan—"

"What's it to Kohan? You're my business, always were; he let you stay on Chanur land, didn't he? If he did that, he'd care less about you light-years absent on a Chanur ship. And right now, what I want—Kohan's going to have a lot of patience with."

He was listening, ears up and all but trembling. "Think so, do you?"

"What's downworld got to offer you? Sanctuary? Huh. Think you'd go crazy on a ship? Unstable? Make trouble with the crew?"

"No," he said after a moment. And then: "Oh, gods rot it, Pyanfar, you can't do something like that."

"Afraid, Khym?"

Ears went down. "No. But I have consideration for you. I know what you're trying to do. But you can't fight what is. *Time,* Pyanfar. We get old. The young have their day. You can't fight time."

"We're born fighting it."

He sat silent a moment. The ears came up slowly. "One voyage, if the crew doesn't object. Maybe one."

"Be a while in port, getting our tail put back together again. Getting navigational details worked out. Then we go out again. A long voyage, this time."

He looked up under his brow.

"It's different out there," she said. "Not hani ways. No one species' way. Right and wrong aren't the same. Attitudes aren't. I'll tell you something." She crooked a claw and poked it at him. "Hani downworld want their houses and their ways unquestioned, that's all. They don't ask much what we do while the goods come in and don't cost outlandish much; they don't care what we do either, so long as we don't visibly embarrass the house. Kara's going to be upset. But he'll live with it . . . when *The Pride*'s light-years out of sight and mind. Might start a fashion. Might."

"Dreamer," Khym said.

"Huh." She got up, flicked her ears and waited to see him settled again. She walked out then, weaving a bit in her steps and figuring she had about strength enough to get to her own cabin and her own bath and her own bed, in that order.

Tully came and went, among his human comrades, and on *The Pride*. He did not, to Pyanfar's surprise, cut his mane and shave his beard and walk about in human clothes: he did go shod, but no more change than that.

For the sake of appearances, she thought; in respect of her one-time advice and the opinion of the Llun (and of Chanur too, that brief time they paid a downworld visit, to afford Kohan time with his favored daughter and a view of their sponsored guests). Tully flourished—grinned and laughed and moved with a spring in his step quite strange in him. He brought a solemn trio of humans off their ship to take notes aboard *The Pride*—Goldtooth attended with his own records—to ask questions and to exchange data until they had some navigational referents in common.

They frowned suspiciously, these humans, but they stopped frowning when they learned precisely where home was—some distance beyond knnn space and kif.

"Got between," Tully said enthusiastically, jabbing the chart which showed hani and mahendo'sat territory, cupping one hand on the hani-mahendo'sat side and one hand on the human side, with the kif neatly between. The hands moved together slowly, clenched. "So."

So, so, so, Pyanfar thought, and her lips drew back and her nose wrinkled cheerfully.

In time, he went, back to his own . . . that last sealing of the lock which marked the separation of the human ship from Gaohn. *Ulysses,* its name was, which Tully had said meant *Far-Voyages.* Nearly fifty humans lived on it, and whether they were related or not, she could not determine.

They prepared to go. She started back across the docks to *The Pride,* to follow—with a smallish cargo, nothing of great mass, but items of interest to humans. There might be a chance to see Tully at voyage's end, but it would hardly be the same. He belonged with his own, that was what, and she did not begrudge him that.

She planned to have use of that acquaintance, Tully—and the captain of this *Far-Voyages.* So, of course, did Goldtooth, with his sleek refitted ship, going with them, while Jik carried messages back to the Personage, no doubt, and the mahendo'sat tried to figure out how to cheat an honest hani out of exclusive arrangements.

But the odds in that encounter were even.